Praise for Folkston

"This book is a long cast on a cool country morning, a story that sets the hook early and keeps the line tight. The modern South is rarely rendered with such seedy, stinky, silly accuracy."

Ben Montgomery — Author of *Grandma Gatewood's Walk* and Pulitzer prize nominee

"When wet-behind-the-ears attorney Ethan McDaniel arrives in Folkston, he's primed and ready for his first real trial, but he's woefully ill-prepared for the entertaining, eccentric (and at times, disturbing) cast of characters he encounters in the small South Carolina town, especially his temporary neighbors at the seedy Sapphire Courts motel. In his delightful novel, *Folkston*, author Brian Livingston creates an impressive literary stew—a rich mixture of courtroom shenanigans, uniquely drawn Southern characters, fishing adventures, cheap bourbon...all seasoned with a healthy dose of humor. Add a visit to Livingston's *Folkston* to your travel itinerary. You'll be damn glad you made the trip."

Scott Gould — Author of *Idiot Men* and *Peace Like a River*

"Folkston is a great example of the good things that indie publishing can produce. The book is an unconventional spin on a classic setup - big city hotshot goes to small town and naively screws things up on the path to enlightenment. Livingston's writing is consistently light and entertaining, and his sense of humor is quirky and endearing. However, he also manages to weave together surprisingly complex commentary on urban/rural tensions in modern Appalachia with the voice of an insider. Livingston reminds me at times of a poor man's Flannery O'Connor. That kind of comparison can feel like damning with too much praise, but *Folkston* is an unmistakably Southern story full of memorably eccentric characters told with an endearing blend of wit and honesty. Recommended for anyone who likes that sort of thing."

Tim Mathis — Author of *The Dirtbag's Guide to Life* and *I Hope I was Wrong About Eternal Damnation*

In this masterful story that deftly weaves together southern grit, humor, and compassion, Livingston explores the ever-increasing chasm between the haves and have-nots in this well-written, astonishing take on unintended consequences.

Jon Sokol — Author and Robert Driscoll Award winner

Folkston

Brian Livingston

Be Living Enterprises

To Maddux
We really miss you

Chapter One

The Folkston County Courthouse dominated Ethan McDaniel's horizon. The building was readily identifiable as the town and county's tallest and cleanest edifice. Its red bricks and reflective windows surged two stories over any other Folkston Main Street structure.

In the corner of the empty parking lot, where he had backed into a space, Ethan straightened his tall, borderline gangly, frame out of the atrocious green coupe the insurance company had rented him for his trip. He ran a hand through his neatly arranged dirty blonde hair as he surveyed the grounds. The courthouse offered ample parking: seven rows of eight spots encased in a ring of parallels, then additional opportunities on the adjacent roads. At that moment, early on a Saturday afternoon, every spot was up for grabs, but come Monday morning, the lot would be overrun with one hundred fifty presumably reluctant jurors, courthouse personnel, and a brood of anxious attorneys. If Ethan arrived early enough, and parked in this spot in the back right corner, he could ensure a peaceful arrival without any unnecessary stress or potentially inappropriate interactions.

This preliminary stop had been one of Mrs. Warland's pro-tips: *do yourself a favor and scope out the parking situation beforehand. Formulate a parking plan, and a backup plan, then anticipate both failing. Lots of courthouses, especially rural ones, have limited or oddly situated parking. Some don't have any. To the extent possible, get to know the courthouse, the viable entrances, the exits. Mark all routine matters off your list of concerns. Trials are already too stressful to start off scrambling for a place to leave your car. You'll sweat through your suit before you make the steps.*

He turned his attention to the courthouse itself; some time had passed since the photographs on the Folkston County website. The red bricks had faded and were no longer quite as crisp; the windows were streaked and watermarked. Altogether, the Folkston County Courthouse appeared scuffed and in need of a shine. To Ethan, the condition of the venue was no matter—this aging government building's sole function was to host the proceedings that would earn him lifetime admittance to the South Carolina Trial Attorney Association, a monumental brick in his professional development, providing access to the SCTAA's vast networking resources including twice yearly conferences and quarterly golf outings. The SCTAA would also serve as a key selling point to future clients, and a desired talking point on his resume, if he were ever to move on from Hamel, Collins, Nagurski & Hamel, LLC. Ethan didn't golf, but he would be happy to learn.

He folded back into the driver's seat, started the car, and exited the lot, navigating the side street to turn right back onto Main. He slammed the accelerator to stay ahead of an oncoming pickup, sending a stack of bulging red binders skidding across the backseat. They smashed into the rear passenger door before dumping into the crevasse. Ethan whipped his head around, checking the extent to which this had scattered his files—it had not—and whether the impact had scuffed the vinyl—also good. He had never rented a car before but felt certain there was a charge for scratching the interior. A row of hanging and freshly drycleaned suits and shirts swooshed against the window behind him.

Folkston was situated in South Carolina's northwest corner about five interstate, highway, and backroad hours from Charleston, Ethan McDaniel's Lowcountry base of operations. He had spent the early parts of his Saturday driving diagonally across the state, making his final approach across the vast plain to the town's east, watching through his windshield as the surrounding mountains sprouted from the ground, first as formless dull blue lumps, then matured into vivid deep green cathedrals, which, at the peak of their majesty, disappeared behind the stalky pines lining the highway. Now that the preliminary matters had been attended to, and suitable plans established, it was time for a brief respite.

Ethan drove east, back down Main Street, turning left just after the wide gardened median containing Folkston's dual purpose *Welcome/Thanks for Visiting* sign. He stopped briefly in front of the sign, denying an incoming minivan the town's friendly greeting as he unfolded a piece of legal paper from the cupholder. After a quick *three-two-one*, he hit play on the stereo, reentering town-bound traffic as the first guitar strains and signature *ooooooooohhhhhhh bbooyyy* kicked off the beloved and, in his life, ubiquitous theme song to *Wettin' the Line with Chuck Palwagon*.

The visuals to Chuck Palwagon's iconic intros changed each week to feature driver's perspective shots of the host rolling into the episode's featured town and, allegedly, following his route to the eventual fishing hole. There were some serious and heated message board debates, including whether Mr. Palwagon drove directly to the fishing hole or even actually drove himself, but a large contingent of the fanbase insisted that one had but only follow the intro footage to find the specific spot where the legendary angler had wet his line. Ethan had watched and rewatched the "Folkston-Lake Marie" episode, and noted the landmarks in order. He double-checked the piece of legal paper where he had transcribed the lyrics, mumbling to himself as he passed the sites:

The Folkston Welcome Sign – *Ain't we jus' in for another one*

Two rows of brick buildings – *Quittin' time, now let's have us some fun*

An old timey gas station – *Hard up but I know how I'll unwind*

Right onto a wooded mountain road – *Hit the water, Lord, and wet the line*

The *Wettin' the Line* production team had been selective in their editing; Folkston was considerably bleaker in person. The opening credits neglected to showcase Main Street's myriad vacant storefronts whose plate windows served only to display *For Sale* signs; others exhibited nothing but dusty shelves and faded curtains. Folkston's occupied spaces were limited to a pharmacy, which had been featured in the intro, a thrift shop, and three antique shops.

Main Street was only enlivened by the town's school spirit. The same Folkston High School Football poster—complete with schedule and flexing, frowning teenager—adorned every storefront. Each window had likewise been tagged with some variation of *Go Eagles, Beat the Cats!* in painted red and white letters.

I guess the locals have to get excited about something.

Ethan tried to assemble a clever crack about how Folkston should show its academics the same enthusiasm.

The featured gas station, Bogie's Pumps, had an old metal sign and a small dining area which Ethan recalled to be unoccupied in the intro footage. *Must be new.* It was here that Ethan caught up to the cheerleader troop responsible for painting the town. Three of them had their paint markers pressed against different portions of the diner window. On the other side of the glass, a fluorescent lit room of grey-headed locals watched with approval. An elderly mob milled about outside the restaurant as well, most of them wearing sweaters in the same shade of red as the Folkston High posters and window art.

Must be a nice place to be a high school football player.

After the gas station, Ethan turned right on the mountain road, driving for some time until the song had long since faded out. His eyes darted between both sides of the road in search of Lake Marie related signage, side roads, or dirt roads, but for ten silent minutes he encountered no signs, turn offs, or any suggestions of nearby water. He had studied the maps; Lake Marie was geographically near, but no official or recognized roads ran to, or really even near it—part of what made it so special. In the event he was unable to follow Big Chuck's specific trail, he had assumed there would at least be signage guiding him to a put-in or picnic area. But there was no mention of the lake.

Ethan pulled over and stopped, humming, *"by wettin' the liiiin-nnnnneeeeee, yea wettin' the line"* absently to himself as he crossed the deserted roadway to survey the woods. Unless he had driven too far, he was directly facing Lake Marie.

But how far is it? Could I walk there? I just need to see it.

In the intro, after travelling an unidentified road, and just as the Fisherman's Rag reached its climax—*oh boy here we go again, hangin' with ol' Chuck Palwagon*—the host drove up on the clear waters of Lake Marie. Unfortunately, neither the intro nor the message boards gave any indication of how he had actually accessed that final approach. The fact that the intro was intercut with shots of Big Chuck fishing, eating, and *gettin' on* with the locals only complicated the task. Ethan walked several yards into the brush, then stopped and considered the risk. He couldn't afford to get lost in the woods on the eve of his first trial.

He returned to the rental and prepared for one last stop. Just outside of Folkston, past the welcome sign, he took a left onto Woodstone Road, following it for about half a mile before stopping on a small rise overlooking a pine forest. The tall trees and green bristles concealed the small grey prefab building which served as Lucas Trash's headquarters. Ethan's extensive trial preparation, however, had made him familiar enough with the surveys, tax maps, and overhead shots to be able to point at the building with certainty. He had also memorized the creeks, hills, and drainage ditches on the property until he was confident he could walk the line between Lucas Trash and Kurt Bickerman's land without map or compass. Ethan supposed he knew the topography of these properties even better than their respective owners.

This land is my clay mine, Ethan thought, *these hills have produced the raw materials which shall be forged into my keystone brick.*

He stood tall and raised his head to take in the landscape and sniff the clean mountain air.

No smell.

He flinched at a whoosh and rattle of leaves behind and above him. Something dark blurred in the top of his vision. Ethan looked up just as a formidable brown bird swooped overhead. He watched the silhouette glide over the trees on its way to the horizon, wondering whether it was a hawk, falcon, or a literal Folkston Eagle. The bird began circling in the skies above Lucas Trash and gave a mighty screech.

Ah, a red-tailed hawk. That has to be a good sign.

Chapter Two

Ethan returned to Folkston and began his search for Sapphire Courts Motel, his home for the next several weeks, which he only knew to be somewhere past the courthouse on the left.

Mrs. Warland's advice about scoping out parking had seemed sound and practical in the firm conference room, but upon locating the actual Sapphire Courts, it proved wholly unnecessary. Sapphire Courts was not simply past the courthouse on the left, it was the next building on the left, separated only by a dismal side street and a dense tangle of unkept brush. Ethan turned left off Main Street in front of the blue and white Sapphire Courts sign—the world plummeted, the rental jolted, screeching as if some giant claw had snatched its metal frame. The searing sound continued for a long second, cutting off only when the rental jerked free of the road's shoulder where Ethan had misjudged the slope and slid slightly askew down the sandy bank into the gully containing Sapphire Courts. When he regained control, Ethan whipped into the nearest spot and leapt out to check the damage.

After confirming the coupe had incurred no observable injury, Ethan stood, brushed off his knees, and inspected his surroundings. Sapphire Courts appeared to occupy Folkston's lowest point; the land sloped down towards it from all directions. The structure itself was dispiriting even by rural roadside motel standards. Two rows of faded blue doors, one on top of the other, composed the two floors. The doors on the second story opened to a tilted exterior walkway. Those on the first floor opened directly to the silt. A cloudy green line about a third of the way up the ground floor doors marked where the structure had previously flooded.

Ethan had done his research and prepared himself for the grim accommodations. He also had a feeling that Margot, the insurance adjuster on the case who made a point of pronouncing the *t* in her name, could have done better—especially if she had bothered to expand her search to neighboring towns. Ethan also instinctively wondered whether the decrepit conditions and obvious flooding issues had led to any lucrative litigation.

As it was, he was here.

Two men—one White, one Black—studied him from the second-story walkway where they had no doubt witnessed his eventful entry. Ethan kept the pair in his peripherals during his long walk to the office, tensing as each leaned further over the railing to better inspect the foreigner; he only breathed again after finally passing underneath the walkway and out of their view.

The office comprised a counter with an aging computer, a small table with barely enough space for a discolored coffee pot, and a three-chair sitting area. Ethan knocked on the counter, waited, then gave several incrementally louder *hello's* and *excuse me's* before deciding no one was coming through the slightly ajar door behind the counter. He checked the bathroom before noticing his key taped to a yellow piece of paper bearing the name *Ethan Daniels* stuck to the window.

Close enough.

He picked it up and once more swept his eyes around the empty office.

I guess they don't require a card for incidentals.

He sighed and set off back to the coupe, steeling himself, eyes locked forward as he once again exposed himself to the men's stares. When Ethan reached the car, he checked the number on the key and located his room: 217. He reverse-engineered the route: up the steps and almost all the way to the right; he would have to pass the onlookers. After lugging his personal and professional effects from the trunk and backseat, he shifted his left hand free to rummage his pocket to mash the lock button on the car key. The coupe beeped behind him as the men again tracked Ethan's progress, black-eyed crows on a cement branch, cocking their heads as he neared. Ethan braced himself for them to begin cawing, but nothing came.

When he arose from the square hole in the second-floor cement, the duo had rotated to face the doors with their propped elbows pointing at Main Street. Ethan angled closer to the bricks but kept his pace steady, his face a practiced lawyer neutral. Upon closer inspection, the men were actually quite young, early twenties at most, at least five or so years his junior. The White youth was shirtless and wastefully skinny. His stomach dove back from his ribs, almost meeting his spine. Hist chest and arms bore several crude tattoos; Ethan made out a pot leaf, but most appeared to be incoherent jumbles. A mullet poof of blond hair haloed the man's head the tips of which bobbed as he took a series of short, sharp preparatory breaths, not unlike hiccups, each time smiling on the inhale. His feet shifted beneath him as if on uncertain ground. His hand tapped his bare side. He grinned hard and wide.

The Black youth, who was taller and frowning, never took his eyes off his companion.

Ethan toed the line between rudeness and vigilance, not staring but not looking away either, while trying to maintain a purposeful, unhurried pace. When Ethan was one step away, the grinning youth produced his closest thing to coherent speech.

"Ha . . . Yo . . . Man . . ."

Ethan flinched, recovering enough to muster eye contact and a fleeting smile, turning over the sounds but failing to make sense of them. The speaker's head continued to bob, his voluminous golden mullet flowing like a lion's mane. Ethan glanced at the second youth who now glared, thin-lipped, at his friend, then turned to offer an unenthusiastic *hello*.

"Afternoon," Ethan responded without stopping. He achieved his door, opened it and slipped in, locking and latching it before setting his luggage on the carpet. He tried to resume normal breathing.

Let's hope I don't see them again.

He looked around the dark room and found the switch. The flickering bulb didn't reveal much, only dimly lighting the bed to his left, the television at the bed's foot, the desk to Ethan's immediate right. In the back, the mirror and bathroom door were left entirely to darkness. The room smelled of moisture.

Well, this is certainly pushing it.

Ethan first inspected the bathroom. The sink and mirror occupied a portion of the main area's backwall while the toilet and shower enjoyed the privacy of their own room—although the door didn't latch and popped open no matter how firmly he closed it. Ethan toed open the toilet lid to expose the flaky brown bowl. He held his breath as he pressed down on the plastic handle: a soft roar as the water twirled down the drain and was promptly replaced.

At least there's that.

He decided to wait on testing the shower, instead returning to the main room where he removed a sleeping bag and pillow from his luggage and spread them out on top of the covers. He knew better than to trust the motel cleaning staff on these matters. He couldn't show up to his first trial with something growing on his face.

Ethan next set his briefcase on the desk and opened it, removing a clear plastic box of thumbtacks and a sheet of paper, his projected schedule for the next few weeks, from a bulging manilla folder. Mrs. Warland had sat with him for an entire afternoon setting it out: ten days of trial each boxed out and divided into morning and afternoon sessions; minute blurbs advised what would be accomplished during each time slot. Underneath each day's schedule was a list of things Ethan was to review and prepare each night broken down to six-minute increments. When it was completed, Mrs. Warland urged her mentee not to get flustered when—she repeated that, stopping to look at him over her glasses after pronouncing WHEN—things got off track. Ethan had said he understood but still obsessed over the schedule. It alone served as the framework by which he could render the next few weeks of uncertainty into something predictable, digestible, and comprehensible. Framework in hand, Ethan stepped up on the desk chair, pausing for a second before tacking it into the wall. With no card on file, motel management would go straight to Margo-*tuh* with any incidentals.

Ethan shrugged.

She won't care if—no, when we win.

He continued pulling out and pinning papers until the manilla folder was empty and the wall above the desk resembled a dangling, ten-tentacled rainbow octopus. *Dectopus*, Ethan guessed. Coordinated snippets of colored yarn branched off each day to connect important points, facts, pieces of evidence, and deposition testimony. Each day, even those in which the plaintiff was presenting its case, had its purpose, every moment was building to something.

Ethan texted Mrs. Warland to advise of his arrival, then called his father.

"Aye! You've made it to the lawless mountains."

"Just set down my bags."

"Did you stop by the courthouse?"

"I did. Had to formulate my plan of attack for Monday morning."

"And how is the hotel? I have to believe the insurance companies put their counsel," Arthur McDaniel loved this word, "up somewhere nice."

"You'd think that. But actually it's . . . um . . . well, technically I think it's a motel. It's definitely not nice."

"A motel? A Folkston motel? With doors on the outside?"

"Yes."

"Is it decent?"

"Decent's a stretch. It's . . . pretty dingy."

"Dingy. How dingy?"

"I don't know . . . substantially dingy."

"How's the carpet?"

"What?"

"I learned this when I used to go on business trips: the carpet is the absolute best way to tell how frequently and thoroughly a hotel room is cleaned. Is your carpet dirty or gritty?"

"I'm still wearing shoes. But the motel is in some weird sand pit, so probably."

"What about stained? Is the carpet stained?"

Ethan examined the thin, variably dark red carpet. "The light doesn't really make it down that far, but it's definitely . . . splotchy."

"Spilled drink splotchy or bodily fluid splotchy?"

"It's hard to say. It just seems to have darker, kinda brown areas."

"Then it's probably blood. That's not a good sign. Can't you call the manager? Maybe you can at least switch rooms."

"I don't think there is a manager. There was no one in the office midday on a Saturday. My key was just taped to the window. And I can't go back outside, there're people loitering."

"Loitering!? What kind of people?"

"I don't know, Dad. The kind of people you'd expect to see loitering about a rural motel. They looked very comfortable on the walkway. I get the feeling they live here. Like one of those 'extended stay' things you see on the news."

"People live there? You mean like roustabouts?"

"It's hard to say. I've never heard that word before."

"Well, do you have to stay there? Is it a clause in your contract?"

"Contract? There's no contract. But I'm not going to pay for my own place."

"I'll pay, son. Roustabouts are a distraction. You don't need distractions during your big first trial. Your mother and I will see if there's another more suitable establishment nearby and get you set up properly."

"Please don't."

"I can't let you just stay there. It might be dangerous. Folkston has a massive drug problem. They just did a big feature on it in the paper. Our church does mission trips up there to help out."

"Dad, I don't want to be *that* associate. I want them to think I'm a team player. That I'm easy. This is what they've picked for me, and this is where I'll stay. Besides, I've got a lot to do today, so I'd really rather just get to work. We can reassess if something comes up."

There was silence on the other end of the phone. "Okay. I think that's a good point. I'm proud to hear you're thinking like that. Office dynamics are incredibly important. As is how you're perceived by your superiors, and co-workers. Just promise me you'll lock your door."

"First thing I did."

"And try not to add any of your blood to the carpet."

"Things will have really taken a turn if I end up bleeding on this carpet."

"Oh! And keep your light off, too. At night. Make it look like no one's staying there."

"That will make it tough to read my case file."

"*Crystal methamphetamine*, Ethan. That's what the paper said they use up there. Meth. The paper said it makes people get real skinny, lose all their teeth, and go crazy. It makes people get violent for no reason." Ethan thought back to the swaying young man with the meager belly. "But I'm certain they wouldn't put you up somewhere where you might be in danger."

"I doubt they did any research. They probably just went with the cheapest option."

"Well, in any event, please steer clear of all that nonsense."

"You're worried about me taking up meth during the trial?"

"Not so much that. I trust you. It's the addicts that are the problem. The paper talked about some no-good junkie who just happened across this complete stranger and—"

"Dad, I really can't right now."

"Okay, okay." Arthur McDaniel swallowed. "So, what's the plan? I assume you're meeting with the other attorneys tomorrow to really fine tune your defenses. Turn the screws on these whiny, over-entitled bastards." Ethan's father had never cursed in front of him during his childhood—it would have clashed mightily with his crisp golf shirts, cheery demeanor, and incessant harangues on useful, immaculate living. When he did so now, in what Ethan assumed was a show of earned adult camaraderie, it clanged artificial and only set his son on edge.

"There's nothing scheduled. I'll be reviewing on my own. I'm not even sure they're in town."

"They haven't reached out?"

"No, sir."

"Have you reached out to them?"

"I sent them an e-mail about a preparatory meeting earlier this week, but they never responded."

"Hmm. I do get the feeling Sterling Colt doesn't play well with others."

Ethan leaned away from the phone and narrowed his eyes at the speaker. "What evidence do you have of that?"

"Well, he was at a big firm, a prestigious firm, for a good while, made partner and all that, but now it's just him and three very young associates none of whom have been there more than two years."

"You looked him up?"

"And Mrs. Nelson."

"Why? They're not even with my firm."

"I wanted to learn more about your case and make sure you're in good hands. Mr. Colt is certainly a very impressive man. Lots and lots of experience. Lots and lots of high-profile wins. Former President of the South Carolina Trial Attorneys Association. But, based on what I can find, I have a sneaking suspicion he likes being in charge and doesn't enjoy being challenged or second guessed. There's safety, security, stability at a big firm and I don't know why else he'd leave it to strike out on his own. Especially after being there so long."

"I've seen him in action, Dad. He's marvelous. A bulldog. A man of action. I think the firm was the problem and he just got tired of the bureaucracy and politics. He does things his own way which, based on what I've seen, is usually the right way."

"If he was in the right, then why did no one follow him out? They couldn't have all been bad."

Ethan had no response to this. He felt himself balling up a chunk of the comforter in his fist.

"In any event," the elder McDaniel continued, "Mrs. Nelson is still at her firm and seems to be on her way to a respectable career. Lots of accolades on her attorney profile as well."

"She's a very capable attorney too, but nowhere near the level of Mr. Colt."

"But neither has responded to you?"

"Correct."

"And you're not going to contact them again?"

"Correct."

"What does Mrs. Warland say?"

"She pretty bluntly told me to keep them in sight but stay out of their way. So I'm not gonna push it."

"But she wants you to be present, right? Learn and report?"

"Her phrase is *dry run*. Take swings from the on-deck circle. She wants me to, as much as possible, pretend like I'm running the trial and get familiar with the process, the turns, and the stress."

"Smart lady."

"I have to agree."

"Have you spoken with her since you've arrived?"

"I just texted her, let her know I'm here, but that's it. I'll check in tomorrow. See if she has any last-minute instructions."

"Smart." A moment of silence; Ethan's mind drifted to his next meal. "So . . . have you seen it yet?"

"Lake Marie?"

"Yes."

"No."

"Damn."

Big Chuck Palwagon was the third man in the McDaniel household, holding court every Saturday morning to transport the McDaniel men to a new lake, a new town, and introduce them to a new set of locals. Two Chuck Palwagon posters, both signed, hung in the garage, standing guard over their fishing tackle. Father and son McDaniel could be bickering to the point of a duel and the mention of *Wettin' the Line with Chuck Palwagon* would bring them to the couch.

"I tried re-tracing the intro, but couldn't find the final turn off. That might be another myth. Or at least impossible in this case. I ended up just driving out into the sticks."

"Ah. I couldn't make heads or tails of it either."

"You're not visiting Folkston. Why'd you even try?"

"To see if I could spot something useful for you. All of a sudden he's just driving up to the water. What are you supposed to do with that? You can't even tell if it's a dirt or gravel road."

"It's gonna be hell being this close to Lake Marie and not being able to get out there. Especially in the fall."

"You'll be preoccupied soon, I'm sure."

"Let's hope. I'm not entirely sure where I'll eat here. The only things I saw were a fried chicken place and a gas station diner."

"What about Chuck's local greaser, Jane's?"

"Jeanie's. I got the impression that's not on Main Street, and I couldn't find anything about it online. That will have to be a different excursion once I know the area a little better."

"You'll figure it out. Talk to the security guards at the courthouse. Find your local." This was a Chuck Palwagon phrase.

"Sure, Dad."

"Locals know best." Another verse from the Book of Palwagon which Ethan repeated aloud. Early in every episode, just after he'd rolled into town while giving a brief description of his next stop through his truck window, Big Chuck would ask a resident fisherman, *his local*, for advice on locations, techniques, and lures. "Ask questions. Form friendships. Scope it out so we'll know where to go when we go up there together. When you're not in trial mode."

"Lake Marie. The legend. Folks had been clamoring for Chuck Palwagon to come here for years and then he had a field day when he finally did."

"Season finale."

"Always the best spot."

"I still think you should've brought your rods. Like Chuck says, the best fishing is unplanned. But I'll let you get back to it. Remember to learn as much as you can because you're building something this week. This trial will be the knowledge foundation on which you construct your entire career."

"I am."

"Every day is another brick."

"Every day is another brick, yes sir." Ever since elementary school, this line had closed every father-son conversation. As a joke, Mrs. McDaniel had embroidered it onto a throw pillow which, much to her chagrin, had found a permanent home on the living room couch.

"That's how everything worthwhile is built: brick by brick. Every mistake, a lesson. Every lesson, a brick. And it's in the hottest conditions that the best bricks are forged."

"Right. That's why I better get to it."

"Of course, of course. You know, it's a shame that town hasn't made a better first impression. If they were smart, they'd have put out the red carpet."

"Red carpet?"

"Yea. They should be wining and dining you. Trying to get you to stay. A sensible, educated, hard-working young man like you could do a lot of good in that little town."

"Thanks, Dad. Love you."

"Love you too, litigator. Give 'em hell."

Ethan had been standing on the thin strip of carpet separating the TV stand from the foot of the bed. He now sat down at the desk to review the dectopus. Saturday wasn't listed. Mrs. Warland had refused to go this far, but Ethan had mentally designated Saturday evening for broad, overarching review, the idea being he would refresh himself on big picture themes before drilling down into the details on Sunday. Despite Mrs. Warland's advice that he remain a passive observer, Ethan was intent on proving himself. He had been present for and briefed every deposition, hearing, and site visit. He knew the case as well as anyone and was determined to find the fabled "smoking gun" that would completely unravel Kurt Bickerman's case. He pulled out the red binder marked *PLEADINGS* and turned to the original Complaint.

First came the crisp, synthesized *pop*, akin to someone pulling the tab on an electronic soda can, which Ethan recognized but couldn't quite place.

A moment of silence.

A few soft clicks.

Then the shooting started. Quick bursts of gunfire separated by the scurrying of footsteps and the occasional explosion. The framed mountain landscapes and fruit bowls rattled on either side of the television. Theme music pulsed underneath the gunfire and death groans. He recognized it as the score from *Cosmic Encounters*, an alien "shoot 'em up" video game he'd played in college. A game that rarely got played for fewer than six hours at a time.

Oh no . . .

Ethan gathered the pleadings binder and retreated to the head of the bed. It was no use. During the quiet moments, he could hear the banter of the background characters and the fake, gravelly crunch of the kill sergeant's footfalls. The intermittent skirmishes rumbled his eardrums. The grenades and beam rockets threatened the drywall.

A peek through the curtains confirmed that night had fallen, and that the loitering youths had departed, or perhaps just moved down the walkway and out of sight. Either way, Ethan had no intention of leaving the room.

I can at least eat during this. Maybe I'll get lucky and he'll only be playing a quick mission.

Ethan slipped to the front of the bed to remove an insulated lunch cooler from his suitcase, carefully shifting the contents until he could lift a frozen chicken wrap he had brought along in case of late-night hunger. He used a pushpin to poke holes in the wrap's packaging and set it in the microwave, pressed the appropriate buttons, turned around, then turned back. The screen had beeped in acknowledgment of his fingers, and now counted backwards from three minutes, but there was no low artificial *whirr* generally associated with the uneven warming of food stuffs. The microwave's interior remained unlit. Ethan opened it, closed it—the countdown resumed but again unaccompanied by light and motion. He hit cancel and restarted the entire process. Once more, the countdown restarted independent of both light and heat.

Ethan removed the still cold wrap.

Fucking Margo-tuh.

He examined the room for other options; finding none, he settled on wrapping his dinner in toilet paper and setting it under the clothing iron, after first confirming it actually got hot. He flipped the wrap at approximately halfway to provide what Ethan considered his best chance at even heating.

When the second side of toilet paper began to smolder, he rolled the wrap onto a napkin and sat back down to review the pleadings, losing his place every time an explosion jarred him to distraction. He briefly considered risking a trip outside to knock on the neighboring door but his father's meth talk, combined with the roustabouts, kept his door closed and locked. In a moment of inspiration, Ethan shredded an additional square of toilet paper, rolled the strips into two balls, and pushed them into his ears.

This will be a war story one day.

You're building something.

Brick by brick.

Screams and a fresh explosion.

Brick. By. Fucking brick.

After a fruitless hour, during which the makeshift earbuds fell, were redesigned and replaced, and Ethan had suffered through a smoky frozen chicken wrap tasting vaguely of bathroom, he threw the binder to the carpet to glare at the trembling wall. Even with the sun having set and the light off, the room remained well lit; some nearby light source made his window glow orange. Ethan flipped on the television, which worked, sifting through channels until he found baseball, something which could be enjoyed, or at least comprehended, without sound.

The booming continued past the ninth inning.

Chapter Three

The next morning, Ethan, despite lacking in both sleep and sustenance, peeled himself out of his sleeping bag at his 6 a.m. alarm, and unspooled his yoga mat at the foot of the bed for upper body day. Once the unidentifiably splotched carpet was covered, Ethan did a set of pushups, a set of abs, then additional pushups. If he were at home, or had Sapphire Courts offered a gym, there would have been more variety. As it was, he simply repeated pushups-abs-pushups-abs until the entirety of his pale top half ached and glistened. He cooled down with stretching, used a cold shower to blanche any residual sweating, then dressed for the day: a polo shirt tucked into khaki shorts. He left the room in search of fresh coffee and hygienically-heated breakfast, pausing to inspect the noisy neighboring room. It appeared to be significantly larger, extending for the building's duration. The door was several steps away from Ethan's; the grey knob and cracked blue paint provided no additional information regarding 218's inhabitant.

Hopefully, he's not a permanent roustabout.

Hopefully, he checks out tonight.

Ethan pivoted to look out over the parking lot. On the ground underneath him, directly in front of the sham office, a semi-circle of large, pinkish bricks cordoned off a small area of marginally healthier grass and a rusted fire ring. The deep black char in the ring suggested recent and frequent use. A streetlight jutted out of the grass just past the office, its upside-down *L*-shape placed the presently unlit bulb at roof level just outside Ethan's window.

That explains the bright night.

Further out, in the skewed strip separating the Sapphire Courts grounds from Main Street a tragically short and physics defyingly front heavy woman held the leash to a tiny terrier sniffing its way through the crab grass. The woman wasn't near Ethan's car, but dragged her dog to intercept him.

"Are you the new boy in 217?"

"I . . ." Ethan hesitated to confirm his room number, and wondered how she knew it. "Yes."

"Nightly or a monthly?"

"Ma'am?"

"How long you rent the room? For nights or for months? Mr. Macadoo, the owner, does both, but nothing longer or in between."

"Two weeks. I'm just in town for a trial. I'm an attorney."

The woman nodded; her short hair didn't budge. "He must've made an exception for you. I'm Deborah." She pronounced it *Duh-bore-uh*. "I've been a monthly for ten years." She laughed too long.

"I'm Ethan." He hoped to get away with just his first name.

"So you're headed to the courthouse?"

"Not today. I think it's closed. It's Sunday."

"That's the courthouse there. It's just over yonder." She gestured to her left.

"I saw it. It's hard to—"

"Just right there. Short drive. You can even walk if you want. You know, depending if you want to. Not too hot anymore. Sometimes though."

"I'm just getting break—"

"If you drive, there is parking . . . it's a big lot . . . it can get full though. If that happens you can park on the side streets. They don't usually fill up . . . sometimes people in suits even park here . . . that's rare though. Been years." She spoke in a slow, uneven, halting manner, going on lengthy expeditions for each new word, holding syllables to bridge the silence. On several occasions Ethan thought she had completed her thought, and started to respond, only for her to jump back in, creating the recurring sensation of being cut off. "I'd say you should walk. Just in case . . . not too hot this time of year. Mostly . . . I go there once every couple months to pick up alimony. Walk there. Alimony is through the clerk of court . . . that's in the courthouse too . . . on the first floor."

Ethan marveled at how frustrating, and boring, Deborah was. His attention turned to her dog, whose matted grey-brown fur was clotted with dirt. It peed on the grass, circled around to drag its low belly through the affected area, peed again, walked through that, and peed once more.

Deborah was still going. "Trial's most likely on the fourth floor. When you get there you have to enter the courtroom through the doors . . . sometimes there is a line. Not always though . . . You can't carry nothin' and the guards make you take everything out of your pockets and go through the metal detector. It's about the size of a door . . . you should be able to fit . . . men have to take their belts off. Might be different for lawyers. I can't say for certain . . . I don't know . . . I ain't a lawyer."

This pause grew into a full stop.

Ethan burst into his parting remarks. "Yep. I think walking is a good idea. I will figu—"

"Do you eat breakfast?"

"It's okay. I'm ab—"

"Because we have restaurants. Breakfast restaurants . . . there's Bogie's just over there. It's right by the courthouse . . . almost . . . no breakfast though." The sun strengthened; beads of sweat boiled up in Ethan's hair, preparing for their journeys down to collar and eyebrow. "—Polly Kin's is good too. My favorite, actually. You should definitely go there . . . they don't have breakfast either. Now Lucious' is great. And has breakfast." She raised a finger. "But it's far. Two towns over. So it ain't technically in Folkston . . . closed on Sunday too."

"It's really okay. I appreciate all the inform—"

"Do you drink coffee?"

"I do but—"

Deborah expounded on the history of Folkston coffee, taking care to delineate between the actual coffee shop, which was closed on Sundays, and the establishments which merely served coffee, many of which were also closed. Down below, the dog picked up a scent which led it meandering through its territory where it finally ended up at Ethan's left sneaker. The dog sniffed the shoe, licked it, made eye contact with Ethan, then drove its tiny teeth into the ventilating mesh around his big toe. Ethan kicked his foot back, but the dog came with it, growling and writhing its billiard ball-sized head back and forth to free the ensnared tooth.

"Frumpy no." Deborah made no move to retrieve or assist.

Ethan set his foot down and leaned over to press down on the mesh on either side, pulling it apart to widen the hole. Frumpy gave a final snarl and violent twist, freeing the tooth. Her head bounced off the gravel then back up to snap at the liberating fingers, then make another run at the shoe. Ethan jumped back and kept walking, keeping two eyes on the mutt.

"Sorry," Deborah said.

"Old shoes anyway. I'm actually just gonna drive and look around. Have a nice day. Bye, Frumpy." He turned his back before she could give the history of Folkston dog bites.

In the name of expediency, and avoiding indecision, Ethan drove directly to a fast-food restaurant on the highway two towns over. When he returned to the parking lot, Deborah had been replaced by an athletic looking older man loading a fishing rod and associated gear into the bed of a miniscule green truck. Ethan examined the man through the coupe's window. He had on a well-worn flannel shirt, unbuttoned to expose an equally faded and stained t-shirt, old jeans, and a weathered ball cap. On many an episode, Chuck Palwagon had pointed at such a man through the window of his behemoth truck and proudly exclaimed *now here's my local.* Ethan exited the coupe, searching for an excuse to initiate conversation as he walked across the lot. The man stopped loading and leaned against the tailgate as Ethan passed.

"You've got out-of-state plates."

Ethan glanced at his plates: Oklahoma, a state he'd never visited. "Oh. It's just a rental. I'm actually from Charleston."

"Charleston? Shit. Don't tell me you beach folk are vacationing here now."

"Only the fishermen, sir." This felt like a good way to bait the hook. "But I'm travelling for work."

"A working man, is it?" The man's smile was well-worn, comprised of a thousand deep lines and creases. *Here's my local.* "And what line of work brings you to Folkston?"

"I'm an attorney."

His local's face darkened. "A divorce attorney?" His voice lost any hints of warmth.

"No sir. Strictly civil defense. I'm actually in town for a trial." To Ethan's relief, the local smile reignited. The man's right hand left his pocket and extended for a handshake.

"Pleasure to meet you. Name's Tuck." He took Ethan's hand in a firm grip.

"Ethan McDaniel." *Here's my local.*

"Do you fish, Mr. McDaniel? I have to assume even attorneys don't work on Sundays."

Here's my local. "I do, sir—"

"Tuck."

"Tuck, sorry. Mostly saltwater, but I'd love to try my hand around here. My father and I have Lake Marie on our bucket list."

"Well then, hop in, let's have ourselves a time."

Ethan's eyes sucked in the scuffed pickup, the fishing rods, the local. "You're going to Lake Marie now?"

"I am."

Ethan's next words were difficult. "Unfortunately, I do have to work today. Trial starts tomorrow, which means lots of preparation."

"Have it your way, son. Hope it's an important trial." Tuck set his tackle box in the bed. A blue coupe dipped into the lot. Both men's heads turned to watch its male driver wavelessly pass by to park on the far side. "Bet they would've shelled out for an older fellow."

"Excuse me?"

"Whoever's paying for you to stay here. At this shit-hole. They wouldn't pull that on a greybeard."

"Oh, it's not so . . ." Ethan couldn't finish the sentence.

"Damn shame. Let me know if you need anything. I'm just down the way." He pointed at the door next to the office. "One seventeen."

"Thanks. Enjoy your fishing."

"Ain't no point in livin' if you ain't enjoying it, son."

The pair disengaged.

On the lot's far side, a fat, bearded man in a much-too-tight t-shirt lifted a series of grocery bags from the coupe and began trudging towards the stairwell. Ethan kept walking, measuring his step to arrive comfortably after the man, who kept his head down, taking no notice of Ethan despite arriving at the staircase only several yards ahead. He hummed to himself; Ethan recognized the tune from the video game.

And here's my neighbor.

Ethan followed him up the stairs and down the exterior walkway. The man stopped at the door for 218 and fumbled through his key ring. When Ethan put his key in his own door, the man started, then looked Ethan up and down.

"Who are you?"

"I'm Ethan."

The fat man looked over his shoulder at the truck exiting the lot. "You a friend of Tuck's?"

"No, sir. We just met. I'm an attorney in town for a trial."

"Sir?" The man checked over his shoulder then squinted at Ethan. "And you're staying here?"

Ethan nodded.

"That sucks."

Ethan could only shrug.

"I'm Garth. Garth Quattlebaum."

"Ethan McDaniel."

Garth studied Ethan for another moment. His brown hair was laughably, and almost certainly intentionally, disheveled. Ethan recognized the logo on his shirt as being from a fictional cereal brand featured in an old sitcom. Ethan wished the man would either look away or resume entering his room so Ethan could do the same. But his dark eyes stayed set on Ethan, his brow furrowed. Then the dark eyes opened all the way.

"Shit man, were you here last night?"

"Yes. I arrived yesterday afternoon."

Garth sighed. "Well fuck, why didn't you say anything? At least pound on the goddam wall. I didn't know there was anybody there. Nobody ever actually stays here."

"Oh, it's okay. I didn't want to intrude."

"Intrude? I was the one intruding."

"It really wasn't . . . um . . ."

"Bullshit. How loud was it?"

"When you were conquering Seran, it sounded like you were using the radial blaster. I've always had better success with the dual laser pistollas."

Garth smiled. "I'll keep that in mind."

"It's really okay, but please don't do it on a school night."

"Ten-four," Garth's smile widened. He laughed to himself. "This conversation would have been much more uncomfortable if you heard what I was doing Friday night. Hoo boy. Would you like to come in for some coffee? Or a beer? I certainly owe you one."

"I'm all set, thanks."

"Or some multi-player? Sounds like you could help me out."

"It's okay. Thank you, though. I really need to get to work."

"It is Sunday morning."

"I have a trial this week. My first trial. So I really need to prepare."

"Dinner then. My treat. Even lawyers need to eat."

"I really don't have time to go anywhere. It's alright."

"Well, how 'bout this?" Garth pushed his door open revealing something approaching a full sized and fully furnished apartment. "Does your room have a full kitchen?"

Garth's apartment was at least three times the size of Ethan's. The door swung inward, nearly hitting the threadbare arm of a deep-set beige-orange couch facing Ethan's shared wall. A flat-screen TV and an arsenal of thick black speakers explained the thoroughness of last night's sound intrusion. Fitted in between the television, speakers, and adjacent walls was a plethora of shelves, each loaded with pristinely stacked DVDs and video games. In line with the couch was a black leather arm chair and, closer to the wall, a bright purple bean bag chair. Everything was in service of the television.

Ethan's eyes followed Garth who had already stepped into the combination kitchen-laundry room. The kitchen was existent but miniscule. A solitary square of formica served as half the counterspace; the lid of the washing machine served as the rest. While the apartment wasn't necessarily clean, it was, to Ethan's surprise, clean enough, and devoid of any obvious biohazards. All in all, Ethan was struck by how much Garth's Sapphire Courts apartment resembled the rooms of his law school chums.

A poster on the far wall caught Ethan's eye: an ultra-rare collectible original run *Dalton Stampede: A Fist in the Darkness* holographic print. Faced head on, the action hero stood bare chested, staring down all who entered Garth's apartment; viewers from either side would perceive an action shot of Stampede mid-leaping roundhouse, his face a strained grimace. In both poses, his iconic feathered blonde hair and chiseled biceps glistened against a wall of flames. The tagline, in big black letters, read, *Criminals Best Mullet Over*.

Ethan proudly owned the same poster.

"That's a great poster."

"Don't I know it."

"I actually have the same one."

"No shit. I didn't have you pegged as a Stampeder."

"It's true. I watch all six movies every quarter."

Garth's eyes narrowed. "Prove it. Which movie is the worst?"

Ethan pointed at the poster.

"Right. And which movie's poster is the most coveted?"

Ethan's hand didn't drop.

"Good on you. Do you proudly display your poster in your living room?"

"No . . . um," Ethan scratched at his chin, "mine's actually tucked in the closet."

"So you're ashamed? That must be stressful."

"It's to prevent unnecessary light damage."

"Tell yourself what you want. I've got mine facing the door so everyone knows what I'm about. Dinner's on then. You can trust a fellow Stampeder."

Ethan hesitated.

"Does your room have a full kitchen?"

"No. Actually, the microwave's broken."

"Of course the microwave's broken. Earl Macadoo's a cheap piece of shit. You come over here around . . . what time do lawyers eat? Six-thirty? And I'll have dinner ready for you. Won't take any time at all."

Ethan looked over the man's apartment once more.

I do have to eat. And it doesn't look threatening. Garth certainly doesn't.

Garth continued. "You let me cook you dinner or I'm gonna embark on the Endless Quest of the Shrieking Sirens. Full volume, the long route."

"I'd love to join you for dinner."

"Wonderful," Garth looked over Ethan's golf shirt tucked into his belted khaki shorts. "See if you can dress down."

Chapter Four

Ethan spent the remainder of the morning and entirety of the afternoon rooting through his case file, honing his outlines until he had them tight and freshly memorized. The hope that his neighbor's knock would never come tip-toed into his mind and took hold; partly because any time spent away from his case file seemed like time wasted, but mostly because when Garth Quattlebaum wasn't standing directly in front of him, he melded into the general shadiness and uncertainty of Sapphire Courts, and thus devolved into a creature whose lair it would be unwise to visit.

The knock came promptly at six-thirty.

"Spare some time for free food?" The man was still disheveled, but did not appear dangerous. "If I have to argue my position, the food'll burn."

"I'm coming. Just one second." Ethan fired off a text to his dad:

I'm going to eat at my neighbor's, Garth Quattlebaum, in Sapphire Courts room 218. If you don't hear from me in two hours call the police.

He shoved his phone in his pocket; it vibrated before he could take a seat on Garth's couch.

"How'd you manage to get the big room?"

"I pay more. This is the Sapphire Courts Presidential Suite." Garth pulled a sizzling cast iron pan from the stove and placed it in the oven. "I let my burgers rest for a bit. Helps 'em rejuicify." The room was thick with the smell of cooked meat.

"Yea, I do that as well. Always good to let proteins rest."

"Alright then. Before you get your mouth all stuffed up, tell me about this trial."

"You don't want to hear about it."

"Big city lawyers are converging on my small, impressionable town, which almost exclusively means trouble. I'd appreciate you putting my mind at ease." Garth didn't speak with an accent so much as a congenial growl. His voice, even in jest, betrayed a violent temper.

"My client runs a trash company—"

"Shit. Stop. Stop right there." Garth pushed his hands down his thighs. "You're here for that bullshit? Your client is Emmett Lucas."

"How did you know?"

"Everybody knows. Every damned soul in Folkston knows. Emmett got a little loose with where he stashed his old trash cans, started storing them on Kurt Bickerman's land thinking it was just woods and nobody would mind. Then apparently out of nowhere Kurt gets it into his head to turn his family land into a mountain resort and, to hear him say it, had the whole thing lined up until the development company visited the property and saw what Emmett had done. They pulled out and now Kurt's trying to get his money out of Lucas Trash. That about the gist of it?"

"That's a big part of the allegations. But there's also the smell. Plaintiff, Mr. Bickerman, claims that's what really killed his land deal."

"Right, right the smell. The smell that fouled up Bickerman's dumb ass Mountain Retreat pipe dream. Well, no one else wanted a fucking luxury resort just outside of downtown bringing snotty ass tourists here to tell us what we're doing wrong."

Ethan noted this; the defense team had been concerned that the Folkston locals were excited about the tourism, jobs, and prosperity Bickerman's resort would bring.

If the jury didn't want the resort in the first place, they will be less sympathetic to Bickerman's claims.

Garth continued, "Hell, Kurt didn't even want the damn thing."

"What do you mean?" This was news to Ethan.

"He's got family, cousins or something, that made themselves a pile of money making downtown Greenville pretty. Word is they're pulling the strings on Kurt to do the same thing here. He went along with it thinking it'd be easy and now he's stuck in the mud with you."

"Kurt Bickerman didn't come up with idea himself?" Ethan had sat in on both days of Kurt Bickerman's deposition during which he clearly and somewhat overly proudly testified that he alone had come up with the idea for a resort and had done the legwork before reaching out to the development company.

The smoking gun! We can impeach Bickerman with his own unambiguous deposition testimony. His credibility will be ruined. Not to mention, the whole development plan will be viewed as outsider meddling.

"That's the word."

"Whose word? How . . . how did you come to know this?"

"Ain't nothing but local gossip. Scuttlebutt. The only thing I can confirm first hand is that Kurt Bickerman is not particularly clever or ambitious." This was not news. Mr. Colt had all but eaten the man during his deposition.

"But do you have any proof? Any evidence?"

"Sure. Let me just get my Bickerman file from the closet. What's it matter, anyway? The deal's dead and the trash cans are gone. Can't you people just move on?"

"Plaintiff is still claiming lost profits from the canceled sale in addition to nuisance claims, trespass claims, and claims for tortious interference with a contract."

Garth mouthed the word *tortious.* "All that over some fuckin' trash cans?"

"Is there someone that would know first-hand that Bickerman's family in Greenville actually initiated all of this? Someone with some documents or e-mails?"

"I'm not sure what you're looking for, but it's one of those things that people in a small town just know. Before all this, Kurt Bickerman's never done nothing outside work but collect birdhouses."

"But who told you all that about his family?"

"Wouldn't tell you if I remembered." Garth said this with a note of finality. Ethan decided to back off but made a mental note to take a more nuanced approach at a later time. "But let me ask you this," Garth continued, "have you fools actually been out to Lucas Trash?"

"A couple of times, yes. We visited the buildings and walked the perimeter. Mr. Bickerman's property too."

"And after multiple visits you nitwits still can't decide whether that piece of land smells?"

"It gets more complicated when you have to prove it. We, the defense, had our expert there to observe, take samples. He opined that there is an insufficient ratio of particulates in the air to result in a detectable odor."

"This is an expert in whether or not something smells?"

"Essentially, yes. He has a doctorate in—"

"Fragrance? I don't care. You got a smart guy with letters after his name saying there's no detectable odor?"

"That's right."

"Well, that's that then."

"But the plaintiff has an expert too. He was out there on the same day, nasally observed the premises, took air samples, ran some tests with his instruments, and came to the opposite conclusion."

"He smelled something?"

"His tests detected a high level of particulates. As such, he opined that the property is prohibitively odorous."

"Prohibitively odorous . . ." Garth scratched his beard. "But did the bastard smell something?"

"That's not exactly how it works. For what it's worth, Mr. Bickerman's attorney has also retained a topological climatologist to explain how the two properties are geographically situated such that any wind-blown particulates from Lucas would accumulate and persist on and over Mr. Bickerman's."

"Jesus. Shit really hits the fan once you lawyers get involved. How about the obvious question: did you smell anything?"

Ethan worked his mouth, scanning the room before answering. "It is a trash company and some odor is to be expected. Mr. Lucas has every right to conduct his business on his property in a reasonable manner. I will say that there was no reason for opposing counsel and his client to make a show of walking around with handkerchiefs held to their noses."

"Okay, enough of all that." Garth removed the cast iron and a previously undetected pan of bacon from the oven and started assembling the burgers. "Are you able to detect this smell? Do you need your expert to confirm that this smells fucking awesome?"

"In my lay opinion, it smells very good."

"No, it smells fucking awesome. I'll sue you if you say any different. So," Garth said setting the plates on the coffee table, "is this really what you've signed on to do, all that extra schoolin' so you can squabble over whether somebody else's property smells?"

"I can't say I had this specifically in mind, but you've got to start somewhere. Mr. Lucas' case is just the first brick."

"First brick? Haven't you already gone to law school and taken that test? First brick in what?"

"It's my first trial. That's a huge career moment. As long as Mr. Bickerman's attorney directly examines three witnesses, we cross at least one, and Plaintiff rests his case on the record, I'll officially be a trial attorney. Technically, the defense doesn't even have to call any witnesses."

"Says who?"

"The South Carolina Trial Attorneys Association."

"I reckon they'd know. And what bricked structure are you building?"

Ethan paused, realizing he'd never actually considered the obvious question to the McDaniel creed. "A career. A legal career."

Garth grimaced. "Ain't that somethin'. A career of bricks. You want a beer?"

"Just water, please."

"Right, right. Gotta stay sober for the trash. Can't smell no good when you're under the influence."

Garth set a glass of water in front of Ethan, keeping a foam-topped, sitcom-themed stein for himself.

Ethan inspected his burger: grease, juice, and melted cheese had already saturated the bottom bun, leaving it a grey mush. On top, the formidably crispy bacon provided the sesame seed bun with significant clearance over any moisture. The patty was clearly the fattier variety of ground beef. He made a quick calculation of the calories, fats, and cholesterol—there would be extra work tomorrow morning. Not wanting to appear rude, Ethan gripped the burger, sending his fingers deep into the muck. In addition to being wet, the beast was too big. Ethan struggled to find an angle at which to finagle it into his mouth. One seat over, Garth mashed his burger into his, coming up with a beard full of grease and wetted bun bits. Ethan tried to more delicately perform the same maneuver; the juice flowed down his cheeks nonetheless. The burger was rare, red in the middle and lukewarm in the mouth, but struck an unnuanced, homemade burger chord which transported Ethan back to his childhood. The restaurant burgers of his adulthood were much more subtle, nuanced, and delicate.

Garth's burger disappeared without ever returning to the plate. "So how does this all play out?" He dabbed his chin and cheeks with a wadded paper towel. "Tomorrow you go in and give your opening ceremony or whatever?" Ethan wondered if Garth deliberately waited for him to take a bite; he smirked as Ethan quickened his chewing and covered his mouth.

"Maybe. Tomorrow we definitely pick a jury and argue any remaining pre-trial motions. I'm not sure what order that happens in. I think it's up to the judge. After all that, depending on the time, we will move on to opening statements."

"You want to practice?"

"Practice what?"

"Your lines. The opening thing. You have a captive local audience. Might as well make use of it. And I'm interested to hear what a Charleston attorney has to say about Folkston."

"I'm not actually delivering the opening statement."

"Okay, sure. That makes sense. So your boss is?"

"Not quite. It's kind of unusual, complicated. For whatever reason, Mr. Lucas cycled through lots of insurance carriers. The insurance carriers are who actually selects the lawyers. So there are three different carriers with time on the risk. Each carrier retained its own attorney. Our carrier only insured him for one year over five years ago. We have by far the shortest time on the risk, if any. Almost no exposure."

"Which is why a young attorney such as yourself is handling the trial."

"Kind of, again. It's certainly a great opportunity for a young attorney to observe some very highly-esteemed attorneys in action."

"Observe?"

"Yes, other older attorneys from other carriers have assumed the defense, including giving the opening statements and examination of the witnesses."

"So, what the fuck did you do all day?"

"Prepare and practice. Try to crack the case." *Which we may have just done here tonight.* "I have to prepare and practice as if I'm doing everything. Prepping an opening statement, cross-examinations, arguments, preparing objections. So next time, when I'm running the show, I'll know what to expect."

"Seems like a lot of a practice for a scrimmage."

"I'm also a second, well, third, set of eyes. An additional set of eyes on the case, on the jury, is always useful. And, at minimum, I'm building my knowledge, my experience. Hopefully it keeps me from making some beginner mistakes when I'm first chair."

"That makes it sound like you're the best flute player. But I get it, the brick thing. How long will all this, the trash trial, take?"

Ethan pictured the dectopus schedule on the other side of Garth's wall. "I've prepared for two weeks. That's assuming there's no significant or unexpected pre-trial motions, no jury issues, no delays."

"So . . ."

"I'm told four weeks is a distinct possibility. Each side has multiple experts. In addition to numerous fact witnesses. Apparently, with that many schedules, there's a lot that can go wrong."

"Four weeks of fancy courtroom fussin' over trash and the smelly resort that never was."

"It could also settle tomorrow. Lots of cases settle on the courthouse steps, or during the trial itself."

"Really? All that fucking work and travel just to shake hands smack dab in the middle of the big finale?"

"It happens. Although it's hard to imagine in this case. We are very far apart." Ethan set his sights on his host. "How long have you lived in Folkston?"

"Born and raised. Thirty-nine years."

"And how well do you know Kurt Bickerman?"

"I'd say . . . why?"

"You might be a useful witness." Ethan wasn't sure whether this was a joke.

Garth put down his beer, leaned his shiny beard closer to Ethan, and cleared his throat. "I will fucking kill you." He straightened. "How's your burger?"

"It's good. It might be too big though. I'm not sure I'll be able to finish." Ethan tried to keep eating as a display of gratitude and enjoyment.

"Well don't force it if there ain't room. I know they don't feed you like this down in Charleston. I hear it's all frilly small plate bullshit." Ethan stopped eating, happy that he hadn't offended his host. These free and convenient meals could prove useful when trial was in full swing.

Ethan turned to Garth's hanging posters, the shelves he'd nailed into the wall, and the mounted TV.

"Do you pay extra to hang stuff? I mean, put nails in the walls and all that?"

"No, I've just been here a minute. If I ever move out I'll have to decide whether I want to patch it all up or just tell Earl Macadoo to fuck off."

"Oh, I put some holes in my wall. Pin holes to hold up papers. Do you think Mr. Macadoo will mind?"

Garth laughed. "Mind? No, he doesn't fuss over anything under a twenty-two."

The idea of bullet holes in the interior walls raised a more fundamental concern. "Am I okay staying here? I mean, is this place safe?"

"Sapphire Courts?"

"Yea. I mean no offense, but . . ."

"It's . . ." The *s* turned into a long sigh.

"That might answer my question."

"It's not as bad as you think, city boy. Most folk here are blue collar workers, retirees, and voluntary invalids. Getting rid of the riffraff is one thing Macadoo actually enjoys doing."

"But I still shouldn't wander around at night?"

"I can't claim to be a well-traveled man but is there any real place where that's a good idea? Have you met any of the other neighbors?"

"Two young guys. The kid with the frosted tip mullet and his friend."

"Ah. Frank and Bobby. Bobby's got the ink and the mullet, but he's harmless. He give you any shit?"

"It's hard to say. He kept starting like he was about to say something but ended up just kind of making noises."

"God dammit. That little bastard was cranking his remaining gears trying to think of something clever. He's a nice young man. A friend, actually. But he tries to be clever and chirp, like he sees the other fuckers around here do. It gets him nowhere. Frank's cool though. Good egg. Mostly keeps watch on Bobby. Was it daylight when you saw them?"

"Yes. Yesterday afternoon."

"Good. I hope to God it don't come to this, but if you ever see Bobby after dark, steer clear. Especially if he's not with Frank."

"Why? What happens when he's not with Frank?"

"Like I said, Bobby's a good kid and he's on the right track, but he's working through some shit. This town has not always been a good influence on him."

Ethan tried to picture the skinny mushroom-topped kid turning into a terror. "Right. I'll keep that in mind."

"Anybody else?"

"Oh . . . uh . . . the woman with the yappy dog. Deborah."

"Oh! You got gored by the The Bore . . ." Garth's eyes closed, his head lilted to the side. "Uggghhhhh. I hope you didn't have some place to be."

"I was just hoping to get breakfast."

"But she kept ya till lunch?"

"Long enough for her dog to bite me."

"Oof. She's a genuinely sweet lady. Works at the little bookstores as they open and close on Main Street. But I do everything in my power to avoid her. I can't claim to be a busy man but I ain't got time for that."

I'll have to avoid her from here on out.

Ethan then thought of another way his new acquaintance might be useful. "Do you fish?"

"Can't say that I do."

"Oh, there's good fishing up here. I was hoping to try it out."

Garth smirked. "You looking to wet the line?"

"You watch the show?"

"I'm familiar."

"Do you know Walter Kerps? That's the local who showed Big Chuck around."

"Sure, I know Walt, or at least I see him around. He lives over on Sparrow Street. Let me guarantee you, you will not see him between here and the courthouse. This is not his part of town."

Damn.

Ethan shifted in his seat, pulling the throw pillow from between himself and the armrest. The cursive script sewn into the pillow's face caught his eye.

YOUR NEXT STEP IS ALWAYS THE MOST IMPORTANT

"Sounds like something my dad would say. Did someone knit this for you?"

"That, my friend, is my fortune."

"Inspiring throw pillows?"

"Exactly. Genuinely inspiring throw pillows. Throw pillows always have these useless platitudes, classless, one-size-fits-all scraps of lazy self-serving, good intent. I really hate 'em. So I'm tearing 'em down."

"By making more of them?"

"Check the back."

Ethan flipped the pillow.

GET FUCKED

My dad definitely doesn't say that.

"I don't think I've ever seen a pillow swear before." Ethan had been happier before he'd known this existed. The big, red-threaded swear word was profoundly unsettling.

"That's the dark side of all those platitudes. Because *get fucked* is what all those sugar shooters are really saying—I acknowledge that you're having troubles and have come to me for assistance but rather than taking one single moment of my time to actually assess your singular situation and craft an individualized thoughtful response, I'm just going to blubber out this meaningless pleasantry, smile like a pedantic asshole, and send you on your way."

"How are you going to make money off this?"

"Exactly what you're holding. A line of throw pillows, one side with the cheery bullshit, the other with the hard truth."

"Is every pillow's underside going to say," Ethan lifted the pillow, "this?"

"There will be some variation."

"My word."

"Remember underneath every moronic pull-string feelgoodery, there's a great big *get fucked*."

Chapter Five

Ethan McDaniel was the proud owner of trial socks: a handsome pair of thin ochre silk over-the-calf formals realized from the proceeds of his first paycheck as a licensed attorney. For his first two weeks at Hamel, Collins, Nagurski & Hamel, he'd spent his free moments researching formal footwear, Charleston formal wear, the mercurial nature of style and fashion—more importantly, which styles endured—as well as the most esteemed and sought after sock fabric and the proper procedure for selecting the consummate business sock. He did not want to stumble into a purveyor and rely on a pushy clerk to thrust upon him some trendy, over-designed foot-shaped slip; he wanted to enter the store, and instruct the clerk.

On the day the funds arrived in his account, he'd driven directly from the office to Allred Purveyors, the zenith of Charleston men's formalwear, and simply said: *The Patricians, please.* The clerk offered Ethan a glass of scotch to sip while he measured his feet and pitched Allred's esteemed loyalty program. His parents had provided everything else: suits, shirts, shoes, ties; but not socks, the socks would be truly his.

The Patricians purchased that day remained in their original packaging, sealed off from the deleterious air by a leaf of clear plastic and several grains of a moisture absorbing compound, to be unsealed only when they could be promptly conferred upon a trial-bound foot.

Ethan's alarm went off at five. At seven-thirty, after his leg day routine—with copious additional jumping jacks to atone for Garth's mammoth cheeseburger—and a thorough review of several hundred pages, he showered, shaved, brushed his teeth, and arranged his hair. When he was dry and ready, he pulled on an undershirt and stationed himself in front of the mirror to equip himself for the trials ahead. One choice item at a time, he assumed his first ever trial wardrobe: a fitted white suit shirt; navy blue suit jacket and pants; a calf leather belt; and, a sky blue jacquard floral tie knotted in a perfect Windsor.

It was time.

He sat down on the bed and unsnapped the plastic seal, softly pinching two fingers to guide the silk gems out of their packaging. The Patricians were delicate in his hands, fine, almost translucent, but whole and without blemish. He brushed them with the back of his fingers, then pointed his toes and, inch by inch, ridge by ridge, adorned his feet in the virgin fabric. When both feet had been anointed, he straightened his legs for assessment. *Perfection.* He slid his feet directly into his shined leather wingtips—the Patricians were never to touch this carpet—armed himself with his briefcase, and exited room 217 onto the dusty, grimy, scratchy, and intolerably scuffy Sapphire Courts exterior walkway.

Ethan surveyed the lot from over the handrail: Deborah and Frumpy were out, but at the far end of the lot and thus posed no threat to his path. He began his commute, relishing the Patricians' breathability, as well as the snugness—not tightness—of his leather wingtips, and the close lightness of his suit which moved in tandem with his stride. The morning was his.

He was halfway up the sandy slope, within spitting distance from Main Street, when Deborah caught him.

"Ethan!" She had scooped up Frumpy to make the sprint, clutching the dog to her chest like a football. Ethan was a little sorry he hadn't witnessed her mad dash across the sand. "Are . . . are you on your way to the courthouse?"

The Bore Ugh. "Yes. I'm actually a little late so I—"

"It's okay. I just . . . I heard that you're a part of that . . . that trash trial. And I wanted to let you know . . ." she paused to catch her breath after the scamper. A minivan passed on Main Street as she leaned over to return Frumpy to the ground. Ethan took several steps back. After one final, and long, inhalation and exhalation, she finished her thought. "I wanted to let you know that I think Kurt Bickerman is a greedy jerk. He has no right to do this to Emmett."

"Thank you, the—Deborah but I really do have to go. Have a nice day."

"Good luck!" he heard her yell over his shoulder.

Ethan hurried out of the lot, stopping at the courthouse corner to assess the scene. A mass of rural humanity clad in t-shirts, jeans, sneakers, and scrunched polyester socks, was smeared across the asphalt. Some clustered in small groups, chatting and kicking the dust; a great many others slouched sideways out of their driver's seats to smoke cigarettes. Ethan scouted his prospects.

A select few of these fortunate souls will be foundational bricks in my career as a trial attorney.

He doubted he would ever forget them.

Sterling Colt was present too, a stanchion on the top step, perched only slightly away but wholly separate from the mob, stiffly postured in a neat, if somewhat conventional, dark suit, two hands clutching his leather briefcase, a bastion of taste and rigidity amongst the paunchy earth tones. Ethan maneuvered towards him, focused on keeping his own back equally straight, and his head directly above it, hoping to appear both confident and unconcerned as he skirted the far edges of the crowd. Mr. Colt's eyes fired up at the young attorney's approach, a statue springing to life.

"Mr. Mack Daniels!" He hit the first syllable—MACK—hard, almost separating the name into two distinct words, concluding with a rather subdued *daniels*. As always, and despite having frequently both heard the name and seen it written, he added an *s*. "Here we are on the courthouse steps to submit our disputes to the people." Sterling Colt radiated intensity; Ethan had to muster the strength just to maintain eye contact with his deep-set eagle eyes.

"Good morning, Mr. Colt." Ethan marveled at how his charcoal suit complemented his lithe frame. The shoes, while well-tended, had obviously carried the man through many grueling and glorious courthouse campaigns. He looked like a general on the eve of what was sure to be a bloody, historic, and successful battle.

"What a day, Mr. McDaniels." He swept a hand across the courthouse doors. "I trust you're ready to see the greatest civil law system in our world's long history put in motion." One hand came to rest on Ethan's shoulder; the young attorney buzzed.

We will be riding into battle side by side.

"I certainly am, sir. I'm ready for duty and eager to see you practice your craft." Ethan glanced at the nearest potential jurors and dropped his voice. "I actually learned something last night which might be—"

"I'm practicing now, Mack. The trial can be won or lost on these courthouse steps. An attorney is arguing his case, building his credibility, every second he is in the jury's presence. One misstep, one lapse in decorum, can undermine your credibility and torpedo your case. That's why we must be kind and courteous to everyone we encounter this morning. And carry ourselves with dignity. Follow me and I'll show you how it's done."

Ethan made a note to bring up Garth's tidbit about Kurt Bickerman's Greenville family at a later, more private, time. For now, he further straightened his shoulders, set his feet together, and brought his own briefcase to his hips. Together, they kept watch over the courthouse steps.

A small purple hatchback parked on the street and Teri Nelson, the other defense attorney on the case, exited and approached for her day of work, taking a similar route around the crowd as that previously forged by Ethan. A rolling briefcase, almost the size of its owner, rumbled behind her, on multiple occasions catching on the crumbling pavement and jerking her small frame backwards. As she neared the steps, Ethan lifted a foot to offer assistance—Mr. Colt beat him to the punch, briskly striding past Ethan to meet her at the bottom step.

I'll be quicker next time, Ethan thought as he watched Ms. Nelson wave her counterpart off, press in the briefcase's telescoping handle, and use two hands to lug it up the steps.

"Good morning, Ms. Nelson," Ethan said. She plunked the briefcase down, taking a moment to straighten her straight brown hair before addressing him.

"We're in trial together, Ethan. We're partners. Please God, call me Teri." She turned to Mr. Colt.

"Good morning, Sterling."

"Ms. Nelson. I'm glad to see you made it safely."

Like Ethan, Sterling Colt and Teri Nelson each represented both Emmett Lucas and Lucas Trash, but via different insurance companies. At some point an agreement had been struck above them to fight the common enemy rather than squabble about time on the risk, forcing a reluctant union. Mr. Colt had made no secret of his disdain for her, or anyone's, involvement in his defense. Ms. Nelson's frigid façade of politeness and professionalism did little to conceal her desire that the old man meet a grisly end in her presence.

"Did y'all hear about the weather?" Ms. Nelson asked.

"No, I'm feeling it though." Ethan brushed sweat from his brow and immediately regretted bringing attention to it.

"Apparently there's a bad storm coming. Some sort of enormous low-pressure front from the west. They're calling for heavy rain and hail tomorrow, high winds, possible flooding, maybe even tornadoes."

Ethan's hands balled in his pockets—he had checked and prepared for everything but the weather. "That shouldn't impact us though, right?"

"We're in a government building. Government buildings love to close. It's their natural state. Especially when opening means forcing citizens to leave their homes in inclement weather." Ms. Nelson checked something in a side pouch then looked up at Ethan. "It depends how it plays out. And what the clerk of court says. Generally, local government officials are acutely reluctant to place their constituents in harm's way."

"Is the county government liable if someone gets injured during a storm on their way to jury duty?"

"I wouldn't want to defend it."

Mr. Colt scoffed. "It should be entirely in the judge's discretion. He alone presides over the trial. It should stop and start at his command. A sure-footed judge would put the clerk of court and the rest of those spineless bureaucrats in their rightful place. An ongoing trial subjugates all other concerns."

The glass doors sprang open, sparing Ethan and Ms. Nelson from any reply. The guards gestured for the attorneys to slip in ahead of the crowd. Ethan entered the building behind the other attorneys, following suit as they placed their briefcases and emptied their pockets onto the conveyor belt feeding the x-ray machine, then walked through the metal detector. Mr. Colt and Ms. Nelson passed without incident. At Ethan's passage, the machine buzzed and flashed red. A tall, heavy-set Black security guard stepped between Ethan and where the rest of the defense team was collecting their things.

"Belt," the man said. A horizontal patch on his chest identified him as *Cordell*.

Ethan's mind blanked. His heart beat at a frenetic pace. He turned towards the conveyor belt. "I . . . I put my things on it. My pockets are empty."

"No," the security guard tapped his own waistline. "Are you wearing a belt?"

"Oh. I . . . yea." Ethan pulled his jacket back to expose his metal belt clasp.

"That's it, then," Cordell said, waving a metal detector wand over Ethan's body. "Sometimes it catches it, sometimes it don't."

"Thank you."

Ethan snatched his things from the other side of the metal detector and rushed to where Ms. Nelson was holding the elevator door, once more straightening his shoulders to stand as stiffly as Mr. Colt. Mrs. Warland had been quite clear on this: follow Mr. Colt's every move, and make none that he doesn't.

Ms. Nelson punched the top button and leaned her brown hair back against the wall. Ethan waited for the doors to slide shut before he spoke.

"Did we know that Kurt Bickerman is just a local pawn for family members up in Greenville?" He figured this was the safest way to phrase it in case this had been a known fact that he simply had missed or forgotten. Mr. Colt remained forward facing, but his eyes narrowed. When no one spoke, Ethan continued. "His family are big time developers up there. He certainly didn't say that in his deposition, but apparently selling the property to a resort wasn't even his idea. It was theirs. They were pulling all the strings."

"I'm aware of the Greenville Bickermans," Mr. Colt said, still without turning. "How do you see this impacting our case?"

"Well . . . it . . . it makes him and his story less sympathetic to a jury if it wasn't even his idea. And it hurts his credibility, since he specifically testified to it being his idea."

"How did you learn this, Ethan?" Ms. Nelson asked.

"I just overheard it at dinner last night at a . . . um . . . local place."

"So you don't have a witness to testify to it, or any evidence," Mr. Colt said.

"No, it's just gossip—"

"You're aware we'd need to find one or the other if we're going to try to act on this theory?"

"But we wouldn't need any evidence to use it on cross. We could just ask Plaintiff about it and see what he says." The silver doors pinged open.

"That's a thought," Mr. Colt said. "See what else you can dig up. And make a note to discuss this point again before Plaintiff takes the stand." That was enough for Ethan; he had a substantive, potentially decisive task. "Now, prepare for battle Mr. Mack Daniels."

Ethan soaked in the courtroom: the lacquered church pews; the scowling portraits; the strange, arbitrarily patterned purple carpet; the judge's elevated perch on the backwall. Mr. Colt pushed open the swinging bar separating the well from the gallery, holding it open for Ms. Nelson, who in turn held it for Ethan.

Ethan had entered the well before for hearings and other preliminary matters, but never for a trial. He took a moment to press his heels into the carpet, turning them back and forth.

I've made it.

Mr. Colt assumed first chair at the far left of the defense table, Ms. Nelson settled on his right, leaving the right end for Ethan who set down his briefcase and removed a yellow legal pad which he laid on the table, squaring its corner with the table's. In front of him, the judge's bench rose like a wood-paneled ivory tower, the elevated epicenter of a tangle of fading chairs and decades old computers separated from the world by a circuit of waist-high faux wood. The witness stand jutted out to the right, raised, but not quite so high as the judge's post. Ethan checked to his left, confirming he was shoulder-to-shoulder with the other attorneys.

The rear double doors popped open and Sires Paulson, attorney for the plaintiff, swaggered in. He was a big, loud, confident, and infinitely friendly man who grinned as he strolled through the vacant gallery.

"Ahh, the three horsemen of my demise." His booming voice overwhelmed the thin carpet and paneled walls, making several trips around the courtroom before departing on its own accord. "I trust y'all have found pleasant accommodations. Although I must say one of the main benefits of home games is that you get to sleep . . . well, at home." Mr. Paulson was a born and bred Folkstonian and son of a prominent lawyer. The defense team assumed his client's case would benefit from significant home cooking.

Ethan had always enjoyed Mr. Paulson and been impressed by the breezy zeal with which he plied his trade. On numerous occasions, this case had required him to mine for information and argue hotly-contested points in a room full of enemies, including the zealously strenuous Sterling Colt, and he had done so joyously and without fear.

All in all, Ethan found him to be a worthy adversary and particularly well-suited to wage war with Mr. Colt.

The defense attorneys stood to take turns saying their opponent's name and shake his huge right hand. Mr. Paulson shifted a box of files to his left arm to do his part.

A woman carrying a second box followed Mr. Paulson into the courtroom. "Sires, don't forget we also have Kurt waiting in the lobby," she shouted.

Ethan recognized the voice and turned to better inspect its owner. He had never met Marissa DePaul in person, but had spoken to her on the telephone at least once a week for the past two years; Mr. Paulson, despite his bravado and verbosity, was not much inclined to answer or return phone calls. As such, Ethan had spent significant time on the phone with Marissa, his paralegal, coordinating discovery, scheduling depositions, and resolving motions. She impressed Ethan with her detailed knowledge of both the case and the legal system, particularly the quirks of filings in Folkston County, as well as her ability to shepherd a somewhat lackadaisical attorney through the finer points of the system. But for context, Ethan would not have been able to identify this person as Marissa DePaul. Primarily, because the woman now walking the aisle was about his age. Marissa's informed and authoritative phone presence had led Ethan to assume she would be much older and considerably more matronly. He was further surprised to see that she had straight, shoulder-length brown hair, a color which did not appear to come from a bottle, and was of firm and athletic construction. The age misconception had allowed him to speak freely with Ms. DePaul, asking questions, and, as the phone calls progressed, make jokes. Ethan was embarrassed to find the actual Marissa DePaul to be alarmingly attractive. She noticed him and flashed a bright smile.

Ms. Nelson's phone buzzed in front of her, turning slightly on the dark wood.

"It's Emmett," she said. "Ethan, could you go fetch him?"

Ethan descended, locating Emmett Lucas standing alone on the steps, smoking. He was a tall, well-statured man who'd spent his entire life in Folkston, highlighted by a three-year stint as the star quarterback at Folkston High. He wore a plaid button down he'd tucked into his jeans and thick mat of grey hair he'd combed straight back for his day in court.

"Good to see you, Mr. Lucas. Are you ready to come up?"

"This is dumber than hell, but I'll see it through." Mr. Lucas crossed the staircase to stub his cigarette into a receptacle. "If I go in there," he pointed at the courthouse, "will you people ever let me come back out?"

Ethan didn't know what to say. "Yes, sir."

They shared a silent elevator ride and returned to the courtroom, Mr. Lucas now leading the way through the gallery exchanging joyless *good mornings* with his attorneys as he approached, and waving at Mr. Paulson.

"You get to sit here, Emmett." Ms. Nelson patted the seat next to her, the one Ethan had so briefly occupied. Mr. Lucas brushed through the swinging gate.

"Is that chair any softer than it looks?"

"I'm afraid not. And the jury will be directly to your right in that box there. So you're front and center."

"Ah, we're in luck then," he replied. Ms. Nelson gave him a questioning look. "That's my good side."

Ms. Nelson allowed a solitary chuckle, shook her head, then looked up where Ethan remained standing at the bar in double dismay: one dismay for having been relegated to the gallery, another for not having recognized this as the only possible outcome. "I'm sorry, Ethan. We'll have to put you in the first row."

Ethan stood silently long enough that Mr. Colt started to turn around.

"That's fine. Of course. If I could just," Ethan pointed over the rail, "have my briefcase. And notepad."

Mr. Lucas obliged. Ethan sat down and stared at the rail separating him from the rest of the defense team. His face felt hot. He focused on long, deep breaths.

This is not a problem. They don't need me up there. I'll be able to observe the jury from here. What they do and do not respond well to. And I can still be involved in the strategy discussions . . . during the breaks.

Marissa returned with Kurt Bickerman, a squat, bespectacled, bald man who waddled down the aisle in a grease-stained seersucker suit. Ethan wondered whether after his deposition, in which he had been thoroughly excoriated by Mr. Colt, Mr. Bickerman had begun to rethink allowing his Greenville family to drag him into the real estate business. Ethan tried to imagine his face when the defense revealed this tidbit to the world. Plaintiff took his seat next to his attorney. Marissa sat in the first row directly across the aisle from Ethan. She gave Ethan a look which started at surprise then, as best as Ethan could tell, slipped into sympathy.

As nine-thirty approached, the clerk of court, her assistant, the court reporter, and the bailiff sifted out to their various stations. The attorneys grew still, moving only to straighten the edges of their paper stacks. After some time, the aging bailiff pushed his earpiece deeper into his earlobe, stood, and announced, "All rise for the Honorable Eustus Grimmaly."

Ethan had researched Judge Grimmaly, tracked down press clippings, and read more than a few of his decisions in hopes of gaining insight into his tendencies and preferences. Judge Grimmaly was yet another Folkston native and had even practiced law with Sires Paulson's father before assuming the bench. He was now in his early sixties, but still possessed a robust and vital frame, accompanied by one of those healthy potbellies which plague old men. He pushed through a backdoor, preceded by his belly and followed by his clerk, and ascended his throne, waving a hand and muttering for those assembled to *please be seated*.

After taking his seat, Judge Grimmaly studied the attorneys' tables. "If those assembled would please take a moment to introduce yourselves, it may save us some time and confusion later on." His eyes ran back and forth over the room. "Well, first, let me ask whether this gentleman in the first row is with the defense?"

Ethan had prepared for a similar moment, had practiced saying his name, his firm, and his client's name in the mirror. He rose to his feet and took steadying breath. "Yes, your Honor. Thank you, your Honor. May it please the Court, I am with the defense, sir. My name is Ethan McDaniel of Hamel, Collins, Nagurski & Hamel. I represent Emmett Lucas and Lucas Trash, Incorporated."

"Thank you, Mr. Daniels. While I appreciate your adherence to the formalities, unless we are actually on the record and Ms. Tremaine, our fearless court reporter, is recording our words for posterity, it's safe to assume that everything you say pleases the Court." Judge Grimmaly flashed a casual, friendly smile. "That being said, it's very nice to meet you, and it is always a pleasure to see a fresh face here in Folkston."

"Thank you, your Honor." Ethan sat down, pleased with his paced, stammer-free performance.

"Good morning, your Honor. My name is Teri Nelson. For the defense, sir. This is our client Emmett Lucas, of Lucas Trash, to my right."

"Good morning, Ms. Nelson. I believe this is your first time appearing in front of me, so it's nice to meet you as well. How are ya, Emmett?" Mr. Lucas flashed an upward pointed thumb.

"Good morning, your Honor. Sterl—"

"I figured that was you, Sterling. It's been some time but we locked horns perhaps twenty-five years ago. Back when I used to fight in the battles instead of simply observing them from the hillside." There was no friendliness in the judge's tone.

"I recall. Thank you, your Honor." Sterling Colt placed his hand on his stomach as he coiled back into his seat.

"And don't bother standing up, Sires, I've heard your distinguished name far too many times." Mr. Paulson grinned and shrugged. "Now, if there is nothing further, I will call in the jury pool and we can get this ball rolling."

"Actually, your Honor," Mr. Paulson now stood. "There is at least one matter that needs to be addressed now."

Judge Grimmaly nodded at Ms. Tremaine, who readied her hands over her semi-keyboard. "We are now on the record. Proceed, Mr. Paulson."

"Well, your Honor, I believe that this jury pool has been tainted and would respectfully move for the trial to be continued, for another pool to be pulled, on the basis of Mr. Ethan McDaniel's improper interactions and, possible favor currying, with the jurors this morning."

Ethan froze at the mention of his name. *What did I do?* He searched his memory of the morning as his heart battered his ribcage. *Did I speak to anyone on the steps?*

The hearing continued around him. "Now, and I'm sorry about this, is Mr. McDaniels this young gentleman in the first row?"

"Yes, your Honor."

"Okay then. And what do you assert Mr. McDaniels did to taint the jury pool?" Ethan fought to hear over the deep, arrhythmic pulsing in his ears.

"As I was driving in this morning I observed Mr. McDaniel talking to a potential juror, a woman, in the courthouse vicinity—" Now Mr. Colt whirled around, crimson rage flushing his face.

The judge lifted his hand and turned to Ethan. "Mr. McDaniels, what say you?"

Ethan found his feet again; this time on trembling legs to a room full of cold, unfamiliar eyes. He tried to steady himself on the rail. He had to look over Mr. Colt to address Judge Grimmaly.

"I . . . I . . . I . . ."

A woman? His mind fought through a swirl of surprise and adrenaline.

"Take a breath, son. I'm just trying to figure out what might've happened. You ain't in trouble yet."

Ethan breathed and retraced his morning. He'd left his motel room and—*Deborah! The. Bore. Ugh.* The image of Garth Quattlebaum tilting his head and grunting those words brought Ethan some small semblance of peace. "Your Honor, the only person I spoke to this morning was a . . . a neighbor, sir."

"And you're certain this neighbor you spoke to was not a potential juror?"

"I . . . I am, sir. I'm staying close. I walked to the courthouse . . . from my hotel. She is a neighbor at Sapphire Courts." Across the aisle, Marissa DePaul's mouth and eyes widened. "Deb—she was walking her dog, sir. Holding it, really. We only spoke in front of the hotel. I certainly never—"

Judge Grimmaly wagged his head, raising a hand as he turned back to Mr. Paulson.

"Mr. Paulson did you actually observe this young man converse with anyone in the courthouse parking lot, or rather, anyone not holding a dog?"

"No, your Honor. Although I can't say I noticed the dog."

"Did you see him converse with anyone on the steps or in this parking lot?"

"No, your Honor."

"And is it your request that we poll each member of the pool as to whether they had any interaction with Mr. McDaniels?"

"No, your Honor. If Mr. McDaniel says he did not converse with anyone, I take him at his word."

"How considerate. I'm going to give you the benefit of the doubt and assume you somehow failed to observe the dog and that your motion was not just an attempt to kick up muck. As to that motion, it is denied." Judge Grimmaly took a sip of coffee. "You may take your seat Mr. McDaniels."

Ethan sat, trying both to still himself and find something to do with his hands. In front of him, Ms. Nelson shifted to examine Mr. Colt for several seconds before turning fully round and resting her arms on the rail to smile at Ethan. *It's okay,* she mouthed, *you're doing fine.*

Ethan tried to smile back.

"Now, with that being settled," Judge Grimmaly said from the bench. "Is there anything else we need to take care of at this point? I would prefer to hear any preliminary motions prior to picking the jury."

"Actually, your Honor . . ." Sires Paulson and Sterling Colt stood up in unison. Both had several additional preliminary motions including dueling motions to exclude the other's experts. The most significant issue was each side's expert opinions regarding the presence of smell. Each attorney based his argument on the grounds that the expert's methods of smell detection and determining particulate density were not generally accepted or scientifically based. Mr. Paulson went first. When his motion was denied, Mr. Colt took on arguing what he had just argued against, and Mr. Paulson repeated Mr. Colt's successful argument in favor of admission. Mr. Colt next argued that Plaintiff's expert should be excluded because smell, or even the lack of it, is within the capacity of the layman and does not require expert testimony and a jury may give undue weight to an expert's testimony regarding it. This too was denied.

These motions consumed the morning and took them to lunch.

Chapter Six

Rampant anxiety and residual adrenaline precluded any attempt at a midday meal. Ethan had not anticipated being singled out by the judge before the jury had even entered the courtroom. He'd certainly never anticipated being on the receiving end of the judge's questioning. It had him in knots.

After awkwardly standing behind the two older defense attorneys while they packed their things, Ethan had withdrawn to Sapphire Courts to review his notes, reassess his predictions, and reassume his decorum. Now, with lunch off the menu, his most pressing concern was the moisture trickling down his sides. He checked the pits of his dress shirt and the backs of his knees for any outward signs, then removed the jacket and both shirts, rubbing his torso down first with a wet hand towel, then a dry one. He opened his laptop to find an email from Mrs. Warland wishing him luck and requesting updates about the morning's events. Ethan filled her in on the opposing evidentiary motions and their outcomes but, after much deliberation, declined to mention the allegations directed at him.

He returned to the fourth-floor courtroom early, waiting outside the thick double doors for twenty lost minutes before a series of metallic clicks and twists signaled the bailiff opening the room. Unfamiliar faces occupied the lawyer tables. A Black woman in a skirt suit hunched over the edge of the defense table. Ethan watched as she twice set her notepad on the sliver of wood left by Mr. Colt's voluminous case file; the notepad slipped off once, was replaced, then quickly fell again before she gave in and set her laptop and papers on top of Mr. Colt's files.

He's not going to like that.

Across the way, a tall, acne-scarred young man in a boxy grey suit rested his hands on what had been, and would again be, Mr. Paulson's chair. The young man was Ethan's age but seemed much more at ease in the courtroom, chatting pleasantly with the bailiff guarding the side door.

As Ethan approached, the back bailiff barked, "All rise!" The chatter ceased. Everybody straightened as Judge Grimmaly took the bench and bid them sit. Ethan slipped into a middle row on the plaintiff's side, noting how the young attorney's wrinkled suit billowed around his lanky frame as he approached the low wall separating the clerk of court and court reporter from the well. Ethan tugged his own tailored suit jacket firmly across his stomach. The woman's suit was better fitting, and showed signs having been recently ironed, but was clearly well-worn. Her hair had been tied back tight at some point that morning, but the stress of the day had allowed a significant number of hairs to mount their escape.

Judge Grimmaly looked over the room. "Are we ready to proceed? Good." He shuffled the papers in front of him. "We are here by specific allowance from the Supreme Court of South Carolina opening this special and previously unscheduled term of general sessions." Judge Grimmaly gestured at the bailiff who opened the side door, leaned in, and said something Ethan could not discern.

An unscheduled criminal hearing, Ethan thought, *I wonder what's going on.*

A miniscule man in an orange jumpsuit shuffled out the door, waddling head down to stand next to the young attorney. The shackles around his hands and arms jangled and clanked in time with his steps. He stopped and looked up at the judge, bringing his head almost level with his attorney's shoulder.

"Hey, that's the Caz Man."

Ethan started, rattling the pew—Garth Quattlebaum had joined him on the row; somehow doing so silently and without detection. Garth patted Ethan on the shoulder and smirked. He wore a blue polo shirt under which a crescent moon of pale belly waxed as he reclined against the back. Judge Grimmaly briefly surveyed the source of the disruption, then returned to the matter at hand.

"Mrs. Baldwin you may call your case."

"Thank you, your Honor, may it please the Court. We are here on case number twenty-two *GS* seventeen dash eight five nine eight that is five counts of Purposeful Damage to Valuable Property Under $2,000. Defendant in this matter is Ronald Cazman Mayberry, Jr. The State asserts upon evidence that on or about May 22nd of this year, here in Folkston County, Defendant did willfully and without permission damage and injure the value of property belonging to Martha Willing—"

The double doors clanked open and Sterling Colt and Teri Nelson entered the courtroom. Mrs. Baldwin and everyone assembled turned to watch Mr. Colt, who was fully engaged in a lecture to his partner, speak at full volume for two sentences while Ms. Nelson gestured emphatically at the proceedings.

Mr. Colt didn't turn until he was finished. "I apologize, your Honor. I didn't realize we were filling the gaps."

"Sit down, Mr. Colt."

After a breath, Mrs. Baldwin continued. "Specifically, your Honor, the Defendant threw a series of bricks through the windows of Martha Willingham's family home while she, her husband, and her two children were inside asleep. Each of the five counts stems from the five separate windows shattered in the incident. This incident occurred at night, your Honor. Defendant has fourteen prior convictions for crimes involving property value. As such, he is being charged under the enhancement statute. The State and the defense have not been able to work out a recommendation on this matter. His record is a significant reason for our impasse."

"That was rude." Garth muttered, throwing a thumb towards the new arrivals who had taken a seat in the rear. "Wonder how *he* would like getting interrupted in front of the judge."

Up front, Judge Grimmaly had turned to the defendant, flying through a series of questions concerning his understanding of the situation, his recollection of the facts, and his satisfaction with his attorney.

Ethan scrutinized the orange clad figure. The Caz Man was a dressed skeleton; his dearth in height surpassed by a dearth in volume. Violent crannies and nooks pocked his face, neck, and arms as if the Folkston soil was sucking his flesh inward and down through the soles of his feet. A lank tangle of greasy brown hair dribbled down the back of his neck. A light fuzz grew down the sides of his face.

Finally, Judge Grimmaly asked, "Do you plead guilty?"

"Yes, sir."

"And do you plead guilty because you are guilty?"

At this, Mr. Mayberry glanced at his attorney, who nodded. "Yes sir, I am."

"Okay, Mr. Franklin. Fill me in."

The man in the ill-fitting suit began speaking. "Thank you Judge, and may it please the Court. Mr. Mayberry is twenty-eight years of age—"

Twenty-eight? Ethan wasn't sure whether he'd spoken the words or just emphatically thought them. *That's my age.* Ethan checked his hands. *How could the body up there be so decimated after only twenty-eight years? He must be wretchedly sick. What else could possibly do that a person?*

The young lawyer continued, "... he has lived in Folkston his entire life, and people here will tell you that, when sober, Mr. Mayberry is as pleasant, honest, and hard-working a man as you could hope to meet. But, like so many in this county and the surrounding region, he is stricken with addiction and when he's using methamphetamine, as he was on the night in question, he becomes the erratic and irrational person that gets the good man in trouble. Your Honor, Mr. Mayberry's actions that night were the actions of an addict."

Methamphetamine addict. The tension left Ethan's chest. *I can't catch that.* He leaned forward. *So, this is meth.*

"Your Honor, I would note that Mrs. Willingham, the victim, is currently in a long-term relationship with Mr. Mayberry's biological father, and the home at issue is where the couple resides. Further, my client was under the impression the family was out of town on a vacation on the night of the incident, and certainly did not mean anybody any physical harm. Nevertheless, Ronald Mayberry stands before the Court today, fully sober, to own up to his mistakes, to request mercy and a sentence including drug and addiction treatment."

Judge Grimmaly nodded again and straightened his papers. "Now Mr. Franklin is your client aware that his fourteen prior property crime convictions allow the State to prosecute him under the enhancement statute?"

"He is aware, your Honor. Although I will say that figure is a bit exaggerated. All fourteen convictions stem from two incidents."

"Be that as it may. The enhancement statute means he faces a significantly longer sentence. With these five charges, I could sentence him to up to fifty years in a state penitentiary. Ten years per charge. Does he understand that?"

"Yes, he does. And I must emphasize, your Honor, that these five charges in truth stem from a single incident. This was in no way a spree of any kind."

"And I get that. That's fine. Does your client understand that a conviction under the enhancement statute means this is no longer a misdemeanor property crime and that he will be convicted as, and indeed be labeled, a felon with all the implications and limitations that carries?"

"Yes he does, your Honor. We have discussed those at length."

Garth grunted and shifted in his seat.

"Okay then. Mr. Mayberry, do you have anything else you'd like to say before I determine your sentence?"

The man straightened to face the judge. "I'm very sorry, your Honor."

Ethan got the feeling this brief line had been thoroughly rehearsed.

"Well, don't apologize to me. I'm here either way. You haven't disrupted my life in any way. You might want to consider the children who likely have trouble sleeping after your attack on their home. Those people, the . . . the Willinghams, have a home, a sanctuary, which you have violated. They can't get that peace of mind back. That kind of damage can be repaired, but it cannot be undone."

"It weren't no attack, your Honor. I turned and ran soon as I saw the lights flick on."

Mr. Franklin put a hand on his client's shoulder.

"Right. Well, I'll move on. Is there any restitution being sought by the victims?" Judge Grimmaly turned back to Mrs. Baldwin.

"No, your Honor. They want nothing to do with this. They just want it behind them."

"Ahem. If there's nothing further, this will be the decision of the Court. I accept the plea and find the Defendant Ronald Cazman Mayberry, Jr. guilty of five counts of Purposeful Damage to Valuable Property Under $2,000. Each count having been elevated to a felony due to Defendant's two or more prior property crime convictions triggering prosecution under the South Carolina enhancement statute. As such, the Defendant Ronald Cazman Mayberry, Jr. is hereby sentenced to four years' incarceration. During that time, and before he is eligible for parole, he is to enroll in and complete the State's inmate addiction course." Judge Grimmaly paused to rub his cheek with his palm. "Is there anything further? Okay then. Good luck to you, Mr. Mayberry. I declare this special term of general sessions closed."

Just like that the hearing was over. The whole hearing, which had determined four years of a human being's life, had required less of the court's time than any of Mr. Colt's or Mr. Paulson's evidentiary motions. Ethan stared blankly as Mrs. Baldwin thanked the judge, who was already on his way out the door, and stepped back to the table, her demeanor unchanged.

Mr. Franklin continued whispering in his client's ear, a feat which required him to walk while bending at both knee and hip, as the bailiff escorted him back to the side door. Mr. Mayberry's vacant face gave no acknowledgement of the sentence which had been levied against him, no indication that he resented the next four years of his life being spent in prison. It was as if he had resigned himself to this fate well before that first brick had shattered Martha Willingham's window.

Mr. Colt was up in an instant, but remained in the gallery, giving Mrs. Baldwin a respectful distance as she typed on her laptop and scribbled on her notepad. He turned to Ms. Nelson to finish their conversation from before the hearing, speaking as if it were he who had been interrupted.

"As I was saying, Teri, despite the state of the town this is not such a bad area. Lake Thompson is a fine lake, as is Lake Sassafras. And, of course, the mountains. There are even some rather scenic, and exclusive, golf courses just to the north. All in all, there's nothing geographically keeping this area from being the next Highlands or Brevard."

Garth leaned towards Ethan and, in his version of a whisper, said, "Are they with you?" Ethan nodded. Garth shook his head. "I don't like the old guy. Do better."

Mr. Colt continued. "I'm only saying that for someone my age, it would be too slow an investment to be of any value. This place needs too much elbow grease. It would simply take too long to acquire the property, squabble with or circumvent the town council, and clear enough of the local riff-raff to make Folkston County an appealing destination. Not to mention that, unfortunately, in terms of amenities, you'd be starting from scratch."

Garth's breathing became more rapid and he hunched forward to grasp the back of the pew. *Clear the local riff-raff*, Ethan heard him mutter, *I'll clear his riff-raff*. Garth's knuckles whitened on the lacquered wood.

"The timeline just wouldn't work for what I need out of an investment. But for someone your age, or Mack Daniels' age," Mr. Colt turned to where Ethan sat in the gallery, doing a double take at the hairy mass next to his temporary protégé, "an investment in the development of this area could provide some real security and comfort for you and your families down the line. And, of course, a welcome getaway for the people of Greenville, or even Atlanta."

This was apparently the end of Mr. Colt's pitch. He clasped his hands in front of his waist, standing for several seconds before ambling up the aisle, through the gate, and turning to the woman occupying his desk.

"Excuse me, solicitor, are you going to be much longer?" Mr. Colt asked. Mrs. Baldwin turned, said something Ethan could not hear, and kept typing.

Mr. Colt pivoted to grimace at Ms. Nelson. "Madame solicitor, if you don't mind."

"Give her a second, asshole," Garth mumbled not that quietly.

Mrs. Baldwin paused and looked towards the near wall, silently counting something on her fingers.

"Congratulations on your conviction. While I do very much appreciate your work, I also have a trial set to resume shortly if you would not mind ceding the desk."

"Back off, big guy. You ain't that important," Garth growled.

Ethan scooted towards the wall.

Mrs. Baldwin kept typing.

"Are you certain these are not emails which may be better reviewed in your office?"

She remained crouched over her laptop, nodding as she ran her finger across the screen.

"Because it is considered a professional courtesy to clear the desk immediately after your matter has been heard." Mrs. Baldwin's hand left the screen, to type anew. Mr. Colt crossed his arms, his voice rising. "*Madame Solicitor*. You are holding up the courtroom's other proceedings."

"What proceedings? The judge is gone. Who is this chucklehead?" Garth said this at full volume.

Mr. Colt turned to face the gallery. "What's that now?"

"I said the judge is gone and there's no proceedings. Leave her alone so she can finish her business."

Mr. Colt smiled, pleased to have a challenger. "Excuse me, sir, are you a judge?"

Garth stood up to answer, unsuccessfully tugging his shirt down to cover his bellybutton. "Can't say that I am. But I know—"

"Are you an officer of this court?"

"No, I am not."

"Then are you an attorney?"

Garth snorted. "That's a proud no."

"Then you have no business involving yourself in any matters being discussed on this side of the bar."

To Mr. Colt's left Mrs. Baldwin plunked one final key, examined the screen for a beat, then pushed the laptop closed. She rose to her full height, about one inch greater than Sterling Colt's, first checking the empty bench before turning to look down at the nuisance, assessing him for several seconds before flicking a confused glance at Garth Quattlebaum in the gallery, and walking away. Mr. Colt evidently thought he was the winner of both interactions; he sat down with his back turned to Garth and began straightening his desk.

Garth sat down, looking surprised to see Ethan so far away. "Fuck that guy. What happens now?" he whispered. "Are y'all back on?"

"Yes. Hopefully, we pick a jury."

"*We* meaning *him*?"

"And Ms. Nelson and Plaintiff's counsel, yes. The jury pool will be sitting here so you'll have to move."

"You'll be up there with that asshole?"

Ethan had to think about this one. "Yes."

"Cool. If that's the case I'll just bow out now. Do me a favor and try not to pick up any habits from that douchebag."

Chapter Seven

The named parties and Plaintiff's legal team returned to the courtroom around one-thirty, moments before a bailiff guided an impatient and visibly frustrated jury pool down the center aisle. The jurors filled the gallery, relegating Ethan to a spare bench pressed against the back wall. Judge Grimmaly assumed his own, more prominent, bench, introduced himself, and commenced the long list of in-depth questions about the jurors' families, their home's proximity to the at-issue properties, their history and familiarity with commercial real estate transactions, their familiarity with the parties, their satisfaction with trash service in Folkston, and their sense of smell. Ethan, who had nearly memorized the jury pool, got a small thrill putting faces and outfits to the list of names, ages, genders, addresses, and occupations he'd received several weeks prior. He noted multiple other Folkstonians about his age who, similar to the Caz Man, appeared to be in the process of being consumed by their hometown.

How many share the same affliction?

After about an hour, Judge Grimmaly paused, leaned over to ask his clerk something, then addressed the room, "Okay then, now, notwithstanding any question that I may have previously asked, does anyone have any reason they believe they cannot serve as a fair and impartial juror in this matter?"

Ethan scrambled to mark the swarm of now standing Folkstonians.

Judge Grimmaly took it in stride. "Okay then, you here on the near left. We'll start here. Yes, you sir." As best as Ethan could tell, he was speaking to a scrawny older man standing almost directly behind Emmett Lucas. "What's your juror number and why do you believe you can't serve as a fair and impartial juror in this matter?"

"One-six-eight. Kip Winchester. I blocked for Emmett every Friday night for two years and I just don't see how I could ever find against him."

"Okay, Mr. Winchester. I don't think it's rude to note that it's been some time since you and Mr. Lucas shared the field so I'll ask whether you and the defendant have stayed in touch?"

"No sir, after school he went and done his thing, I done mine."

"I see. Folkston is a small town, and these types of connections are hard to avoid if we are going to fill those twelve chairs to your right. So, that being said, is there any other reason you feel you can't serve as a fair and impartial juror?"

"There's a storm set to come tomorrow. Would rather not be out in it."

"I understand that as well. I'm gonna keep you on. But let me assure you we'll address the storm later in the afternoon."

Mr. Winchester sat down. Judge Grimmaly turned to a nearby young woman whom Ethan had noted as well-educated and a strong candidate. She said she was the sole caretaker for her kids during the day; Judge Grimmaly let her go without further inquisition—a half dozen additional jurors popped to their feet. Next was a woman who claimed to be blind but admitted to having read the juror notice and driven herself; then a man who claimed to be deaf but answered Judge Grimmaly's questions clearly and without hesitation. Several additional people claimed chronic, but undiagnosed, back issues of such severity that they could not possibly sit for eight straight hours—these Judge Grimmaly kept but comforted with a promise of frequent breaks.

Ethan marked their numbers.

Finally, only one juror, a forty-two year-old manager at the local factory who to this point had provided invariably calm and well-reasoned answers to Judge Grimmaly's questions, remained standing. He was a member of several Folkston preservation societies; Ethan desperately wanted him on the jury.

"I'm number fifty-four, Carl Nuner, your Honor."

"Okay Mr. Nuner, why do you feel you can't serve as a fair and impartial juror in this matter?"

"Well, your Honor," Mr. Nuner took a deep, hoarse breath; Ethan's stomach dropped. "Because I'm tired of foreigners who ain't got no concern for Folkston coming here and trying to make a quick, dirty buck, and it makes me sick to my fucking stomach when idiots like this man," he pointed at Kurt Bickerman, "get duped into helping them. Now, I'm not some kind of simpleton but—"

"Sir—"

". . . this moron has to know—"

"Sir, let me stop—"

"Whatever greedy fuckers he has pulling his strings will make sure he won't see a dime."

"ENOUGH!" Judge Grimmaly slapped his desk. "Now if you can't control yourself I'll hold you in contempt and have my bailiff escort you to the detention center." Judge Grimmaly, seeing that he'd been understood, breathed and leaned back in his chair. "I've heard what you said and won't make Plaintiff waste one of his strikes. You may go."

Ethan's disappointment at the departure of juror fifty-four was mitigated by the number of the remaining jurors nodding their approval at his remarks. He noted their numbers as best he could.

I'll let Mr. Colt and Ms. Nelson know at the next break.

The break never came; immediately after juror fifty-four's exit, the clerk of court stood and started calling numbers.

"Ninety-six."

Juror ninety-six, a matronly middle-aged woman in a white shawl, stepped to the front of the room and faced the attorneys. She had nodded along with fifty-four.

"Please present the juror," Mr. Paulson said.

Mr. Colt stared the woman down.

Pick her. Pick her! She's perfect.

Mr. Colt checked his notes, then once more set juror ninety-six in his sights. "Please excuse the juror."

Juror ninety-six took two steps towards the jury box before the clerk of court stopped her. "Ma'am. Ma'am! You've been excused."

"Oh . . ." the woman froze mid-stride.

"You are free to go."

"Oh!" Her face brightened as she scampered for the exit, having to be reminded of her purse. Once outside, Ethan heard her squeal with delight.

One by one, the numbered stepped to the front of the courtroom. Both plaintiff and defense used all ten of their exceptions, sending an additional nineteen people home. It took thirty-four names, and twenty minutes, to fill out the twelve-member jury panel and provide two alternates.

When everyone was seated, Judge Grimmaly swore in the jury.

"Now as we've all heard, there's some threat of a particularly bad, dangerous storm hitting Folkston sometime this evening. While our judicial system is very important, and these parties deserve their day in court, your safety," he swept his hand across the jury panel, "and the safety of our court staff, and even the safety of the assembled attorneys, is of the absolute utmost importance. Accordingly, I believe Mrs. Marsh, our elected clerk of court, has some instructions for you as to how we will be proceeding."

Mrs. Marsh stood up, smoothing her dress as she spoke. "There is a number on the back of the sheets which have just been handed to you." Her voice started shrill, but relaxed as she continued speaking. "If you call it after six-thirty tonight, and follow the prompts, you will get a message letting you know whether the courthouse will be open tomorrow. We will try to make the decision as early as we can but, if necessary, y'all may have to call again tomorrow morning."

With that, Judge Grimmaly dismissed the room and everyone filed out. Ethan made a quick stop at the rail by the clerk of court to get his own copy of the number, which she provided with a jolly *oh of course, honey*. Ethan jogged to catch the elevator with the rest of the defense team.

"I think y'all picked a good jury. I had almost all of them marked in green on my list."

Mr. Colt seemed not to hear; Ms. Nelson looked up and nodded.

"Thanks, Ethan," she said. "I guess we'll just have to see."

"Are y'all . . . we meeting tonight?"

"It will depend on the storm, Ethan. I'm not particularly keen on getting lost in the country during a typhoon. If there's no court tomorrow, which is my bet, I'm not going to leave my hotel, so you just enjoy your night."

"Is there anything you'd like me to work on?"

"No. Stay safe. Try to relax. And stay out of trouble."

Chapter Eight

E than navigated the cracked sidewalk back to Sapphire Courts, stopping at the bottom of the slope. For the first time, he took a moment to really inspect the front façade in daylight; something about the windows caught his eye. While standard as-you-would-expect curtains adorned most rooms, hanging blankets lined the windows of others. As Ethan neared, he saw the blankets were of the thick, cheap, heavy, and incidentally completely opaque, variety which one would usually pick out of a bin or a wire rack at a department store.

They must've nailed those to the wall. Why would anyone do that? It's about as ugly as anything I've ever seen.

The designs varied; Ethan recognized cartoon characters, national park maps, pop stars, and portions of the emblems for several Carolina sports teams. The stillness of the hanging blankets, and the thoroughness with which they concealed their rooms' innerworkings made it feel as if they concealed some monster. Ethan looked away.

Must be an unfortunate local thing.

He returned to his room, closed the curtains, and undressed, replacing the suit to its hanger, then rolling his dress shirt and stuffing it into the portion of his suitcase reserved for dirty clothes. He had packed enough suits to make it through the week before he had to repeat; it had been his intention to re-wear each shirt, but the first day of trial had induced significantly more sweating than anticipated. Today's shirt's role in this matter was over.

The Patricians, which were never meant to be tossed about with lesser clothes in a laundry machine, had come with a special formula powder wash. The proper course was to handwash them with spring water in a galvanized tub—although the packaging noted that tap water and a sink would serve in a pinch. Accordingly, Ethan handwashed the Patricians under the faucet and hung them on the towel rack to air dry. He had just situated himself at the desk when Garth knocked on his door.

"This storm's horse shit. They do this every year and nothing happens." He picked a skin of flaky paint off the doorframe. "But, just in case, I'm making a grocery run. Figured you might be in similar need and would like to join."

Ethan was loath to leave his preparations, but food was a necessity—as was Garth's open access to food heating devices. "I could use some provisions."

"Great. Let's roll."

Ethan used the first part of the car ride to fill in an attentive Garth on the jury selection and his six-thirty call.

"I'd ask you for the names of the jurors, but I reckon you wouldn't give them to me anyway. I also reckon I'd know if somebody close drew the short straw. That's probably good for you. After your boss' showing today, I might be inclined to thumb the scale in favor of Bickerman. Going on about how Folkston ain't nothing but an investment opportunity and we need to clear the riff-raff. We're fine without y'all. It was y'all that gutted us and made sure we came out this way. Don't think that's over by the way. I ain't done with that pompous jagweed."

Ethan did not wish to explore Garth's threat; it may prove beneficial to sincerely plead ignorance later on. "But you said you do know the defendant from the plea?"

"Very well. I used to babysit the Caz Man when he was a pup. He was a good kid, cute kid, smart kid. Pretty much sucks to see him get swallowed up by all that bullshit."

"Didn't they say he's addicted to methamphetamine?"

"Him and every other skinny little fucker."

"Then, well," Ethan searched for the right way to say this but didn't find it, "he can't be that smart."

Garth took it in stride. "I understand the point you think you're making, but let me assure you, you don't have the first fucking clue what you're talking about. You learned about meth on the news and in anti-drug presentations at school. These kids learned about it from friends, siblings, and parents. Maybe you're young and folks around you are having fun on it and want you to join in, or you'll find other folks that are already hooked, hopeless and low, they just want someone doing it with them. Other folks are making money off it, usually to feed their own habit, and they can make a pretty good pitch and know when to strike. If you're around it long enough, meth finds its crease and takes hold. Once it gets ya, it's hell gettin' off." Garth parked the car and gestured for Ethan to exit. "Caz Man in particular was wide open for it. His parents were hopeless addicts. My mom would send me over there to watch after him when they went on their benders. Then his mom OD'ed when he would've been in high school. That's when his dad cleaned up his act, figured his shit out enough to start a new life with sweet ol' Martha on the good side of town. Got himself two new kids to whom he's a tremendous father, if I'm not mistaken. But, once a fucker always a fucker, pulled himself up, but didn't bother to reach back for his kid."

They entered the store. Garth lifted one basket from the stack, inspected it, and selected the second one.

"A four-year sentence isn't too bad though. He'll still be young when he gets out. If he completes that drug treatment he'll be clean and on his way."

"I envy the childhood that permits such optimism. But the time is the least of Caz Man's problems. He'll serve maybe two years depending how he behaves and it may well be the most stability he ever sees. Maybe even give him a chance to kick the meth. Although prison ain't great for that."

Garth stopped talking and waited for Ethan to ask. "So what is his problem?"

"He got himself tagged with the enhancement. That means that as of lunchtime today, the Caz Man is a felon, which is a life sentence, a nail in the coffin for a kid with a shaky foundation and no education. With background checks, he won't be able to get a decent job. It even cuts off his access to government assistance and makes it harder than hell to find decent housing. So he'll end up living amongst criminals. Probably working with or for criminals. Pretty much guaranteeing he'll turn back to crime."

Ethan's Criminal Procedure professor had spent a day on the stringent limitations on felons but had noted that the lesson would not be on the exam; Ethan spent the hour catching up on the baseball season. He figured it best not to admit this to his Sapphire Courts neighbor.

"I've never seen meth before. Or a methamphetamine . . . user. Do they all look like that?"

"No. That was a sober young man who'd been clothed, fed, and bathed. So what you got in the courtroom with all the padded chairs and suits was just this side of the world cracking the window to give you a sniff. Let me assure you most of the fart is still in the car." Garth picked up a package of steaks, poked each one, then turned them over, grunted, and tossed them on top of the chicken thighs. "But enough of that. Ain't nothing to be done about it tonight. What's your plan if you make that six-thirty call and find out you have the day off?"

"Tonight will just be an extra night of preparation. Why?"

"I need to know how much food to buy. And beer."

"For tonight?"

"Yea. For my storm party."

Ethan recalled the explosions and rattling walls of his first night in Sapphire Courts.

"Please don't."

"Don't give me that. Storm or no storm you are a non-participant in a bloated overhyped trash squabble. I mean, other than your brick thing, how invested are you actually in this trial? Or actually, answer this: will these precious proceedings proceed any differently if you're hungover?"

The honest answer was another thing Ethan did not want to admit. He considered saying *I'm a young attorney trying to build my knowledge and experience* but it tasted corny.

"So, no," Garth continued when Ethan failed to respond. "And do you get paid any more if you work every night?"

"Actually, no. Once it went to trial it converted to a flat—"

"There you have it. You're useless. You're free. Let's boogie."

"Garth—"

"You're a young man in a strange town. I aim to make you feel at home and that won't happen until you wake up bleary-eyed. So, I'm buying four big-ass T-bones. I'll butter these bastards and fry them up with some potatoes like you ain't never seen. You suck up all that grease then try to tell me you feel like sweating over some papers. Storm steaks. Thunder potatoes. So heavy and filling you'll sleep through anything."

"Seeing as I don't really have any other appealing options, I'll eat dinner with you. But afterwards I'm returning to my room and getting back to work."

"As you wish. Or, rather, if you say so. Be forewarned, we'll almost certainly pick up a couple other dingbats as well. They're the ones bringing the total to four. We know how to have a good time, how to find relaxation in the face of overwhelming burdens. We'd be happy to teach you."

Garth pulled back into Sapphire Courts; Ethan once more noticed the blankets.

"What's the point of covering the windows with blankets? Is it just cheaper than replacing the curtains? Or is it something else?"

"Something else."

"Is it like a local thing?"

"I can't say for certain, but I doubt it." Ethan started to get out before noticing Garth's hands remained on the wheel. "You got time for a tour?"

"A tour of what?"

"The rest of the fart."

Garth exited the lot, driving back through Folkston, past the welcome sign.

"So what you're showing me isn't in Folkston?"

"No, it is. But they tried like hell to make it look separate. We're going to Cochran's Mill. It came into being as a textile mill community. Work for the mill then rent your home and buy your food from the company. That was fine and Folkston welcomed the commerce. Until when I was a kid and the mill closed. As you might expect, most of the employees left to find work elsewhere. Those that stayed became a problem. No mill meant no work, no work meant no hope. So they took to drink and drugs. And even that was relatively fine. Drink yourself to death. OD in your home. Keep it indoors and off Main Street. No one's problem but yours. Then came meth."

Garth turned right down a road that was more pothole than asphalt.

"Meth charges people up and sets them out on the streets. Meth, and the desperation to acquire more meth, leads to violence, theft, vandalism, prostitution, and general destruction. That's public. That's expensive. That's a problem." After a thick strand of trees, Ethan found himself riding through row upon row of single-story tract homes varying only in color and level of decay. The weather was perfect on a late September afternoon, but the streets were lifeless. "I'll slow down, but I ain't gonna stop. You take a look at the windows and tell me what you see."

"Blankets," Ethan said as they passed one house with fully covered windows; the porch had collapsed under the accumulated weight of perhaps a dozen rusted lawnmowers.

"Meth fucks with your sleep something awful. To the extent you sleep at all, it tends to be during the day. And the sun can be a real son of a bitch when you're trying to sleep and standard two-ply curtains aren't up to the task. So the afflicted learned to stagger on down to the store and steal the cheapest, thickest blankets they could get their hands on."

"So every house with blanketed windows is a meth house?"

"The mark of disease."

"And Folkston wanted to distance itself from this?"

"First, the town council moved to make this area its own town, or at least unincorporate it. When those both got shot down, they settled for positioning the new sign to give the appearance that Folkston isn't associated with this hellhole."

Garth led them around the perimeter of Cochran's Mill past decrepit house after decrepit house, blanket after blanket after blanket, until they arrived at the mill itself. Ethan gaped at the four-story structure spanning two blocks. The red bricks had been stained, first by the smoke of industry, then decades of neglect. Tangles of ascending vines wove their way up the façade, disappearing into the shattered windows. This vacant blackness horrified Ethan. If the blanketed windows were an indicator of sick people, the darkness inside Cochran's Mill harbored the disease itself.

"Why would anybody stay here?"

Garth sighed. "I don't know, man. Lack of resources. Lack of options. Lack of gumption. Misplaced pride. A chance to play the victim. That mill was the foundation of their lives. Who knows what people do when that disintegrates."

Chapter Nine

They returned to Sapphire Courts for the second time to find the two youths, now both shirted, stationed on the exterior walkway. The pair snickered as Garth and Ethan exited the coupe.

"Garth man, who's your friend?!" the blonde shouted.

Garth looked up at them and raised his pointer finger, muttering at Ethan, "I'm not yelling across the lot at these jackrabbits." Garth approached like a schoolmaster stalking towards a pair of back-of-the-class hooligans. They straightened, their smiles curving all the more.

"You two met Mr. McDaniel this weekend?" Garth asked.

"Yea man." The blonde youth really gave the *man* room to breathe.

"Did you speak to him? Introduce yourself and welcome him to Folkston?"

"There wasn't time, man. He just cruised by."

The second youth was wearing a black t-shirt tucked into crisp, creased jeans; compared to his companion's outfit—khaki cargo shorts and a ratty, bacon-necked t-shirt—he appeared almost formal. He stood straighter as well; his friend, even while standing at mock attention, bent forward at the shoulders as if leaning out to greet life's next moment.

Garth pointed at Ethan. "Mr. McDaniel is our guest. He's an attorney in town for a trial. And you two strapping young fellows, steeped in the rigors of southern mountain hospitality, presumably capable of basic human interaction, are tasked with making him feel welcome."

"Couldn't think of nothing to say," the blonde said.

"Don't try so goddam hard. It's not a contest. Just say *hello how are you? Welcome to Sapphire fucking Courts.* Don't try to chirp and be clever like those other terd waffles."

"I wasn't chirping, man."

"I know you weren't. Chirping would've been better. If you would just be nice and stick to the standard, generally accepted greetings, then you wouldn't end up standing there like a fucking redneck bobblehead. Now, shake Mr. McDaniel's hand and introduce yourselves."

The taller Black youth extended his hand first. "Frank Besch."

"Pleasure to meet you, Ethan McDaniel."

Ethan turned to where the blonde was wiggling on his feet, almost bursting to thrust his hand towards him. "Ethan McDaniel."

"Robert Canterbury, Jr. The good ones call me Bobby." Bobby's eyes shined a joy and gentleness unlike anything Ethan had ever seen.

"Great," Garth said. "See, that's all it goddam takes. Now the three of y'all can enjoy simple mature interactions for the duration of his stay. But if you'll excuse us, it is my intention to spend this storm in the sweet embrace of inebriation."

"Cool, man. Can we come?" Bobby asked.

"That depends, do you have work in the morning?"

"No, man. Mr. Howard closed the foundry for the storm."

Garth turned to Frank, who nodded confirmation. "Do you have any bullshit on you? This is a booze-only event."

"We're clean." Another glance, another confirmation. Ethan was beginning to understand what Garth meant when he said Frank looked after Bobby.

"Cool," Garth nodded several times and grinned. "Let's get it on."

The three locals went directly to Garth's apartment; Ethan embarked on a brief side quest to dump his own limited wares on his bed before joining them. Frank had already reclined in the overstuffed chair while Bobby sank into the bean bag, gangly legs sprawled across the floor. Ethan took his place at the near end of the couch as Garth distributed the first round of beers, placing one on the coffee table in front of Ethan.

"In case you change your mind."

Garth flipped on the television, muted it, and started scrolling through the channels.

Bobby rolled on his side to look at Ethan. "You don't drink, man?"

"I still have work in the morning. Court, the trial, hasn't been cancelled yet. I'll know for sure at six-thirty. Although I'm really just here for dinner either way." Ethan checked the clock on the wall, recognizing it from the bedroom of a young, mischievous boy in a famous cartoon. It was currently just past six.

"Why, man? If you ain't got work you should hang with us."

"That's a good point, Bobs," Garth said returning to the kitchen. "A great point."

"You are an attorney?" Frank set Ethan in a penetrating stare.

"I am. Civil litigation."

"Insurance defense?"

"Some construction, too. But for the most part, yes." Ethan was surprised Frank knew this term—he had never heard it prior to law school.

Frank nodded. Ethan thought he discerned the slightest trace of a grimace. "What type of trial?"

"It's that goddam trash trial," Garth yelled from the stove. "Kurt Bickerman is claiming Emmett Lucas' land is too stinky for him to sell to the resort developer folks."

Bobby snorted. "Oh man. Too stinky. How do you prove that? Are you gonna jar up some air and hold it under the judge's nose? And then the other a lawyer, like, holds up their own jars?" Bobby mimed each movement as he said it. "Because I've got good jars, man. They close up tight. We could collect tonight."

Ethan shook his head. "That's not really how that works."

Frank reassumed the reins. "I am going to be an attorney. I'm at Folkston Tech now. But I'm moving to Columbia in January to finish my degree at USC. Then USC Law."

"That's great. What kind of practice are you looking to get into?"

"A worthwhile attorney could've helped my dad from losing his job, his life. I want to help people who've made mistakes. Keep it from derailing their lives."

"Oh, that's great." Ethan assumed this meant criminal defense. "I went to USC. My firm has a Columbia office. Definitely let me know if I can help."

Frank leaned back in his chair.

"I'm going with him, man," Bobby said. "We're getting the hell out of this town."

"Are you going to school as well?"

"Hell no, man. I'm gonna be working. Supporting both our asses." Bobby cackled. Frank shrugged.

"What kind of work?"

"Whatever I can find. The hard kind for sure."

"Good. That's very good."

Ethan recalled Garth's special pillow and lifted the nice side in front of his face.

"Get fucked, man!" Ethan had to double check that Bobby was reading the pillow and not directing this at him.

"Have you collected any more platitudes, Garth?" Ethan asked. The sizzling steaks filled the room with the smell of meat and browned butter. There was also something in the microwave.

"Since last night? No. But I keep a list of the particularly irritating ones. It's in that drawer by your knee."

Ethan jostled the reluctant drawer open and removed a yellow legal pad. A wandering vertical line divided the first page into two sides. In the top left, Garth had written *horse shit platitudes* with *Bad Ass P.W.A.s* on the right. Ethan scanned the list, reading them aloud.

God has a plan - - - God says get fucked.

This too shall pass - - - Shit happened. Shit's happening. Get fucked.

Everything always works out in the end - - - Someone will probably benefit from this. Get fucked.

It doesn't matter whether you win or lose, only that you try - - - You lost. Get fucked.

Tomorrow is another day - - - Today sucked. Get fucked.

The list went on, but Ethan figured he got the idea. He set the pad on the coffee table.

"The platitudes aren't the only selling point," Garth said. "They'll be stitched with the highest quality materials on the highest quality materials. And my pillows will be durable, comfortable, fashionable, and stain resistant. Fashioned in classic timeless styles to match, and accentuate, any décor. Feel free to add some platitudes if you have any. You seem like the kinda guy who'd be full of them. Like that brick nonsense."

Ethan furrowed his brow, unwilling to subject the McDaniel motto to Garth's criticism. "Don't shit where you eat?" he offered.

"I'm actually rather fond of that one. First off, it says *shit*. And, secondly, at least that's sound advice. So, in acknowledging the presence of a place to eat and the existence of shit, somewhat addresses a specific set of circumstances. For Platitudes with Attitude I'm really focusing on the trite and completely meaningless."

Ethan tried his hand again. "If you can't *change* the people around you, change the *people* around you." He tried to inflect to clarify the phrase's meaning.

"What the fuck does that mean?" Garth asked.

"Like . . . if you can't make the people around you better, find better people to have around you."

"Oof. That's so lazy you can't even tell what it means. And on the back?"

"Your friends suck. Get fucked?"

"Lose the question mark. I love it. Write it down."

"Yea man!" Bobby shouted, high-fiving Frank. "We're gonna be rich."

Ethan returned the platitudes to their lair then checked the clock again before pulling out his phone and the scrap of paper with the court's number. "Alright gentlemen. Moment of truth."

He dialed the number, listened, said *Jury Duty* twice, pressed *1*, listened, pressed *3*, listening again before putting the phone back in his pocket.

"What's the verdict?" Garth asked.

Ethan looked around at the three strangers leaning forward in their seats, waiting for his answer.

"Cancelled. Stay safe, shelter at home, and, if possible, call back tomorrow for updates."

The strangers cheered. Bobby leapt to his feet, pumping his fist like a golfer, then thrusted his open hand in the air. It took Ethan a moment to realize that he expected Ethan's participation. He stepped over to fulfill his manly duty.

"Now you can drink that beer, man!" Bobby repeated it before he could respond. "Drink that beer! Drink that beer!" It became a chant. Garth joined in, stomping his feet on the linoleum. Frank contributed too with significantly less enthusiasm. "DRINK THAT BEER! DRINK THAT BEER!"

Ethan's face reddened; it had been some time since he'd been cheered. He couldn't suppress the full-face smile boiling up from his core. That smile was gasoline to their flaming enthusiasm, extinguishing any internal resistance.

What the hell. Anything I would've done tonight I can do tomorrow. This barely even counts as a missed brick. I can also loosen them up and press them on Bickerman's Greenville family.

Ethan cracked the beer and lifted the can to his lips. The crowd roared.

Just make sure not to overdo it.

Garth came round with a plate of steak and potatoes for each attendee. Waves of browned butter sloshed against the meat as he set them down. Ethan waited for Garth to look away, then used a napkin to soak up the excess.

"Now, let's put on a goddam movie so we don't have to make any more decisions. Any suggestions?"

"Something good, man. Don't put on something shitty."

"Happy to oblige, Bobs. Any suggestions?"

Ethan's eyes drifted to the poster on the wall. "Dalton Stampede."

"That's the one. Bobs, hop up and pick out the first one."

"*Gravity's Elbow*," the room said together. Bobby popped off the bean bag chair in one fluid motion.

Garth set a case of beer on the floor between Ethan and Frank. "I hate missing the good stuff just to fetch a damn beer. So, it's *Gravity's Elbow* right into *Naked Punch*, then *Infinite Duress*, if there's time *A Fist in the Darkness*. We'll dropkick this bitch ass storm right back to where it came from."

Frank broke the seal on eating the steak and Ethan followed suit. Those still seated devoured their steaks, pausing for sips of beer as Bobby fumbled with the DVD case and then the DVD player. Finally, when only limp tangles of potato skin remained on Ethan's plate, the intro credits to *Gravity's Elbow* rolled. Bobby plopped back into the bean bag and quickly caught up.

The influx of red meat made Ethan thirsty. He opened a second beer.

Gravity's Elbow starts with a bang. A carful of vaguely ethnic bandits roars down a desert highway trailed by an expanding plume of dust. A long metal cylinder lays across the laps of the bandits in the backseat. The group laughs and cracks jokes—until Dalton Stampede's thicket of blonde feathered hair appears in the rearview mirror, whipping in the wind as his iconic Harley Davidson Roadster closes the distance. After Mr. Stampede dispatches the grunts, and *just* after he tosses a rattlesnake into the head bandit's face, four men in Folkston cheered and high-fived.

"Bourbon!" Bobby said, miming flinging a snake.

Frank and Garth exchanged a look and must have agreed because Garth responded, "Bourbon it is. What better way to celebrate the best intro ever put to film," Garth nodded at Ethan, "and a new friend, than a glass of the South's finest."

Garth went to the kitchen and poured four glasses of dark brown liquid out of a plastic bottle. They would be the first of many.

Eighty-three glorious and unparalleled minutes later, Dalton Stampede appears to be in dire straits. The lead villain, Loathsome Joe, has ensnared Stampede in a straightjacket to subdue his ferocious punches and devastating kicks, and imprisoned the hero in a white cinderblock room. Joe, striding about in front of his control panel, speaks to Stampede through the thick glass window serving as the room's fourth wall. Ethan had often questioned why the supposed genius would have designed his lair such that the most prized prisoners were but one good smashing from accessing the control room, but it did not detract one spinning elbow from his viewing.

Loathsome Joe draws near the conclusion of his speech. "So you see, Mr. Stampede, the entirety of humanity recognized a need for action." He walks up to a TV screen, hands clasped behind his back. "But *I* am the only one with the strength, the force of will, to do anything. Thanks to me, and me alone, tomorrow you will see a world free of problems. Free of strife."

"The only thing I see is a madman, a killer, a thug," the hero growls.

"You and I are quite different, Dalton. You cling to the past. The status quo. All your actions, your so-called *heroism*, are intended to preserve homeostasis. No matter what that is or where that may lead. Meanwhile, I . . ." he points at the screen showing a horde of manic citizens fleeing from some unseen terror. "I put my talents to use in service of a different goal. A better goal. I . . ." he rests his hand on the screen, "did this."

He steps to another screen: people run and scream amidst the chaos of a blossoming atrocity. "I did this."

The room was full of screens, examples of his insanity.

"I did this. I did this. People everywhere are saying that something must be done. *Oh somebody please do something.* Well, *I* am the one who did the thing."

Joe's inattention doesn't go unnoticed; slowly, the entangled badass shifts towards the window, eyeballing the far wall then looking back at the villain.

A running kick pulverizes a waist high cinderblock. The brick above it loosens, dropping one spot. Through a feat of karate, acrobatics, and editing, Dalton Stampede hooks it over the toe of his snakeskin boot and back flip catapults it through the glass; before it lands, the brick collapses the villain's knee with a crunch Ethan knew to be celery, chilled then snapped.

Bobby popped to his feet again, pointing at the screen. "That's the move, man! I wanna do that!" He swung his leg back and forth.

"Bobby . . ." Ethan detected actual concern in Garth's voice.

"I know, man. I know." Bobby sat down.

Back on screen, the well-muscled Stampede kicks through the remaining glass to stand over the fallen villain.

"You ain't done nothin' yet."

With that, the hero puts an offscreen boot through the villain's head, headbutts the killswitch on the control panel, which also inexplicably serves as the lair's self-destruct button, saves the girl, escapes, and rides off into the sunset.

Four men in Folkston slapped hands, took another shot of bour-bon, and braced themselves for the sequel.

Men. Action movies. Bourbon.

It escalated into a late night, one ass-kicking gem from the *Stampede Saga* after another, each one impossible to resist; each one requiring the consumption of several beers and, after particularly chin-shatter-ing, temple-busting spinning elbows, joyous shots of bourbon. Ethan waited for a gap in which to subtly probe about the Greenville Bick-ermans but was reluctant to talk shop during the films. At some point there was oven pizza.

Ethan was only able to peel himself off the couch prior to the unendurable *A Fist in the Darkness*. He slurred his goodbyes then, before opening the door, turned to face his still seated companions. The bourbon had relieved him of his nuance.

"It's just . . . I can't believe . . . Kurt Bickerman's family over in Greenville is trying to develop Folkston. I mean, what are people saying about that?"

"Zip it, lawyer boy," Garth said from across the couch. "No one wants to be your witness."

"That's fine." Ethan nodded, then cast a different line. "Do any of y'all fish? There's great fishing up at Lake Marie."

"I fish, man," Bobby said. He was splayed out face down on the bean bag chair like a starfish on a rock. "My dad takes me."

"Oh, maybe we could go some—"

"Go to bed, Ethan," Garth interrupted. "It's been a fun night."

Chapter Ten

E than woke up bleary-eyed. His temples pulsed as he tried to run through the night before; he wondered how much he had forgotten.

Did I get, and lose, anything useful about Bickerman?

He had a feeling he hadn't. He rolled away from the sunlight invading through the curtains, pulling his pillow over his eyes and listening for the sounds of an almighty storm. A bird chirped nearby.

A phone rang, not his cell phone, this was too clangy and shrill, reverberating through his skull like marbles on the sidewalk. He slapped at the bedside table until locating the bulky room phone and pulling it under the comforter to his ear.

"Yes?"

"Ethan?"

"Yes, this is . . . yes."

"It's Marissa DePaul. From Sires Paulson's office."

Ethan jolted upright.

Shit. There's going to be an off-day mediation or settlement talks. Or, worse, Judge Grimmaly, that sure footed judge, has somehow put trial back on for the day.

"Yes. Yes. Hi. Good morning." The sheets had come up with him. He pushed them down, away from his face and mouth. "What can I do for you?"

"There's nothing to worry about. I didn't mean to scare you. Court's still cancelled but, on that note, since it's actually nice out, I was wondering if you wanted to go for a hike."

Ethan blinked. His stomach bounced. "A hike?" He checked his phone; but for the predicted storm, he would have been due in court ten minutes ago.

"Yes. I heard where you're staying and thought about you having to sit cooped up there all day and, well, this seemed the hospitable thing to do."

Ethan rubbed his temples, reluctant to reveal why a hike seemed unadvisable. "Could we maybe get coffee first?"

"Sure. Of course, breakfast too. Sorry, I didn't mean to wake you."

"Oh I wasn't . . . it's no problem."

The pair arranged for Marissa to pick Ethan up in half an hour. He showered, vomited, brushed the alcohol off his teeth, vomited, brushed that off his teeth, and dressed for an outdoor adventure—not before ripping the wrapper off the motel's plastic cup and setting up by the sink to gulp down the old tasting water. He sat by the window to watch for Marissa's arrival.

Almost exactly one-half hour after Ethan had put down the phone, a white SUV descended from Main Street into the sands of Sapphire Courts. Ethan bolted out the door and down the stairs, waving at a startled Deborah, pointing at the car before she could start on another list. A gritty mist settled on the paint as Ethan approached the car. Marissa pointed at the passenger seat.

"I brought you a coffee and a breakfast sandwich. Coffee's just black now but I have some creamer packets."

"Black's fine. Thanks." Ethan took a testing sip. It wasn't well received.

"I was wondering if you were as bad off as you sounded."

"I'm fine. I was just startled at the call. And being woken up."

"Is that so? Would you like to eat here or on the road?"

Ethan looked around the parking lot: Frumpy was pooping on the second step. "Go. We should go."

"I was hoping you'd say that." Marissa put the SUV in gear and exited the lot.

"Thank you again for the invitation. I'm not sure what I would have done with myself otherwise. It would've been a long day at the desk."

"Of course. It'd be a shame for you to come all this way and not see the mountains. How are you liking Folkston so far?" Marissa's brown hair was tied back in a ponytail. She appeared completely at ease with the relative stranger in her passenger seat. Ethan had to admit she was even more attractive in her athletic gear.

"It's good. It's a . . . um . . . pretty town."

"What did you do last night?"

"Nothing too much. Just went over to my neighbor's for a bit."

"Oh no. You hung out with someone who lives at Sapphire Courts?"

"Yea. The guy next to me is actually pretty cool. We just watched old action movies. Ate steaks."

"Watched old action movies, ate steaks, and slugged moonshine?" She smiled.

"Is it that obvious?"

"You smell like my dad on Christmas."

"Just beer and bourbon. I may have gotten carried away. I got excited when we liked the same movies. I think they did as well."

"It's fascinating how easy it is to bring men together."

Ethan pulled a piece of biscuit off the sandwich, laid it on his tongue, and rewrapped the remainder. The road tilted, rising into a curve around the mountain. Ethan's stomach lifted and sank; a ball of pain rattled around his brain like a nickel in the dryer. The SUV's interior felt hot. Stifling warm air stuffed his nose, suffocating him, making him feel heavy, slow, and unstable. He let his forehead fall against the window glass, hoping it would be cool; when it was not, he lugged it back nearly upright. The SUV rolled over the first mountaintop and began to corkscrew down. Ethan finally made a pass at swallowing the biscuit, it made it halfway, then reversed course. With a panicked force of will he fought it back down, wondering what the fallout would be if he threw up in Marissa's car; she had been kind so far but he had to imagine she would take that personally. It would no doubt make it to her employer, then Mr. Colt.

"Are you okay?"

They passed a brown sign for an upcoming overlook. Ethan pointed at it.

"Uh oh. Absolutely. Right away. You just hang in there, bud." She eased onto the off-ramp, pulling up parallel to a picnic table. "Okay go sit, or lay. I'll park and be right there."

Ethan leaked out of the passenger door, stumbling to the bench without lifting his head. A cool breeze caressed his face as his world steadied, somewhat. The vehicle parked somewhere behind him; footsteps approached.

"Your biscuit and coffee are on the table by your head. I'm also giving you my water bottle. It has an electrolyte mix which may be of some assistance. I'm going to go some distance away, put in my headphones, and enjoy the view. I'll announce my return so don't be shy about doing what needs to be done."

There were a couple metallic noises by his head then the footsteps grew faint.

Ethan lay on his back, trying to relax and endure the moment, maintain equilibrium. Eventually, he gave in, plodding to the woodline for the purge.

I wish she was an old lady.

When he again retreated to the bench, he felt steady enough to unscrew the water bottle and pour some onto his sour tongue. He swooshed, spit, swooshed again, and swallowed. Chills ran through his body, his body hair standing on end as his vitals embraced the nourishment. He tugged off another piece of biscuit, sucking on it before sending it down. By the time Marissa shouted her return, he had forced down half the biscuit and water and coffee sufficient to sit upright in relative peace.

"Feeling better?"

"I'm upright. Although a hike may be out of the question."

"No worries. Hiking kinda sucks. It was just the least datey way I could think of getting you out during the daytime. I hated, hated, hated the idea of you, or anyone, thinking Folkston was just Sapphire Courts and the crumby courthouse. This is a nice spot though. If you turn around, slowly, you can see it."

Ethan shifted to the bench's intended sitting position. In front of him was a sweeping green plain fading into the horizon.

"Can I sit too? Or is there danger in the area?"

"It's safe."

"You stayed intact?"

"No. But I managed to distance myself from . . . this spot."

"A true Charleston gentleman. What do you say we sit here for a while? You can finish that biscuit and get back on your feet."

"I very much appreciate you suggesting that." Ethan laid back down.

"Who were your drinking companions?"

"Do you know a lot of the Sapphire Courts crowd?"

"More than I'd care to admit. Sires does a fair deal of criminal defense work. Sapphire Courts houses a fair deal of the criminals. Also, I grew up here so a lot of my classmates have done stints in Sapphire Courts as they circled the drain. I can probably tell you who's actually dangerous and who's just fooling."

Ethan listed the names of his drinking companions.

"I know two. *Of* two really. Bobby Canterbury was a couple years behind me all through school. He's just fooling about being dangerous, I think. He was the crazy hyper kid in school. The kid climbing trees and trying to do backflips off the monkey bars. I think he was a wrestler or something. I remember him getting some accolade in one of our assemblies and doing a cartwheel on stage. Garth Quattlebaum was a sheriff's deputy. Maybe even a detective."

"Really?" It was hard for Ethan to imagine his disheveled neighbor in any uniform, or even just well-fitting clothes.

"He didn't tell you that?"

"No. But I guess I didn't ask. So he's not a cop anymore?"

"Correct. I'm not sure what happened but he was the arresting officer on a couple of Sires' cases when I first started. All of a sudden, both were dismissed. Same day."

"Nobody said why?"

"Nope. But, generally, when the solicitor's office quietly dismisses a cop's cases wholesale it's a pretty good sign the guy did something unprofessional, dishonest, or altogether shitty. So you're keeping good company there."

"They've all been very nice to me."

"That's how they get ya. Or maybe they recognize one of their own." She smirked. "That must've been a wild night for you. You don't seem like the kind of guy who leaves his bubble very often. And the Sapphire Courts crowd must be way outside your bubble. I mean, who do you commiserate with in Charleston?"

"Mostly friends from law school."

"My point exactly. How was it?"

"Honestly, from what I can remember, pretty great. It's been a while since I've stayed in, gotten plastered, and watched old action movies. It's kinda all I've ever wanted."

"Better than a night out in Charleston? Definitely less expensive."

"Damn near free. Do you ever come down to Charleston?"

"I have actually. Many times. I'm certainly not above getting all dressed up just to go out and drink frilly cocktails. But I'm glad it's not my normal. It's exhausting."

"What is your normal?"

"What you did last night sounds like good fun. I can do without the shitty movies, straight bourbon, and presumably lousy beer but I'm a fan of the organic, easy, stationary hang."

"I can let you know the next time the gang assembles."

"I don't like it enough to do it at Sapphire Courts."

They stopped talking. Ethan enjoyed the view, the breeze, and the greasy biscuit, as feelings of health blossomed in his gut. He breathed, looking across the horizon in what he estimated was the direction of Lake Marie.

"Can you see the lake from here?"

"Which one?"

"Lake Marie."

"No. And oh no. Are you one of the lame-o wannabe adventurer fishermen?"

"Because I know Lake Marie?"

"And you refer to it as *the* lake. So you're a fan of the dumdum bandwagon show and you think Lake Marie is one of those mystical outdoor utopias."

"I watch it with my dad. The Lake Marie/Folkston episode is one of the best ever."

"So I've heard. After that episode aired, we got flooded with floppy hatted tourists stopping at the gas station to ask for directions to the lake. None of them have any idea the destruction and displacement it caused."

"Destruction and displacement? It's a lake."

"Not a natural lake. It should be the Folkston River."

"I know. Most lakes in the South used to be rivers." Ethan only knew this because in the episode Big Chuck fishes by the dam, where he pulls in a good-sized striper. "They constructed it to produce hydroelectric power for the area."

"Area is a loose term. That dam doesn't produce shit for this area. Each and every watt of electricity produced by that dam gets shipped off to Greenville and beyond. The state and federal governments decided that the Greenville-Spartanburg metropolis was destined to be the jewel of the region and they only needed additional electricity to make it happen. So they decided here, right here, was the place to build it. They even named the dam Wedgewood after a Greenville bigwig. Did Mr. Bandwagon mention that?"

"He doesn't usually go into that much detail."

"So he didn't mention Hermantown? That there were people living where the lake is, an entire community, a whole town of jobs, homes, families? He didn't mention that their own government flooded them out because it thought another place would bring in more tax revenue?

Or that all those people fought and lost to keep their homes? That their government sank one town to help build another?"

Chuck Palwagon had neglected to mention Hermantown altogether but Ethan figured it was best to let her say her piece.

She paused and took a breath. "Sorry. That's one of my rants. A lot of those folks are still around and are still very bitter about how that went down. It rubs off on you."

"I'm sorry. I didn't know."

"How could you? Why would you? That's the trouble with stuff like this. All you want to do is fish peaceful waters, which is entirely fair, but it stirs up some deep resentment around here. Which is fair as well." She sighed and shrugged. "Everything is at something else's expense. What builds for one destroys for another. Usually by the time you figure it out, it's too late."

Ethan thought for a second. *I'm building a career. That's not hurting anyone.* He decided against responding.

Marissa picked a flower and dropped it. They watched it seesaw to the ground. "Are you up for a town walk? It's relatively flat and I'm restless. I'll show you the prettier parts of Folkston. That's important to me."

"I think I can handle that."

"Great. Meet me at the car in ten seconds."

Marissa guided the SUV out of the mountains, passing the courthouse before turning right into a quaint residential zone: rows and rows of charming, if presently out of style, brick one-story ranch homes on neatly apportioned lots with well-tended lawns; the exact style of home currently being gutted, or torn down altogether, as a part of Charleston's fervent modernization. Marissa parked in front of a particularly immaculate specimen.

"So this is the nice part of Folkston?"

"One of them, yes. There's also the lakeside scene, waterfront on Lake Thompson, but that's mostly out-of-towners. You know, second homes."

"I didn't know Folkston was big enough to have multiple nice parts."

"We have it all, Mr. McDaniel. The good and the bad. The affluent and the indigent. Douches and cabooses."

"Garth already drove me around Cochran's Mill."

"Of course he did. I'm glad I'm balancing that out."

"That's a pretty nasty caboose."

"It's actually not too far from here as the crow flies or if you cut through the woods, but you have to go back to Main Street to find a connecting road. This house," she pointed at the red brick, "belongs to the esteemed and most honorable Judge Eustus Grimmaly."

"Judge Grimmaly lives here?"

"In the home he grew up in. Do try to veil your surprise."

"I'm sorry, I . . ."

"Don't worry about it." They exited the car and started walking away from Main Street, passing two women walking their households' overweight dogs. Marissa waved and called one of the women by name without stopping to chat.

They meandered through rows of neat, clean homes, Marissa occasionally stopping to tell a story about a home or point out a friend's childhood residence, taking several turns until Ethan lost track. Marissa had a bounce to her step, a slight bob that became more pronounced during quiet moments when she lost herself in the breeze and autumn sunshine. She swayed her hips, opening her hands to corral the cool air, each step finishing with a light spring of her toes to propel the next. They made a final turn, which as best as Ethan could guess, led directly out of town, and kept on. After a while, the grid straight road began to drift left as Folkston surrendered to the trees.

"Where are you taking me now?"

"I heard about something going on back here. I want to check it out while we're in the area."

Her posture stiffened. The bounce left her step; she now paced in a more determined manner reminiscent of her courtroom gait. Eventually, they came to a brick church.

"Fuck me. They're here again."

The street-facing façade, white steeple, and sidewalls were tidy and well-kept, but as the whole structure came into view, Ethan observed a chunk missing from the back corner; coal black scorch marks stained the adjacent bricks. A crowd of people milled about the churchyard, shuffling between white tents and the black hole. The people were uniformed in matching white t-shirts tucked into jeans; most wore the same branded ballcap. Marissa and Ethan stopped to observe. Ethan recognized the emblem on the hats and shirts.

"I know that church. Mount St. Mercy is a big Charleston church. It's only like a five-minute walk from my apartment."

Marissa didn't respond.

"I didn't know they did stuff like this, domestic mission trips or whatever. That's pretty cool." Ethan noted silently that he lived a place that provided aid and his tour guide lived in a place that required it.

One of the missionaries, a fit older man dressed for labor in creased khakis belted under a spotless polo, noticed them and approached.

"Here we go," Marissa muttered.

"Good morning!" The man stopped to shake each of their hands. "I suppose y'all are wondering what these strange people are doing in your town." His grey hair was as neatly coifed as Ethan's on trial days.

"You're here to rebuild Gary's base of operations."

"If Gary is Pastor McCann, then yes, that is exactly what we're doing. We are rebuilding his church. He wrote to tell us about his unfortunate fire and the destruction of his tabernacle, and helping him rebuild seemed the least we could do. We're hoping to be done by this weekend so we're truly blessed to not have lost a day to the storm."

"Y'all are from Charleston," Ethan said.

"We are indeed."

"I'm from Charleston too. I pass your church all the time. I'm just up here for work."

"Good for you, son," the man looked Ethan over again, smiling as if seeing him in a new light. "Please stop in some time and join us for worship. We have lots of events and programs for young professionals such as yourself."

It had been a long time since Ethan had been to a non-holiday service but the impassioned smiling face made it hard to say no. "For sure. Of course. I'll make sure to check y'all out." He needed an avenue to silence. "It's great what y'all are doing here."

"Oh, it's our pleasure. We love coming up to this beautiful area and doing what we can to help. There's so much to be done and the people up here need a guiding hand. Would you two like to join in? We have plenty of shovels and, more importantly, ice cold lemonade." Behind him, the entire group seemed to be sipping said lemonade as two men dressed in faded colors mortared bricks onto the ruins.

"No, we would not," Marissa said.

"Well, okay then." The man took a second to form a response. "If you'll excuse me, I don't want the other angels to think I'm not carrying my weight. Nice to meet you son, ma'am."

Marissa darted off back towards town, leaving Ethan to watch the man rejoin a group standing in the shade under a tent. He scrambled to catch up.

"Pompous asshole. Here to help the people of Folkston find the Lord my ass. And before you ask what it's like to live in a place shitty enough to warrant the attention of domestic missionaries, I'd like to remind you of the area we just traversed."

"They're just here to help."

"Help themselves. Those *angels* don't give a shit about Folkston."

"They're rebuilding a church *in Folkston*. Why else would they be doing that?"

"Because it's easy and it makes them feel good. Them. Folkston must be on some list because once or twice a year those goodly godly folks show up to preach something that don't need preaching or fix something that don't need fixing. We've had obscure sidewalks repaved, a retention pond dredged, our sign cleaned, our sign replaced, and seven damn gazebos erected in the park. This is the third time they've rebuilt that church. The missionaries love it. They rent houses on Lake Thompson, or stay in ones they own, bring their own food, bring their own contractors, and descend into town to do their worthless work. It's truly impressive the extent to which they accomplish nothing."

"They're rebuilding a church."

"Barely. That *church* wasn't a victim of lightning or bad wiring. No one ever went there to pray or find Jesus. It's a meth den. The spot that blew out is a storage closet where Pastor Gary McCann cooks and deals meth. Before he blew it up."

"The Pastor cooked meth in the church?"

"Every day except the Sabbath. It was, and thanks to the inexhaustible generosity of your Charleston church crowd will again be, a one stop shop. He cooks it. He deals it. He shoots it."

"The congregation of Mt. Saint Mercy is rebuilding a meth den?"

"More like tampering with a crime scene."

"They don't know that right?"

"No, they're too self-righteous and dismissive to ever learn anything like that."

"If it keeps blowing up . . . how has he, Pastor Gary, not gotten caught? I mean, you know about it. Why don't you do something?"

"Because he's got a good last name, is a pastor, and isn't all that dumb. He only deals to meth heads that wander in through the woods. He doesn't mess with dabbling teenagers from Sparrow Street. The mill folk trek in and he gives them their fix. Sires and I hear about him all the time from our court appointed clients. They joke about it, call it *a pilgrimage*. Then they try to roll on him to save their own asses."

"Why don't you tell the police?"

"We've tried. But when you're as firmly entrenched on the side of goodness as Pastor Gary McCann the blow to knock you off has to be really fucking square. The sheriff's office isn't super keen on launching an investigation into a pastor with no record and coming up empty. Especially based on the word of a defense attorney and his desperate criminal clients. So, they don't investigate. No investigation. No evidence. The church burns and the world turns."

Ethan looked back over his shoulder. "So those angels from Mount St. Mercy are really rebuilding a meth lab?"

"In His name."

Chapter Eleven

Marissa returned Ethan to Sapphire Courts shortly after noon, once more plunging her spotless SUV from Main Street into the pocked, dusty lot. Ethan thanked her for the morning adventure and apologized once more for the lack of a hike.

She smiled. "It's okay. I finally got to show a Charleston boy all the good his people do up here. Just know that you owe me one."

A chorus of cheers greeted Ethan's exit. He checked the second-floor railing but found it unmanned. The cheering crescendoed as Ethan, his hangover rallying, slugged up the stairs. Bobby, Frank, and Garth were slumped outside Garth's apartment, sitting against the brick wall with their feet splayed across the cement.

"Way to go, lawyer boy! Taking Folkston by storm!" This was Bobby.

"Oh that was just . . . why are y'all sitting out here?"

"Too hungover to stand," Garth said without moving his head. "Which begs the question: how did you pull that off?"

"That? That was nothing. She works for an attorney in the trial and picked me up this morning to go for a hike so I wouldn't have to hang with you lowlifes all day."

"Is that so?"

"Pretty much, yes."

"How'd you do on the hike?"

"I threw up on the ride out."

"Bully for making it that far. Bobby lost his pizza on his floor."

Ethan looked at Bobby, who did seem spryer than his companions. "I blew chunks, man!"

"Frank won't admit it but he lost his somewhere around the lot. I'm not sure how but I know he didn't keep it down." Frank could do nothing but gently shake his head, eyes closed against the sun. "We're going to spend our day in recovery." Garth rubbed his belly. "What's on your docket today, barrister?"

"I guess I'd better—"

"Wait, let me guess, get back to work."

"Trial resumes tomorrow."

"Allegedly."

Don't say that, Ethan thought. He closed his door and stationed himself at the desk with two cans of coffee he'd procured during the grocery run, opening his case file to Plaintiff's deposition. His eyelids sagged down. His head tilted forward. He emptied the first can of coffee, started the second, blinked, and rubbed his eyes.

Q: When do you first recall perceiving an odor on the property at 787 Woodstone?

A: I can't say precisely. It must've been when . . . can I have some water?

Break While Deponent Obtains and Drinks Water

A: Okay, sorry, thank you. What was the question?

Q: When do you first recall a smell on the property?

A: Oh yes, of course. When was that? I apologize but this water is warm. Is there any chance of getting chilled water?

Break While Deponent Obtains Chilly Water

Ethan jolted awake. His jaw ached where it had been pressed askew by the desktop. The general feeling of illness and exhaustion had subsided, but his stomach screamed for the repayment of missed, and lost, meals. He checked his stores: low fat chips; organic granola bars; low sodium soups; and decided to walk to town for a more satisfying burst of blood sugar.

The upper walkway was vacant. Ethan kept his head down as he left the stairs for the lot.

This would be the time to drive around and find Jeanie's but I'm not up for it. It's also probably closed. I'll just have to eat whatever I come across.

He tried to picture Main Street and any potential restaurants or general food purveyors. His mind felt heavy and slow.

"You going to dinner?" It was Deborah—The Bore, ugh—approaching from the grassy strip. In his distracted state, he had neglected to check the perimeter for patrols.

"No." Ethan waited until she was in the shade to look up. Frumpy prowled the crab grass; he shifted back to remain out of leash range. "Just stretching my legs."

"We have good dinner. *I* think it's Folkston's best meal. There's . . ." Early in the list Ethan wondered how he missed all these wonderful establishments over the past few days; later he felt certain Deborah's list of restaurants exceeded the number of viable structures. More hermit crabs than shells.

"It's really okay. I'm eating in tonight. I stockpiled for the storm so—"

"Oh, the storm, the storm. Everybody was talking about the storm. Not me, though. I didn't buy nothing. Every year that Dick Bailey, that WSMP weatherman, does this. I think he just likes the attention.

And getting people all riled up. Last year it was an ice storm in February. The year before . . ."

This was too much. Deborah's second endless list incited a fervent protest in Ethan's belly which, in its opinion, had tolerated enough mistreatment. Now it demanded proper care. Ethan needed to feed it. But the words kept coming. Ethan's stomach well understood that Ethan's deeply ingrained politeness was the only thing standing between it and nourishment and decided to push the issue: his body grew heavier, the sun brighter, as his stomach cranked at the control knobs for his inner ear, upping the volume and isolating the The Bore's shrillest and most nasally tones, contorting the woman's voice to something approaching fingernails on a chalkboard.

I can't do this. I'm going to have to yell at this woman. It's not my fault. I didn't start this. I'm not keeping it going. I have no other choice. She's making me do it. She has no claim on my time. And I've been more than tolerant before. On several occasions. And I've been humiliated for it. Now this is dangerous. I might die.

Ethan's mouth had just opened when there was a shout.

"KEEEEYYAAHHHH!"

Ethan turned to see a gold and beige missile blast off the second story railing, rolling on impact with the sand to pose in a superhero crouch. Bobby Canterbury stood up, flipping his glowing hair back to strut the final few yards.

"Sorry I'm late." Bobby turned to Deborah. "Ethan and I were just about to head out for dinner."

Deborah glanced at Ethan, mouth working as if physically chewing Bobby's words.

"Well, not dinner Bobby, remember I have food in the room. We're just going for a walk. Maybe getting drinks."

Bobby stood silently grinning long enough for Ethan to worry he'd missed the implication. Finally, he perked up. "Right man, drinks. Sorry."

Deborah's mouth stilled. "Where y'all going? We have . . ."

"—Bobby hasn't told me yet." Ethan leapt on Deborah's words. "He says it's a local treat. An institution, I think you said."

"You taking him to McGillicutty's? That place is too rough. You could go to—"

"Don't want to ruin the surprise." Bobby latched onto Ethan's arm and started towing him away. "Now you have yourself a nice night Debs." When they were just questionably out of earshot, Bobby crooned: "Thhheeee Boooooorrrrreeeee," then burped. "UGGGH-HHHHHHH!" Ethan checked on the song's subject, who appeared wholly consumed in conversation with her mouthy mutt.

"Thanks. She caught me flat-footed."

"Ain't nothin' man."

"I definitely owe you a beer."

"You're my buddy, man. I can't stand by while you suffer in the clutches of The Bbbbooooooorrrrreeee . . ." Bobby once more let his neck droop and jutted out his chin, "ugggggghhhhhh." He laughed at himself, a genuine, warm honey giggle that Ethan couldn't resist. Ethan was surprised at the growing warmth in his chest triggered by Bobby calling him a buddy. "I probably shouldn't get a drink now though."

"No problem. I am actually out for food though. Just didn't want to tell Deborah that and get tagged with an endless list."

"She knows a lot of spots, man. Where you gonna eat?"

"I was just going to walk and find something."

"Nah man. I'll take us somewhere good. Don't you worry. Just let me think for a second."

Bobby palmed the light poles as they passed, letting his fingers slip off just in time to reach for the next one. There was joy in his movements, a child completely safe and at ease on his home turf. It was hard to imagine him in a foreign and potentially hostile city like Columbia.

They finished passing the courthouse.

"Oh yea man. This is an easy one. There's no way you've had Gruber's yet. Fried chicken sandwich and some fries."

"That sounds like exactly what I need. Are they open with the storm?"

"Yea man. Grubes never closes."

Ethan followed Bobby to the exterior walk-up counter, where Bobby ordered two fried chicken sandwich combos with fries before the teenager working the booth had even turned to face him. Ethan started for his wallet, but Bobby stopped him.

"I got this one, man."

"Oh no, you already saved me from—"

"Garth would want me to pay. Frank too."

Seconds later, the cashier handed Bobby two dinner plate sized lumps of tinfoil.

"There's a quiet place to eat up here. Local secret." Bobby nodded down Main Street and the pair continued their journey. At the Folkston welcome sign, Bobby turned right into the bramble creeping up Main Street's shoulder. Ethan followed, the thorns tearing at his pants, as the local led him down no discernible path.

"Where are you taking me?"

"The water pit."

"Water pit?"

"Yea, it's a pond I guess. Water pit is just more fun to say."

"Water pit . . . You come here often?"

"It's more of a high school spot. But yea, all the time back in the day. Cops don't like messing with all the thorns so they usually leave you alone."

After about fifty yards of vines and pricklies, and some steep terrain, Ethan heard the sound of moving water. A few more burr and nestle steps and the pair emerged onto a pebbled, streamside clearing. At the bank's far end, the stream pooled into a cul-de-sac sized pond.

A fishing hole. I've discovered my own local who's taken me to his own fishing hole.

Ethan tried to picture Chuck Palwagon tramping his hefty frame through the vines and pricklies. Bobby stopped, tossing Ethan his shiny lump of food, before folding to sit in the sand.

"This was the high school move, man. Pick up some Grubes and hang out here for hours."

"You and Frank?"

"Nah, Frank didn't come around until later. But he wouldn't have had time for this kind of shit. He's always working. Frank and I met at the Courts."

"So he moved to Folkston?"

"Yea from somewhere in the midlands. Pine-something. His mom died and his dad lost his job so they started moving around."

"Jesus, what happened?"

"I don't really know, man. Frank doesn't talk about it ever. She was sick, I think. His dad was a truck driver, but after she died something happened and he couldn't get a job driving anymore. Came up here to work at the plant. Always work at the plant."

"Shit." Ethan knew enough to assume it had been a DUI as that's essentially the first question in any wreck case involving commercial drivers: has the driver ever been convicted of any driving offenses involving alcohol or other intoxicants. Insurance companies absolutely do not insure drivers with DUI convictions. The policy had always made sense to Ethan on its face, but he had never considered it under these facts: a father grieving his deceased wife. It suddenly seemed severe.

"Frank's pretty blown about the whole thing. Whatever the problem was, he's gonna become a lawyer and fix it."

Ethan unwrapped his chicken sandwich and fries both of which had steamed to mush in the foil. Still, the salty grease buoyed his blood sugar and spirits. Bobby sat cross-legged, facing the water with his tinfoil platter in his lap. When he was done eating, he took to launching a series of pebbles over the water. They cleared the considerable water to thunk deep into the opposing brush—an impressive distance for someone with their butt cheeks in the sand.

"Did you play baseball?"

"No way, man. I can't do sports where there's that much standing around. I gotta be moving all the time or I get distracted and start messing around, digging, dancing, or singing, or whatever. Gets the coaches all riled up when you don't pay attention." Ethan remembered watching little leaguers play in the dirt while the ball dribbled past. "That's why I wrestled. Once the ref blows the whistle, it's pretty much all action. No time to get distracted."

Bobby sprang to his feet and, without explanation, waded in the water out to his knees and looked around him like a bird on the hunt. "There we go." He leaned in and snatched something shiny from the depths. For a second, Ethan thought it was a trout. "Almost always cold beer here."

He detached one from the six-pack and tossed it to Ethan. The can was frigid.

"Whose are these?"

"No telling. But what's left here is fair game. That's tradition." Ethan checked the lid for signs of rust, wiped off some ooze, and opened it as Bobby dropped the remaining five back into the water pit with a splash and commenced sloshing back to shore.

"You're not going to have one?"

Bobby stopped, now only ankle deep, looking back at the rippling water as if the thought had not occurred to him. "No, man. I really shouldn't. Frank doesn't like when I drink on work nights."

Ethan sensed a topic that didn't require further investigation. "Were you born in Folkston?"

"Only place I've ever lived." Bobby plopped into the sand next to Ethan.

"How was that? I mean, it's very small."

Bobby pushed a wet hand though his hair; it stuck behind his right ear. "Awesome, man. I was always exploring, climbing trees and shit. Plus, there's a lot of nooks where nobody's watching you. Easy to hang out without folks getting on your ass all the time."

"Nooks like here?"

"Exactly, man."

"You're lucky. That was hard to do in the city."

Bobby looked up. "No shit?"

"Everywhere we played was someone's backyard or basement. In high school it was a high stakes game just finding a place to take a girl. It took a great deal of planning and more than a little luck."

"Should've brought them here. This is a great spot."

"It's about five hours from Charleston to the water pit, plus a walk through the stickers, so that would've been a tough sell. And a lot of time to have to explain away." Ethan enjoyed a long sip. "Was this where you brought your girls?"

"No." Bobby shifted to sit cross-legged again. "I mean, this is a good spot for that. But I went elsewhere, man."

Ethan finally asked the question that had been chewing on him since he'd first heard the water rushing. "Does this feed out of Lake Marie?"

"Maybe. I've never been much good at knowing stuff like that."

"That's legendary fishing, Lake Marie. My dad and I are hoping to make a trip up here to try it ourselves."

"Sure, man. My dad's got a boat up there. He goes out all the time." Bobby's dad then. That was a natural connection. *The Canterbury's, together, could be my local.*

"You're really lucky to have a dad with a boat on Lake Marie. A lot of folks in Charleston, everywhere really, would kill to have easy access to that water."

Ethan stopped talking, waiting, hoping for Bobby to extend the invitation to go fishing on his dad's boat. Bobby threw a final pebble; this one didn't clear the water. "You mind if we get moving, man? I'm freezing from fetching that beer."

"Yea. Sure. Let's do it." Ethan chugged the remainder of his beer and burped. Bobby laughed and so did he.

They returned to Main Street. Ethan brushed the bristles off his clothes as Bobby checked both ways, lost in thought. "I got an idea man. Follow me this way."

Ethan followed, feeling like he was visiting his nephew who always made a point of giving Ethan a detailed tour of his playroom and backyard, pointing out his favorite toys and where he played with them.

They turned right off Main Street, went about a hundred yards, and came to the sign for Folkston High School.

"You're taking me to school?"

"It's closed, man, for the storm, but there's this window that's been broken since my dad's time. You can jimmy it out and, at night, or when it's closed, the school is yours. If they haven't fixed it."

Ethan followed Bobby around the faded brick building to a chest-high window with a bent frame. "Ah! Shit here never changes." Bobby slid his fingers into the bend and pulled the window ajar, then stood aside and motioned for Ethan to climb in.

"I think I'm a little old for this. It's a tough look for adults to get caught sneaking into closed high schools." This arrest would be uncomfortable to explain to Mr. Colt, Mrs. Warland, or his father.

"We won't get caught. You're with a master thief, man. Just harness your inner Stampede. If we have to, we'll just bop our way out."

Bobby jumped and, in one fluid motion, slipped his body inside the window, landing noiselessly within. Ethan took a slower, noisier course, wriggling over the frame and through the window, then sliding down onto a desk. The room appeared either to be a little used office or rarely visited storage area. Despite his earlier confidence, Bobby checked each way twice before committing to the hallway. The lights were off; only the fading rays of sunset lit the hallways.

Ethan kept both ears cocked for approaching footfall as they twisted and turned into the bowels of the school. Eventually, well after Ethan had lost his way, Bobby stopped by a relatively innocuous interior door.

"This is the spot, man." Bobby opened the door before Ethan had the chance to read the placard. The interior was pitch black.

"It's very dark."

"Yea, I know man. You gotta step in before I can get the light."

Ethan did so and Bobby closed the door. There was a heavy click and a trio of huge caged onion bulbs above them groaned to life, revealing a wall of athlete portraits to Ethan's left and racks of trophies to his right.

"The Folkston High School Athletic Hall of Fame."

The Hall of Fame was little more than a closet which happened to be stuffed with trophies. "Why is this the spot?"

"We used to get stoned here and make up stories about the old dudes in the pictures with the funny names." Bobby ran his fingers over the nearer, black and white photographs. "Buck Gently. Fritz Burroker. Dats Nieto. Mickson Match." The infectious cackle punctuated each name. "There's a couple of my dad's friends up here too. They're just fat old beer drinkers now."

Ethan drifted down the wall, wondering what drove Bobby to get stoned in this interior closet at his high school when he had a perfectly good and secluded water pit. His eyes ran over the collection of spry young wrestlers, football, basketball, and baseball players. Towards the far end of the room, just when it was becoming clear that square footage would necessitate the school raising its bar for athletic recognition, Ethan came across a familiar name under a bumpy faced, crew cut blonde wrestler:

Robert Tucker Canterbury, Jr.
Most Valuable Wrestler
Sophomore

"Was this all just a ruse to show me this?" Ethan tapped the photo.

"Show you what?"

"This picture, Bobby. That you were the most valuable wrestler."

"What are you ta—" Bobby stopped in front of the picture. He pushed back his hair, forgetting his hands on top of his head as, mouth agape, he gawked at the photograph. "Oh man."

"MVP as a sophomore. That's quite the feat." Ethan checked the rest of the wall for another Bobby portrait. "I don't blame you for showing this off."

"I didn't know, man. I guess I haven't been here since that season ended."

"They didn't have a ceremony or anything?"

"Maybe. That was my last year."

"Of wrestling?"

"No, man. Of school. I stopped going."

But your bricks . . . "Were you kicked out?" Ethan thought this was a safe bet for a kid who made a habit of getting high on school grounds.

"No, man. I just stopped going." Bobby continued scrutinizing his photograph and plaque.

"Why?"

"Season ended. I only went for wrestling and I didn't feel like going back."

"Your parents didn't make you?"

"Coach called a couple of times but, other than that, nobody said nothin' man." Bobby's head drooped, just for a second his blonde hair covered his face, then his head was upward and he was back in motion, working over the pictures. "Yes! Here he is, man. This guy could've been the next Dalton Stampede."

Ethan stepped over to inspect Bobby's find.

Derrell "Whomp" Bludgeon
Middle Linebacker

They returned to Sapphire Courts in darkness. Bobby alternated between repeating his favorite names and long fits of giggling. He was capable of producing a wide range of noises, movements, and facial expressions, and put each skill on display as he performed the names.

"Deeewww-EEEE CROAK-er . . . POW Urrrgghhhlllllly . . . Buhh-Aaa-RUN Fields."

Ethan couldn't contain himself. Bobby's clean, unfettered, and above all loud laugh did not exist amongst his young professional circles; each name, each fresh outburst of laughter ambushed Ethan's sensibilities, overwhelming his inhibitions and demanding participation. Ethan's own guffaws achieved unprecedented tenors and ferocity.

A figure watched them from the second-story walkway. Bobby looked up and waved. "Frank! How you doin' man?" Ethan wasn't sure how he recognized his friend with only the aid of a distant street light.

"Where have you been?"

Bobby bounded up the stairs before responding, "I've been showing Ethan the sights, man. I took him by the school and the water pit."

Ethan emerged into the crosshairs of Frank's scowl. "Have you two been together all evening?"

"Yea. He saved me from Deborah then walked me around town."

"Where?"

"Just like he said the pond thing and the school."

"You stop anywhere else?"

"Nope. Well, Gruber's."

Frank relaxed. "Okay, that's fine. I'm glad y'all had a nice time."

"Nothing to worry about. He was just showing me around."

"Alright men. I'm hittin' it," Bobby said clapping Ethan on the back. "See you clowns tomorrow. Frank, Ethan."

"Good night, Bobby." Frank and Ethan watched Bobby go into his room. When the door was closed, Frank leaned in close.

"Did you stop anywhere else? Did you go to the Mill? Did you meet anyone?"

"No, it was just the two of us."

"Did y'all do any drinking or . . . anything else?"

"I had one beer that he pulled out of the pond. But he didn't. I don't even think he had any water."

"Okay, good. Good night, Ethan."

"Good night."

Chapter Twelve

The next morning, a sober Ethan reinstituted his morning exercise routine with extra push-ups and jumping jacks to mitigate the cheat day. Next came case review, then shaving, showering, and selecting the next pre-arranged outfit off the hanger. Once more, he saved the Patricians for last.

Still awesome.

He paused on the walkway to locate Deborah: she was out there, directly blocking his path to the courthouse. Ethan stalled, watching as Frumpy sniffed the same collapsed pack of cigarettes for five minutes before picking up what appeared to be a chicken bone and leading her owner back inside. When he heard the door close, Ethan made his move.

Today only a small scattering of jurors, presumably fourteen, dotted the courthouse steps. Ethan kept way back, finding refuge in the shade of a fledgling tree growing in a grass island near the lot's entrance. To Ethan's left, Mr. Paulson peered through the windshield of his minivan, his lips moving as he studied the jurors' interactions. Sterling Colt surveyed the lot as well from his perch on the top stair, his back every bit as stiff and straight as the pillar to his right.

"Your boss is intense."

Ethan jolted, first at someone being so near, then at the horrifying prospect of that someone being a juror.

"I'm over here." Ethan located Marissa standing on her own grassy island in the shade of her own tree. "Don't worry. It's just me."

"I'm not sure how I missed you."

"Must be that hawk-eyed, eagle-nosed, short-sighted lawyer trial day focus. How are you feeling today?"

"Much better, thank you. I behaved myself last night."

Marissa nodded. "Are you being overly cautious because Sires called you out for talking to potential jurors?"

"Yes. That wasn't great."

"I wouldn't take it personally. Sires just wanted to see how ol' Eustus was feeling, and obviously piss your boss off."

"My boss isn't here."

"Sorry, I mean Captain Gargoyle. The sneering robot."

"That's Mr. Colt. He's with his own firm."

"Yea I know, but I bet if I asked him, he'd say he was your boss. Teri's too. Perhaps the boss of all defense attorneys everywhere. But Sires was just abusing you because he wanted to split the team up. Gargoyle has a nasty temper and is quick to judge. By accusing you of talking to jurors, Sires already set him against you. Gargoyle doesn't trust you. He thinks you're a weak spot in his case."

"That's not true." *I hold the smoking gun. I have valuable information about Bickerman.*

"He didn't even pretend to give you the benefit of the doubt. And that's after he saw firsthand with his own stony eyes that you didn't talk to anyone. We all saw him snap at you before you'd even said your piece. We don't even have to get into them casting you off into the gallery."

"Why are you telling me this?"

"Because it's hot and there's no harm in it. You're getting burned by the way, sweaty too. Join me in the shade." Marissa's sapling was much more substantial, providing significantly more coverage than the paltry collection of leaves above him. Ethan rubbed a hotspot on his forehead and obliged. "You weren't up for another wild night with the Sapphire Courts crew?"

"I did actually hang out with Bobby again. He showed me around town."

"All my work undone. Did he take you back to Cochran's?"

"Nope. Just went for a walk down Main Street and ate some Gruber's."

"That's almost just as bad. Whatever insurance company is paying you clearly doesn't give one single damn about your comfort or safety."

"They have a bottom line to worry about. Attorney's fees add up. In addition to any potential payout. However, unlikely."

"They may end up paying out for your funeral. Sires can represent your estate if something happens to you because they put you in harm's way. That could be a big payout."

"Hopefully it doesn't come to that."

The glass doors opened and the jurors formed a line.

"Okay." Marissa passed her hand downwards in front of her face, taking on a more serious expression. "Game time. Game face. Get away from me, enemy." She turned and walked away.

When the last juror had disappeared inside the glass, Ethan counted to fifty and approached, this time pulling aside his jacket to display his belt to Cordell when the metal detector beeped around him. As Cordell wanded him, Ethan studied the building's utilitarian interior. The floor had the same cheap, thin looking purplish carpet that lined the halls of Ethan's high school. The walls had been painted, or papered, in something between off-white and grey. Directly in front of Ethan was a framed picture of the Folkston County Courthouse on its opening day; Ethan recognized this as the photo he had found online. To the right of that was the door to the Clerk of Court whose office appeared to extend all the way to the building's far end. Ethan had been sent on enough courthouse fact-finding missions to know this extra space housed Folkston County's physical court records. To Ethan's left, past the stairs, and protected by a sheet of plexiglass and an aging administrative assistant, was the solicitor's office. Four different prominently displayed signs guided entrants to the second-floor for Family Court. The Bore Ugh was right: the courthouse was a one-stop shop.

Ethan took the stairs and assumed his place on the first row of the gallery. Ms. Nelson turned to him and put on a smile.

"Good morning, Ethan. How are you?"

"I'm well, thank you. Good morning, Mr. Colt."

Mr. Colt addressed him while writing, somehow speaking without stopping his pen. "Good morning, Mr. McDaniels. I have a very important task for you today. Please keep a keen eye on the jury during my opening. I'd like to know how they respond to my different arguments. Their reaction may decide how we structure our defense."

"Of course. Yes sir." *See, he trusts me.*

Ethan checked across the aisle—Marissa was deep in conversation with Mr. Paulson as their bespectacled client watched, concerned, from the adjacent chair. Ethan leaned in close over the bar to confer with his co-counsel.

Ethan crept through the swinging bar and knelt between Mr. Colt and Ms. Nelson to whisper, "I just want to remind y'all that, in case Mr. Bickerman gets called today, we can go after him about his family in Greenville pulling the strings on his resort plans. If he admits to it we can impeach him with—"

"We cannot go after him with something for which we don't have any evidence."

Ethan took a breath, measured his words, and pushed forward, "But if cross is anything like his deposition you'll be able to pull anything out of him." Ethan thought this a particularly deft maneuver. "We can at least mention his family and plant the seed in the jury's mind that outsiders were involved."

Mr. Colt turned fully round to face Ethan.

"It's not a bad idea, Sterling," Ms. Nelson said.

"No, it's a great idea. Mr. McDaniels, you draw me up a quick line of questioning and I'll review it as I can prior to Plaintiff taking the stand."

Ethan sat back down, biting the corners of his mouth to keep from smiling as he began his first draft.

Emmett Lucas trudged in moments before nine, slumping his denim clad body in the chair to Ms. Nelson's right.

"Another day gone," he muttered. She patted him on the back.

Judge Grimmaly entered precisely on the hour and briskly took the bench.

"I trust that those assembled came through yesterday's trials unscathed." Judge Grimmaly smirked. "It appears our local weatherman, Mr. Bailey, has outdone himself yet again. Mr. Bailiff, please bring in the jury." The lawyers barely had time to stand before the jury streamed in from a backdoor.

"Good morning, ladies and gentlemen. It's nice to see everyone survived yesterday's weather delay, or as I prefer to call it, weather-*man* delay." Judge Grimmaly paused for laughter. "In the spirit of expediency, we will now commence with each party's opening statement. Mr. Paulson, the well is yours."

Ethan tapped the timer on his watch.

"Thank you, your Honor. Ladies and gentleman of the jury and fellow Folkston residents, my name is Sires Paulson. I was born and raised here in Folkston in a house on Wickam Road just a few hundred yards from where we are now assembled. My father, Donald Paulson, practiced law here for fifty years, representing this area's residents in all manner of criminal, civil, business, and family matters. He could've gone somewhere else, moved to one of the cities and plied his trade in Columbia or Charleston and almost certainly seen more personal economic success. But my father stayed here because, as he told me just about every day, *the people of this region are our family. It is a small population but it possesses the values that built this nation. These people deserve better than this country, even this state, are giving them.* It's safe to say my father never quite got over the government building that dam. So I joined my father's practice when I was twenty-five and, as you may have guessed, have now taken up my father's mantel. My client today, Mr. Kurt Bickerman," Mr. Paulson used two massive paws to gesture at the seated man, "is another southern gentleman who cares about this region's prosperity. Kurt Bickerman is a man intent on bringing wealth and prosperity to this town and this county."

Ethan took notes and monitored his watch: Mr. Paulson spoke for eleven minutes thirty-six seconds. He was casual and informal, at certain times leaning on rails or resting his hands in his pockets to stroll by the jury, whose heads, Ethan noted, turned with his movements. Mr. Paulson took care not to speak directly negatively about Mr. Lucas, who was also a beloved figure, but laid out in detail how he had overstepped his property, improperly and illegally stored trashed there, leading to what he termed *a most unpleasant odor*, and how these actions had thwarted Mr. Bickerman's attempts to bring jobs to Folkston County. When Mr. Paulson was done, he thanked the jury and sat down.

Judge Grimmaly spoke. "We will now hear the defense's opening. Mr. Colt."

Ethan marked the time on his notepad and restarted his timer.

"Thank you, your Honor." Mr. Colt paced towards the jury. "My name is Ster—" everyone in the courtroom jumped; those not already facing that direction turned to the rear as the doors burst open. Sterling Colt stopped too, twisting to watch openmouthed as Garth Quattlebaum, clad in a formerly white but now urine yellow business shirt which dangled untucked over fraying khakis, amble down the aisle and take a seat four rows behind Marissa.

Ethan gaped, horrified that Garth may acknowledge him in some by waving, pointing, or, God forbid, saying his name. But Garth paid him no mind, stretching his arms across the backrest just as the heavy doors finally rattled back into position. The heads slowly turned back to Mr. Colt who, now a brilliant shade of red, was the last to take his eyes off the intruder and look up at the judge. Judge Grimmaly lifted a hand at the attorney.

"Is that a Quattlebaum I see out there?"

Garth pointed at himself, started to answer, then stood up. "Yes sir. Garth Quattlebaum. I'm Ray's boy."

"Mr. Quattlebaum, the next time you enter this courtroom, please take care to either do so silently or during a break."

"Yes sir. Sorry sir. Dunno my own strength."

Judge Grimmaly motioned for him to sit then, with the same hand, motioned for the opening statement to continue. Mr. Colt took a long breath and smoothed his suit before refacing the jury.

Sterling Colt briefly introduced himself, Ms. Nelson, and Mr. Lucas, then plowed into his argument, stamping out his words like a typewriter, his hands hitting three marks: at his side; fingers touching in a triangle at his chest; or, pointing at the jury. His voice rose and fell as he detailed Emmett Lucas' life and legacy in Folkston, emphasizing the integral daily service his client had provided for over thirty years. The jury appeared to follow Mr. Colt this far. But, after establishing this base, he went on the offensive, vilifying Mr. Bickerman as a traitor to his town and his proposed buyers as intruders looking to exploit Folkston's natural beauty to no local benefit, condemning their plan to crush a local institution, Lucas Trash, for the mere potential of selfish personal gains. Mr. Colt vowed to defend Emmett Lucas from such attacks and stated his intent to show the jury that, not only was there no smell emanating from the Lucas property, but also that the property sale fell through for a variety of other reasons, not limited to Mr. Bickerman's own incompetence, hinting more than once that Mr. Bickerman filed this suit to avoid having to confront his own failure. It was during the Colt offensive that the jurors' heads began to drift down to their laps. Ethan checked on Garth, who alternated between grimacing and shaking his head. After twenty-three min-utes and twelve seconds, including the Quattlebaum delay, Mr. Colt thanked the jury and sat. His eyes locked on Garth as he took his seat.

Mr. Paulson called his first two witnesses: both county officials who testified to the metes and bounds of the properties and their respective histories. Garth left halfway through the second, tiptoeing out when Mr. Paulson had paused to check his notes. Ethan used the breaks, of which there were many, to prepare a clean looking draft of a line of questioning about Kurt Bickerman's Greenville family. When court adjourned for lunch, he handed it to Mr. Colt, standing at attention as the older attorney looked it over.

"This is good, son," Mr. Colt said, patting Ethan on the shoulder. "Rough and ready. But very good. I might be able to do something with this." Ethan smiled all the way back to Sapphire Courts.

When Kurt Bickerman took the stand after lunch, he and the jury endured three hours of uneventful direct examination before Mr. Colt stood to deliver his cross-examination. Ethan surveyed the twelve blank faces in the box.

Just you wait, Ethan thought, *you're really going to hate him soon.*

Mr. Colt started off re-touching and pushing on some preliminary matters. Ethan tried to predict how he would make the turn, deliver the blow.

Will he start with something innocuous like 'are you at all related to the Greenville Bickermans, the ones who did such a great job, and made a fortune, renovating that downtown?' Or will it be more direct, ambush style like 'now isn't it true that your more intelligent and successful Greenville family were pulling the strings on this development?'

Ethan's anticipation grew until, in the end, Mr. Colt sat down without mentioning family or the city of Greenville. Ethan watched him organize his papers as Judge Grimmaly adjourned the proceedings with instructions to reconvene tomorrow at nine. Ethan calmed himself, thought things through, then leaned over the bar as the other defense attorneys were packing up.

"I think that went really well. Is there anything you need from me for tomorrow?"

Mr. Colt finished locking his briefcase and looked up. "What did Bickerman testify was the initial reason he became interested in purchasing his property?"

"In his deposition he said—"

"Not his deposition, please. What did the jury hear?"

Ethan's heart jumped, or stalled. "Yes sir. I have that . . ." He flipped through his yellow legal pad.

"This is an important detail."

"Sorry, sir." Ethan placed his thumb on the relevant notes. "He said that he was looking to use it as a storage yard for his other business. The tire business."

"Is that his exact testimony?"

"It's not word for word. He spoke quickly so I—"

Mr. Colt pushed the final piece of his case file into his briefcase. "Ms. Nelson and I are convening for a dinner strategy session this evening. We could certainly use your notes."

"And you," Ms. Nelson added.

"Absolutely."

"Good. Ms. Nelson will give you the details. Bring whatever notes you may have made."

They watched him exit the courtroom before Ms. Nelson filled Ethan in on the time and restaurant.

Marissa waited to walk out with Ethan.

"Y'all are in trouble now, McDaniel. Sires done set the trap and Captain Gargoyle stepped right in it."

"I actually think we got exactly what we needed."

"Nope. We have you exactly where we want you. What do you think about that?"

"I think it's inappropriate for us to discuss the current proceedings."

"You're right. Especially since *I'm* actually involved."

Chapter Thirteen

Ethan knocked on Garth's door; when he didn't answer, he called Mrs. Warland on the walkway.

"How'd day one go?"

"Well, I think. Pretty much according to plan so far. They say it smells. Mr. Bickerman is not particularly sympathetic so I don't think Sires made any ground there."

"Perfect. And you're going to dinner with Sterling and Teri tonight?"

"Yep. Thanks for setting that up."

"It'll be a learning experience for sure. Sterling's scorched earth litigation policy is truly something to behold. And it will keep you out of trouble."

"Are you concerned about me getting into trouble?" For a moment he worried she'd somehow heard about his binge drinking two nights prior.

"No. But it's best to be extra careful when in a trial with Sterling Colt."

Ethan also called his dad but caught him fishing rod in hand and was only able to give him the briefest of updates. He went inside, changed, washed his socks, and reviewed his notes.

The restaurant was two towns over; apparently neither older attorney had seen any acceptable accommodations, or eateries, in Folkston, or their adjusters were simply less miserly than Margot with a T. Still, Ethan was driving to his first in-trial strategy meeting; he checked no fewer than twelve times whether his legal pads were in the manilla folder on the passenger seat. He also tried to manage his expectations as he had a feeling his main and perhaps only responsibilities would be the provision of trial notes and the taking of preparatory notes.

The restaurant, Ristorante Rotondo, was a square building relying on a combination of faux stonework and off-white stucco to provide the serenity of an Italian villa. Through the plexiglass doors, the interior was dark, red, and loud. Ethan was twenty minutes early and sat down by the hostess stand, examining the various photographs of robust men and women presenting the camera with bottles of olive oil and blocks of hard cheese.

Eventually a very local girl with jet black hair and purple eye liner noticed Ethan in the entryway. "Are you with the lawyers?"

"Yes."

"We got y'all in the party room."

She led Ethan through the crowded restaurant to a door marked *Stanza de Festa*; she opened it and stood aside. Mr. Colt and Ms. Nelson hovered over the near end of an oval twelve-person banquet table. Folders and exhibits lay in neat rows, covering the entire surface except for a single untouched charcuterie platter on the outer rim.

"Good evening."

"Mr. McDaniels."

"Ethan."

"Is there anything y'all need back here," the server asked, "or should I just shut the door?"

"A wine list, please," Mr. Colt responded.

"Absolutely."

The door closed and Ethan spoke. "Anything I can help y'all with?"

"Be ready to hand us exhibits from the far end as they come up."

Ms. Nelson raised her head, raised her eyebrows, and nodded at a chair. "You're welcome to speak your mind if you think of anything."

"Of course," Mr. Colt added. "We can always use a third set of eyes."

"Absolutely." Ethan positioned himself at the far end of the table. Two red balloons, presumably leftovers from an earlier birthday party, floated in the corner behind Mr. Colt, their brightly colored ribbons dancing in the air conditioning.

The server returned with a wine list, offering it only to eldest attorney, who pointed at a wine low on the list of reds. "This will do, thanks."

The pair apparently had already been there for some time as they had already summarized the first two witnesses' entire testimony and the first portion of Mr. Bickerman's. Ethan kept quiet, following along on his notes.

The server returned again with the bottle and three glasses. Mr. Colt poured three, setting one in front of each of his colleagues. Ethan waited for someone to take the first sip. Ms. Nelson gulped hers down, stared at the bottle for a second, then walked the glass to the far side of the table. Ethan took a sip, enjoyed it, but decided against openly complimenting it.

They pored over Mr. Bickerman's testimony, word by word, for another two hours. Nobody mentioned food or touched the charcuterie plate. Other than the occasional sip of wine, Ethan did not eat. When they finally finished with Plaintiff's testimony, Mr. Colt poured himself a fresh glance, sat down, and looked at Ethan.

"I did not pursue your line of questioning with Mr. Bickerman today."

"It's okay. I understand. I thought it still—"

"Your proposed questioning was good enough. But we've got a strong case on the facts. And he gave us what we needed. I didn't want to get greedy, to risk overextending. My credibility with the jury is of the utmost importance. I cannot allow myself to appear as if I'm grasping at straws."

"I certainly understand."

"Good. That's good. I'm glad we're on the same page. So, Mr. McDaniels, what do you anticipate Mr. Paulson doing tomorrow?"

"What do I anticipate?"

"Yes." The low light through the red wine gave Mr. Colt a sinister affect. "Ms. Nelson and I appear to be at odds."

"Well, he has to call the buyer at some point. But that's not extremely useful because the buyer's never testified directly that he pulled out because of the smell."

"I'm not asking you to think aloud."

"Dr. Clarkson. His expert. First. To prove, or opine, as to the presence of a smell and his measuring of the particulates in the air which he believes can be traced to Lucas Trash."

"So you side with Ms. Nelson?"

"I agree with her, yes."

"And how would calling Dr. Clarkson at this point aid Mr. Paulson's trial strategy?"

"Establish scientifically the presence of smell so later Ms. Polly, the neighbor, will close it off by testifying how the smell overwhelms her property and alters her daily routine."

"Ms. Polly is a crazy, radical, old hermit whom Sires is entirely unable to control. She will almost certainly utilize her time on the stand as she utilized her deposition: as a platform to spout her paranoid homegrown political nonsense." During her deposition, Delia Polly had testified that she noticed a smell coming from Mr. Lucas' property; however, she did not think he was the source but rather believed the county was poisoning the land in an attempt to get rid of her because of a high school heartbreak she had allegedly inflicted upon the now Folkston County director some thirty years prior. "Sires would be wise to limit her testimony and bury her in the middle. Call her first thing tomorrow morning and he can get her on the record but, by the end of the day, the jury will have forgotten her nonsense. He will certainly not use her to close." He sipped his wine and grimaced. "I can count. I'm aware you two have out voted me. But we will proceed under the assumption that Ms. Polly will testify tomorrow morning, when her useful testimony can be proffered and her quirks and abrasiveness can be forgotten. I believe that Dr. Clarkson, steady, well-spoken and reputable, will be Paulson's final witness to serve as the button and summation. We will proceed under that assumption."

He looked up, daring one of the younger attorneys to disagree. Above and behind him, the two balloons squeaked against the ceiling.

The trio started preparing in earnest for the cross-examination of Delia Polly, making sure to utilize phrasings guaranteed to trigger her paranoia. Two hours later, the hostess opened the door to announce that Ristorante Rotundo was closing for the night. Ethan assisted in collecting and re-ordering the files. The hostess returned with a box, offering it to Ethan for the charcuterie. The edges of the meat had dried and curled during its time in the war room, but Ethan was well past hungry and figured it would serve as a late and salty dinner which required no heating element. The two older attorneys left as he ushered the reluctant meats and cheeses off the wooden platter and into the styrofoam. Ethan was halfway through the door when the hostess spoke again, "Y'all didn't finish the wine. I can recork the bottle if you'd like to take it home."

Ethan didn't see the harm in it, and said yes.

He returned to Folkston and Sapphire Courts, noting the circle of old men sitting in lawn chairs under the corner street light as he sloped into the parking lot. He parked near the entrance, far away from the laughter and shouting, well remembering Garth's warning about venturing out after dark. He tiptoe-jogged up the stairs.

A low pair of eyes awaited him at the top. Ethan yelped and stopped, seizing the handrail to stop from falling forward.

"It's just me."

Ethan squinted, just able to make out Frank sitting against the brick wall. "Jesus. You scared me. What are you doing out here?"

"Waiting on Bobby."

"Y'all going somewhere this late?"

"No. He's just not home." Frank's legs extended across the walkway, calves twitching in his pants as his toes tapped the banister rail. His fingers fussed on the cement.

"Where did he go?"

"Generally, when he's not home, at work, or with me, it's because he's out getting himself in trouble."

"I thought he wasn't an addict anymore."

"Always an addict. He's working hard but shit still sets him off. Mr. Howard laid into him today because Bobby poured the metal too hot, blew the molds, and wasted a whole morning. Bobby doesn't know how to take shit like that."

"That's enough to make him relapse?"

Frank continued. "He's very sensitive. But if he doesn't pull his shit together, all-the-way together, his people in this town, that way of life, are going to eat him before I can get him out." He slapped the cement. "Fuck!"

Ethan couldn't formulate a response that didn't taste saccharine on his tongue. Frank muttered on. "We have work tomorrow. If he misses, Mr. Howard will fire him. If he gets arrested again for stealing shit, or breaking shit . . ." Frank stopped speaking and shook his head.

"Anything I can do to help?"

"No. I won't sleep anyway. Not until he comes home. Out here I'll know as soon as he does so. And what condition he's in."

"Alright I, um, I'm sorry. I'm sure Bobby's fine."

"This is how it is. You go enjoy your wine."

Ethan had forgotten about the bottle of wine in his hand. "Oh that's . . . can I bring you something? A pillow or a blanket? Wine?" Ethan raised the bottle.

"No."

"Okay," Ethan waited. "Good night, Frank."

"Good night, Ethan."

Ethan returned to his room but did not go to bed—Bobby, the vital laugh and blossoming smile, was out there potentially wilting. Ethan cracked the window and pulled the chair close, to pass the time he reviewed his notes from Ristorante Rotundo.

The circle of men, situated almost directly under Ethan's room, laughed and traded jokes, drowning out any other noise the Folkston night may have produced. Ethan picked out Tuck's dusty, unfettered drawl.

That's my local.

Ethan's mind devised ways he could join the men down there and earn his invitation to fish Lake Marie. His eyes drifted up from the legal pad as the men's conversation grabbed his attention. After some coaxing, one man started on a story.

"So, I woke up to something rattling in the kitchen, grabbed my Winchester, and went down to check on it." The speaker was unfamiliar and hard to decipher through the booze. "I get down there and there's wums-his-face, Marty's kid, Bo, standing in my damn kitchen, clutching my damn toaster to his damn chest. He's just as wide-eyed and jittery as all hell. So I can figure what he's been up to. And now I've spooked him by turning on the lights so he's froze up like a deer in the headlights. So I said to him, very calmly, *Bo put down the damn toaster and leave.* The little bastard don't do nothin', just stands there staring back at me. Then he looks down at the rifle pointed at his chest. So I stand there for a minute, just letting him wrap his pickled brain around his predicament. Then, after a while, the idiot looks back up at me and says *I ain't Bo, Mr. Grimball, I'm someone else.* I said *I know your daddy, Bo. Known him twenty-five years.* So now he has that to consider, so he furrows his brow like he's thinking real hard, and finally says *no sir, Mr. Grimball, it aint me.*"

This sent the men into a riot. Several repeated the line: *It aint me, Mr. Grimball. It aint me. Promise!* When it got quiet, Mr. Grimball continued his story.

"With that the sucker bolts, toaster in hand, blowing down the hall and through my screen door and starts off tearing through my pasture and, God only knows why, right into the barn. I holler up to Beverly that everything's alright but to call the sheriff then I set off after him. I like that toaster. So now I'm creeping through the barn, thinking I'm gonna have to whomp this biscuit with my rifle, when I hear this whimpering coming from Eliza's stall. I peek over the rail and there's Bo crumpled on the ground holding his chest next to my toaster. Best I can tell he jumped in the stall to hide, scared Eliza, and she whomped him herself." The men cackled in the night.

"You got yourself a guard donkey, Ward. First one on record." This was Tuck. "I mean what kind of idiot—who in the hell is . . . is that you Bobby?"

Ethan perked.

"Evenin' sirs," a new voice, younger and familiar, said.

"Shit son, what are you doing sneaking out of the woods in the night like a damn . . . now what's that thing called . . . a damned bigfoot."

"I was restless man so I went for a walk. Ate my dinner down at the water pit."

"Well come have a drink young man. Ward was just telling us about when his donkey kicked Marty's boy."

"Bo told me about that. It's a good one man. But I can't. I got work in the morning."

"One drink never kept a man from working."

"The first one's not the problem." This sounded like a Frank line. "It's late and I'm beat anyways. I can hang with y'all Friday night."

"Every night's Friday night when you're living right," Tuck said, "but go on, I wouldn't want to get you in any trouble with your daddy."

"It's not like that. I got work, man. I'll catch y'all another time."

Ethan leaned closer to the window as Bobby came up the steps. "Frank! What are you doing out here? Couldn't see ya."

"Where have you been?"

Bobby repeated what he had told the men then said, "Mr. Howard got on my ass today man. I got restless and had to walk it off."

Frank's toned softened. "I'm glad you're home."

"Me too, man. I'm on fumes. Gotta get down quick if I'm going to work tomorrow. Can't be fucking up anymore."

"That's what I like to hear."

They exchanged good nights. Ethan listened to them close their doors before shutting his own window and going to bed.

Chapter Fourteen

The next morning Ethan entered the courthouse with the entire defense team, joining them in the elevator before following the three older adults down the aisle, stopping short to take his place in the front row of the gallery. He watched them pass the bar to their seats at the table.

Sires Paulson kicked off the action by calling his expert, Dr. Clarkson.

If this gave Teri Nelson any satisfaction, she gave no outward indication of it. Although he remained silent, the back of Mr. Colt's neck reddened as he pushed aside a stack of papers and tugged a fresh legal pad from his briefcase. His neck remained red for an hour and a half of questioning, at which point Judge Grimmaly lifted his hand and called for a quick recess before scampering through the backdoor.

Ethan leaned over the bar. "Is there anything I can do to help y'all?"

Mr. Colt turned. "No. Well, yes, actually, Mr. McDaniels, I believe you might be better positioned to observe the jury's reactions from further back."

"Sir?"

"You can help me, us, by sitting further back. To better, and less conspicuously, observe how the jury reacts to the remaining testimony."

"You want me to sit further away?" Ethan's eyes searched out Ms. Nelson, who looked sympathetic but merely shrugged. Mr. Lucas was leaning back in his chair with his eyes closed.

"From where you are, you can't see the jury any better than I can."

"Yes. Of course. I think I will be able to observe them more discretely, more completely . . . from further back."

"Good. Please do so."

Ethan gathered his things and moved closer to the exit, turning back about halfway to see if this was far enough to satisfy Mr. Colt, but he seemed to have forgotten or lost interest in this development. On the other side, Marissa did turn, giving Ethan an inquisitive look. Ethan averted his eyes and sat down.

If this is what Mr. Colt wants, then observing and noting the jury's reactions to Dr. Clarkson's testimony must be very important.

When Dr. Clarkson's examination resumed several minutes later, Ethan scrutinized the jurors who at all points appeared to vacillate between boredom, disinterest, anger, and sleepy—one older woman nodded off entirely. It made for tough note taking: *Juror #1 appeared unsurprised when Dr. Clarkson opined that the property was inundated with smell inducing particulates; Juror #2 appeared unmoved when he opined that the particulates were of a variety generally emitted by residential garbage; Juror #7 appeared indifferent upon learning . . .*

When Mr. Paulson had elicited everything he needed out of his expert, namely the presence of particulates in the air on the property sufficient to cause a pernicious stench and consistent with the presence of residential and commercial trash being improperly stored nearby, he thanked his expert and sat down.

After Judge Grimmaly's blessing, Sterling Colt stood for the cross-examination.

"Good morning, Dr. Clarkson, if you don't mind, I do have some foll—"

The rear doors crashed open and, once more, Garth Quattlebaum entered. This time flaunting a vibrant pink t-shirt depicting a female punk singer Ethan recognized as being two decades deceased. All heads turned including Mr. Colt's, whose thin lips convulsed at the bottom of his twitching, crimson face. His distended eyes continued their assault Garth long after he had taken his seat and, with a final nestling wiggle, rested his hands in his lap.

Judge Grimmaly spoke first. "Bailiff," he turned to face the security guard, "please escort Mr. Quattlebaum out of the courthouse. See to it he does not return today."

The bailiff passed Mr. Colt who now spoke. "Your Honor, I must respectfully request that this ludicrous man be held in contempt or, at minimum, put on notice from disturbing this trial a third time. Otherwise, we—"

"That won't be necessary, Mr. Colt. I'm quite certain we've seen the last of Mr. Quattlebaum."

Garth stood when the judge said his name and now waited for the bailiff to see him out. When the bailiff reached him, he shoved his hands in his pockets and strolled out without further incident.

That night the defense team reconvened in Ristorante Rotondo's war and party room.

"That beast, that buffoon, in the pink shirt. What did Judge Grimmaly say his name was?"

"Quattlebaum, sir."

"Quattlebaum," Sterling Colt spat the name. "Do you know this man? He was seated next to you the other day."

"I don't sir." *Although I do drink his beer and use his microwave.* "He must be a local eccentric. He sat next to me on his own accord."

"Ah. Well, I pressed the guards and that utterly useless clerk of court." Mr. Colt paced around the table, thrice passing the balloons which, now deflated, lay crumpled on the ground. "They all claim to have no authority to prohibit his access to these public areas except as ordered by Judge Grimmaly."

"Who only explicitly banned Ga—him—for the day."

"Exactly. It's home cooking, McDaniels. This whole town appears to be against us. So, here's what we are going to do. You," Mr. Colt stepped behind Ethan's chair, gripping his shoulders with both hands, "young man, are going to station yourself just outside the courtroom doors. You are going to guard those doors and make certain that degenerate does not further disrupt these proceedings."

"You want me to sit outside the courtroom?"

"Sterling, that's ridiculous," Ms. Nelson said. "Ethan has no authority to stop someone from entering the courtroom. What do you expect him to do? Fight the guy?"

"I expect Mr. McDaniels to do whatever it takes to benefit the defense."

"Sterling, he has a right, and a responsibility, to be physically present inside the courtroom. Same as us."

"He also has a responsibility to aid in this case's defense. His client, our client, will benefit from me being able to question witnesses without having my thoughts scattered by that buffoon . . . that . . . that furry man. We'll keep him well apprised."

"Sterling, this is ridi—"

"Mr. McDaniels," Sterling Colt's long fingers tightened around Ethan's shoulders. "Are you up to the task?"

"Sit outside the courtroom and watch the door?"

"Precisely."

You already banished me to the gallery. "Sure. Yes sir. I can do that."

"Perfect. Thank you, Mr. McDaniels. You're doing a great service to your client. In a trial, every role is important."

"It's actually just McDan—"

A knock at the party room door signaled the arrival of Emmett Lucas, present, much to his own dismay, to be further prepped for taking the stand. The defense team tabled the Quattlebaum dilemma for the time being. Mr. Lucas arrived at, and remained at, a simmer throughout his attorney's thorough and extended direct questioning. It was during the mock cross-examination that he finally boiled over.

"Mr. Lucas," Mr. Colt, a stickler for realism in his rehearsals, roamed the party room as he delivered his lines, "did I hear you testify that you've owned the property at 785 Woodstone for thirty-five years?"

"I said thirty-three."

"So, is it fair to say that you are well acquainted with the property?"

Mr. Lucas nodded.

"Now, Emmett, the court reporter will need to record your verbal response. So please provide a verbal answer."

The local glanced at Ms. Nelson, who nodded, then grunted, "Yes."

"Thank you. Then, is it fair to say you know the metes and bounds of the property, where it ends and abuts the adjacent properties?"

"Yes."

Mr. Colt grimaced. "Now, Emmett, what Ms. Nelson and I are afraid of is Plaintiff using your knowledge of the property against you. Saying that you knew you were placing the receptacles on his property. Perhaps doing it intentionally to keep the smell off of yours."

"It's the truth. I know my property."

"I'm certain that you do. But that's a large area out there, and there's little in the way of landmarks. There are no clear delineations. It's simply woods and brushland. It wouldn't be unthinkable that you misunderstood the line."

"I know exactly where the damn line is. You don't own a property for thirty-three years without figuring that out." Mr. Lucas answered without taking his eyes off the table.

"But how could you have known for sure? Are you an experienced surveyor? Did you ever go out there with levels and a tripod?"

"No, didn't have to." Ethan and Ms. Nelson exchanged a glance as their client's tone darkened.

"Did you ever walk the lines? Or try to locate the boundary pins?"

"No, didn't have to."

"Well, have you ever even studied the land survey?"

"No, because I didn't have to." This was a growl.

"Because if you did have uncertainty—"

"There's no uncertainty!" Emmett Lucas slapped the table and shot to his feet. "I know my damn property."

Mr. Colt did more than remain calm; he seemed to relish his role as the cooler head and, over his trial partner's soft objection, continued pressing his client. "Now Emmett, no one is trying to shame you. Just listen to me. If there was any uncertainty, we could imply that you simply stored the bins on what you thought was your property. Somewhere out of the way, but, as far as you knew, yours. That would look much—"

"I don't give one damn how it looks. I'm not saying something unless it's the truth."

"It wouldn't be unreasonable if you—"

"I don't need you tellin' me what's reasonable."

Mr. Colt briefly looked taken aback, then angered. "We're here on behalf of you and your insurance company. It's in your best inter-est—"

"I certainly don't need you tellin' me what's in my interest."

"Then could you take us out there right now and show us the lines?"

"Way I am right now, the mood you put me in, I can't recommend you going out alone with me."

Emmett Lucas stood up and exited the party room.

About an hour later, Ethan left the party room with a congealed fried appetizer sampler and another one-third bottle of red wine. He decided to warm his belated dinner in Garth's functioning microwave.

As the appetizers spun and warmed, Ethan asked the question which had been bugging him since Marissa had mentioned it. "Did you used to be a cop?"

"Are you asking me a question you already know the answer to?"

"I heard you used to be a detective for the sheriff's office."

"That is correct. I was one of Folkston's Finest."

Ethan tried to formulate his next question in a polite, unintrusive way. "Why did you leave the force?"

Garth's fingers disappeared into his beard. "The stadium announcer for the Folkston High football team is Bill Marks. Has been for about fifteen years. Folkston High's first home game is always in the end of August. On August twenty-fifth, five years ago, I pulled Mr. Marks over for speeding. Since I was a detective, I wasn't routinely running radar at that point, but he was swerving and it was clear he was piss drunk. I got him stopped on Townes Road and, as I approached his vehicle, he exited and charged me shouting something about bacon. He and I went to school together so I recognized him and requested that he calm down. He pushed me. I repeated my request, so he slapped me, at which point I assisted Mr. Marks to the ground. Some time later, he sued the sheriff's department and I lost my job."

"If he charged you and slapped you, why did you lose your job?"

"Well, you lawyer folks got involved and it became clear I hadn't followed proper protocol. Since I was a detective, had been for some years, it had been a bit since I'd pulled someone over, especially in a squad car. I wasn't used to them being equipped like spaceships. In all the excitement of pulling over a classmate, I forgot to turn on the camera and none of it made video. As you can imagine, Mr. Marks' statement differed on the particulars from my account."

"But why did he sue in the first place? It doesn't sound too bad. If he was drunk and speeding and the aggressor. Seems like he would want to bury the incident."

"Well, something about the manner in which Mr. Marks came in contact with the ground caused his jaw to break. Ground knocked out a good deal of teeth as well. Put him on a fluid diet and caged his golden voice for the season."

"Oh . . ."

"Bill's back in the booth but he still has a tough time with *s*-heavy last names."

"What do you do for work now?"

"I carved out a little business as a freelance security consultant. Insurance companies lower the rates on retail stores, warehouses, and storage yards if they've been inspected and approved by a certified security expert. That's me. I walk through stores, warehouses, and stockyards, make a couple comments about their fences, locks, personnel placement, camera systems, check a few boxes, and go home with a check."

Ethan had encountered such consultant's reports on some of his cases involving retail loss.

"Now let me ask you something," Garth said. "Did that old fucker really call me a degenerate?"

"Those were his words. He also called you the furry man."

"The Furry Man," Garth smirked and made his hands into claws. "And now you're to defend him from me?"

"It is my sworn duty." Ethan took a bite out of a lukewarm mozzarella stick.

"I thought your duty was to use five-dollar words and make buying rice more complicated."

"I can't be trusted with that. That's big-time stuff." Ethan tried to calculate how many pushups were in a fried ravioli.

"Are you up to the task? I mean, do you really think you can handle the Furry Man?"

"You do seriously need to stop. Mr. Colt requested that you be held in contempt and you've given Judge Grimmaly sufficient reason to do so."

"Contempt, eh?"

"Yes. He can put you in jail for civil contempt."

"Oh, boof. Judge Grimmaly ain't gonna put a Quattlebaum in jail for boppin' the doors. I bet he hates that jack pony just as much as I do."

"Well, Mr. Colt can push the issue. And this is all on the record. You're interfering with a court of law."

"And what's so bad about a night in jail? It's not like I have a dog that needs feeding. Or a woman that needs . . . does Pony," Garth was apparently calling Sterling Colt *Pony*, "know about our relationship?"

"No, he does not know that I use your microwave. He certainly doesn't know I bring you his wine and appetizers."

Garth grinned. "Well, ain't you nothin' but a no good, two-faced, spineless, oathbreakin', finger-crossin' double agent. Yes, let's do keep our rendezvous from your fearless leader." Garth chewed on a soggy piece of bruschetta. "So, do you intend to fulfill your duty?"

"And defend Mr. Colt from you?"

"Yes."

"I'd very much rather you didn't put me in that situation."

Chapter Fifteen

On Friday morning, Ethan took the elevator alone and, per Mr. Colt's orders, stopped at the courtroom door then stepped to the side to sit on a bench. Mr. Colt soon passed with an exchange of names and a nod. Ms. Nelson sat down.

"How are you feeling?"

"I'm okay."

"Good. Don't let . . ." She pursed her lips. "Did Emmett say anything about his familiarity with the property lines in his deposition?"

"He did. Sires pushed him on it. Mr. Lucas was adamant that he was aware of his property lines."

"Okay, good. So we're locked into that. Thanks, Ethan." She patted his shoulder. "I don't know how well you'll be able to hear, but if you think of anything useful, don't hesitate to come tell me."

The day began with Mr. Paulson's direct examination of the would-be buyer. Ethan found that if he hunched, and ignored the blossoming spasm in his lower back, he could hold his ear to the crack between the doors and hear the proceedings reasonably well. The examination had gone on for about an hour when the elevator doors opened. The Furry Man had arrived at the gates.

"So this is the stage for our final battle." He rolled up his sleeves, smiling big enough for his dimples to show through his beard. "All roads led to this, McDaniel. It was always going to be me and you. We are . . . inevitable.”

“Please don’t do this, Garth. Even if you’re fine with jail, Sterling Colt is a very powerful and persistent man. He may well take this out on me.”

“He’s already kicked you out of the courtroom. The only thing left is to send you home.”

This barb hit home. Ethan had a hard time convincing himself that his legal experience was being utilized, or increased, in his current assignment. Trials were increasingly rare; Sterling Colt was depriving him of a premium brick.

“C’mon, don’t already look so defeated,” Garth said. “You don’t have to be enthusiastic but at least glower at me while I monologue and explain my evil plan. I mean, don’t you at least want to know how I do it?”

“Do what?”

“Keep bounding in right when that pony fucker is about to open his mouth.”

“I guess I hadn’t considered it.”

“It’s quite simple really.” Garth assumed a standard nasal and grandiloquent villain whine. “You see, we are not so different you and I, McDaniel. We both reside at Sapphire Courts. We are both pious devotees to the teachings and swift justice practiced by the master Dalton Stampede. But while you use your geographic proximity to the courthouse to show up on time. I see it for what it truly is, its true potential.” Garth gave up on the speech. “By having my buddy, Stan the bailiff, let me know whenever it sounds like big pony may be up to speak. He texts me and I run over and listen by these doors. And when the time is right . . .” The Furry Man put his ear to the door crack.

“Seriously, please, Colt can ruin me.”

"Oh Heavens! You really think that human bummer in there is both capable of and willing to disassemble the dubious brick by brick career you've been so carefully constructing?"

"Exactly. He can destroy everything."

"That old bag can't mess with your bricks, McDaniel. If he was half as important as he thinks he is, he wouldn't be up here in Folkston arguing about fucking trash." Garth assumed a more heroic, rebellious tone. "And I for one do not recognize the right to rule of this renegade horse turd. His reign is premised on naught but violence and fear." He then abandoned this tone as well, speaking almost as an aside. "You want me to hit you first? Blacken your eye so you stay on his good side?" He raised his hands like a boxer.

"I really doubt he gives points for effort. He just recognizes success and, in this case, failure."

"Then I'll spare you that."

"Thanks."

"Ethan, you just relax and watch this play out, your big baddy in there is tangling with Folkston now. Folkston doesn't abide his bullshit. It will strip him down and show him for what he really is." Garth put his ear back to the door. "Have I ever told you how fun this is?"

"It's pretty clear you're enjoying yourself."

Garth held up a finger, pressing his ear closer to the door. "Quiet. It sounds like Sires is closing up."

"I do feel obligated to warn you, again, that he is powerful and petty."

"The Furry Man has no reason to fear him. For the Furry Man possesses something he can only ever dream of."

"Free time?"

"Precisely, my young friend. Oodles and oodles of free time. And I'm not stopping until I've taught this old fucker a lesson."

"What lesson?"

He looked down at Ethan, lowering his voice to a cinematic snarl. "Don't fuck with someone with nothing better to do."

With that the Furry Man cocked his arms, palm punching each door on the press bar, sending them careening to the limits of their respective hinges. Mr. Colt's red face and stiff posture flashed through Ethan's mind. Several moments later, Garth reemerged in cuffs being escorted by Stan the bailiff, whose bald head glowed like a cherry as he tried to contain his laughter.

Ethan heard his resolve break in the stairwell.

Chapter Sixteen

Tuck was in the far side of the lot when Ethan returned, pulling a rod and tackle box from his truck bed. Ethan slowed his pace as he passed; when Tuck failed to notice him, he approached directly.

"Good day on the water?" Ethan asked.

Tuck looked Ethan's suit up and down. "Damn sight better'n yours."

Ethan thought about his day in the hallway. "Can't argue that."

"You can't catch your dinner in no dusty law barn." Tuck leaned into the cab, returning with a red and white cooler. "Although you can steal someone else's and just as likely lose your britches." Tuck slid the cooler open, revealing a fat, purple-grey catfish scrunched into a chunky *J*. "Ain't that just the prettiest thing you ever did see?"

My local. "Is that dinner?"

"That's the best dinner there is, son. You haven't lived until you've had my fried catfish."

Lake Marie catch. Local chef. The dream.

"I'm sure. I bet it's incredible. Finger-licking even." Ethan's imagination ran wild: the authentic and flavorful recipe that had been honed by Tuck's father and his father and his father . . . he probably had several blessedly lucky children putting it to daily use.

"Out of this world." The local closed the cooler. Ethan saw he was red-eyed and staggered as he tried to restraighten. This only added to his charm.

"Well, I won't keep you from it. Enjoy your bounty."

"You don't have to worry about that, son."

Ethan lumbered up the stairs, pondering his next two days of freedom and the most natural, unassuming way to catch Tuck leaving for his next fishing expedition. He stopped next to his door, remembering the fate of the Furry Man. Garth had gotten himself arrested and now, in all likelihood, sat alone in jail. Ethan wasn't sure how to feel about it as Garth, somehow, had seemed unperturbed at the prospect.

The lunatic had actually done it. He knew it would probably end with him in jail and he did it anyway. It was as foreseeable as it was avoidable.

Ethan had bookmarked this free night as a potential opportunity to eat at Jeanie's, where Chuck Palwagon had famously broken bread, but after a demoralizing day, was not up for the solo adventure. He decided to lean into his melancholy by disrobing, washing his socks, and peeling open a pull-tab can of room temperature chicken noodle soup. He was scraping the bottom when there was a bang on the window. Ethan reached over and pulled the curtains to reveal a one-dimensional nipple flattened into a pink squid's eye against the glass. Above it swished a frothy mushroom of two-tone blonde hair and one of the biggest, yellow-toothed smiles Ethan had ever beheld. Behind it, Frank wore a more modest smile. Bobby dropped his shirt and pointed at the door.

"We're going to the store, man. Thought you might need some stuff for the weekend."

"I don't know, maybe. It's been a rough one. Which store?"

"*The* store, man. Halyard's."

"Halyard's . . ." Ethan considered this: he hadn't frequented a low-quality-low-budget-high-inventory Halyard's since purchasing his college futon there and, unless he also purchased a microwave, or a hot plate, it would not solve his hot food conundrum. However, it was an activity and Folkston's Halyard's promised to be a cultural experience. "Sure, if y'all don't mind me tagging along."

"I don't mind. You mind, Frank?"

"Do not mind."

"We don't mind, man."

"Did y'all hear about Garth?"

"No, man. What happened?"

Ethan recounted Garth's string of courtroom malfeasances and his exit in custody. Bobby side-hopped to face Garth's door, unleashing a barrage of thundering knocks.

"Garth! Garth! Garth!" He stopped, waited. There was no response. "Shit, man. I guess he's really in the pen."

"The man knows what he's doing," Frank said. "Civil contempt is a one-off thing. Barely even shows up on your record as long as you pay the fines on time."

Ethan had expected a somewhat bigger reaction but they both simply turned and moved on towards the stairs. He followed the pair to a beige late model sedan, which he assumed to be Frank's, and took his place on the vinyl backseat. The interior was faded and immaculate.

"It's two towns over. Now's the time to bail if you ain't got time."

"Friday night in a friendless town. I was just going to take it easy."

"Ain't friendless, man. You got us."

Frank started the car and they were off. Bobby fiddled intently with the radio; only settling on a song after they had been on the road for at least ten minutes.

"They got a Halyard's near you, man?"

"Pretty sure they're everywhere. At least in the South."

"I love this place. I get my food here. I get my beer here. I got my television here. I got my slippers. I got my robe. Work boots. My jeans. That mondo bag of jerky." He tapped Frank's shoulder. "That tub of cheese balls. The good ones. Everything. Is this where you get your stuff, man?"

"Um, it's been a while."

"He's an attorney, Bob." Frank guided the car into the immense parking lot. "He probably shops at one of those expensive places with the chalkboards and wooden crates."

"It is much closer to my apartment."

"I gotcha man. As long as you're shopping somewhere." Bobby nodded, again slapping Frank's shoulder as he parked the car. "I told you he lived in an apartment."

"Yea but I bet his apartment has a pool, a fitness center, and doesn't double as a motel." Frank looked back at Ethan, who nodded.

"Woah." As they traversed the expansive asphalt flats, Bobby did his best Deborah impression, endlessly listing Halyard's merchandise as the doors slid open around them. At the entrance, he shouted, "GILBERT!" and embraced the startled, but smiling, octogenarian greeter. "Frank, you remember Gilbert? This guy gets it, man."

Frank and Ethan nodded at Gilbert, but declined his offer of a coupon booklet.

"You guys ever play that game here man where like one guy hides and the other people try to find him?"

"You mean hide and seek?" Ethan asked.

"Yea man. Let's do that. We can shop after you find me. I'll hide first."

Bobby bounded down the center aisle before anyone could respond, head on a swivel for potential hiding spots.

"Every time," Frank said as Bobby disappeared behind the Household Essentials. "He's lucky they don't remember him."

"Who?"

"The employees. They used to have to chase him out of here with some regularity."

"For playing hide and seek?"

"For shoplifting."

"Bobby is a thief?"

"*Was* a shoplifter, yea. Only here, I think. He was a terror though. They even had his picture up when I first moved here. And that's hard to do. You have to earn that. Unfortunately, his hair makes him pretty easy to pick out. And Bobby Canterbury was already the least stealthy culprit in the history of crime."

"But he seems to love this place."

"I doubt he ever fully considered that he was stealing from Halyards. Doing the business harm. He grew up with everyone around him *lifting* from Halyards so he just thought that was part of the experience. Nobody ever explained it to him and, even now, I don't think he's actually bothered to connect the dots. All his buddies made a game of lifting merchandise from here, even his dad, so young Bobby did too. Then when he got older, it became about the meth. Stolen daily essentials are a great stand in for cash." Frank snorted and flexed his fingers. "It was hell getting him to stop."

"Meth or shoplifting?"

"Both. I moved to Sapphire Courts next to an empty apartment. After about two weeks Bobby came home from the detention center where he'd done twenty-eight days for shoplifting." Frank pointed at the linoleum floor. "He was dried out, clean. We hung out a couple of times right off the bat. I liked him and got him a job at the foundry. That's good. It keeps him busy and tired. Most of the other workers are older and don't mess around with any hard shit. We started hanging out with Garth pretty soon after that. He's good about getting Bobby having fun but keeping him out of real trouble."

"Garth who is currently incarcerated."

"The same. Together we chased off most of Bobby's doper friends. Now, except for the occasional relapse, and very bad night, he's going pretty steady."

"That's good to hear. I like Bobby."

"He's easy to like, and very lucky, at least compared to most poor Folkston kids. He wakes up happy, positive. The way he's constructed his emotional triggers have to be pulled so, even when he was using heavy, he never—well, rarely—woke up in need of an emotional boost. But when those triggers get pulled the whole fucking dam breaks and he becomes a goddam hurricane. Anything is on the table. I lose sleep thinking how lucky we are that he didn't get caught during a couple of his benders. But, as I was saying, being generally happy, upbeat made it much harder for meth to fully take hold."

Ethan thought about the plea he'd seen earlier in the week. "Does Bobby have that property crime enhancement thing?"

"Not yet. As I understand it, they could've slapped it on him for that last shoplifting but the solicitor hoped twenty-eight days would get the point across. No other felonies yet. So there's nothing on Bobby Canterbury's record that can't wash away with a couple years of hard work and good behavior. I guess he's also lucky nobody's ever gotten hurt, or convinced him to do something serious. But," Frank stopped, staring at something playing on one of the display televisions, "if he walks out of here without paying for a pencil, the solicitors office will without a doubt pursue it as a felony. That's more often than not a full stop. Likely serious time and a permanent black mark."

"Sounds like he's doing well though. And he only has to make it until y'all go to Columbia. With a good support group like you and Garth, I bet he makes it."

Frank worked his lips before answering. "He'll get distracted soon, if he hasn't already, usually either starts hoarding candy or sniffing around the lingerie section. We should get our shopping done now. What do you need?"

"Nothing. I'm just happy to get out of that room. You?"

"I'm here for much the same reason parents make their kids play after school sports: it keeps them occupied and out of trouble."

"Does Bobby's dad help at all? Bobby's mentioned him a couple times."

"No, he does not. And don't ever mention him. Bobby's dad is his surest trigger."

"Really? His dad?"

"To any extent they were ever actually together, Bobby's mom left his dad when she tried to straighten her life out. His dad would use Bobby to get back at her. I think he only ever showed up to rub it in Bobby's mom's face that he, not she, was the fun one that Bobby loved. He would take Bobby fishing, go to movies, maybe to a party or a bar, and then, when the man got tired of playing dad or had to actually be a father, he would dump Bobby back on his mom and disappear. Bobby adored him, still does, he is his hero; it was like having Dalton Stampede show up at your doorstep and take you fishing. Hell on his poor mother, of course."

"Bobby says they still go fishing sometimes."

"That's a Bobby dream. That old fuck hasn't taken his son fishing in years. He was still hitting Bobby up whenever he needed a fishing companion or a drinking buddy but that slowed down when I came into the picture and started trying to straighten Bobby out. The man didn't appreciate competition for the role of Bobby's father. It stopped altogether when Bobby told him we're moving to Columbia. His dad cursed him and called him an ungrateful traitor, which naturally sent Bobby on a horrific bender. I didn't see him for forty-eight hours. Ended up digging him out of a basement in Cochran's. Even when that was dealt with, I was worried Bobby would back out, decide to stay here." The conversation struck a nerve, and Frank couldn't seem to stop the words from coming out. "Bobby's got the only father in the world that's resentful of his son trying to get his life together. It's hell just trying to keep Bobby from missing work every time that fucker offers him a drink. It's actually tied to why you're here now. It was Bobby's idea to ask you. He doesn't like people to be alone, especially if there's something he can do about it. It makes him feel like he's abandoning them."

"Have you ever met Bobby's father?"

"All too often. But that fucker would never have a conversation with me."

"Why not?"

Frank pointed at the back of his hand.

"Because of your . . . oh . . ." Ethan's stomach turned. "Fuck."

They rounded a corner in silence. Ethan could not think of a way to shift the conversation without it sounding abrupt and artificial. They had now traversed the entirety of Halyard's main perimeter rectangle of wide main aisles, with no sign of Bobby, and thus began sifting through the offshoots. They wound up in *Household Essentials* amongst the pillows and blankets. Frank picked up a tassled pillow, read it, and turned it to Ethan:

DON'T LET THE WORLD DRAG YOU DOWN
YOU LIFT THE WORLD UP

Frank smiled. "Garth would really hate that."

"You got a marker? We should write *get fucked* on the back."

Frank selected another and read it aloud. "Thankful. Grateful." He turned it over to its blank side.

"Fucked," Ethan added.

They laughed, continuing to pull pillows off the racks to deride the clunky scraps of saccharine soft talk. A tightly bound blue blanket caught Ethan's eye. The words *love* and *strength* bowed out over a fold. Ethan lifted it to read its label.

Finally a blanket that keeps your soul warm
THE HEART BLANKET
Snuggle into this ultrasoft plush blanket and envelop yourself in its words
of strength

"Frank . . . have a look at this."

Ethan straightened a corner, the material was heavy and soft. He read the first message aloud:

*LOVE WHAT YOU **HAVE***
*OR YOU'LL MISS WHAT YOU **HAD***

Below it read:

SOMETIMES HAPPINESS
STARTS WITH A SMILE

"Oh no," Frank stammered.

"It's lousy with them. There must be a hundred on here."

"This might be the worst thing I've ever seen. We should get it for Garth. It could be his welcome home from jail blanket."

"It might send him back. Let's do it."

They collected Bobby, whom they easily located eating animal crackers under the bra display, and made their way to the checkout.

"I'd like to pay," Ethan said. "I owe Garth for a couple dinners now."

"No," Frank responded. "Bobby gets to pay. That blanket is cheap and he's already eaten most of the crackers."

Ethan decided against pressing the issue so, as Bobby explained the condition of the jug of animal crackers to the dead-eyed clerk, Ethan took in the Halyards. Somewhere along the line someone had explained to him that you could tell whether someone was shoplifting because shoplifters always either walked with a purpose or purposefully attempted to give the impression of casual ambling. Ethan checked his immediate vicinity but could detect no shoplifters; everyone he observed seemed to be at Halyard's to socialize. Groups clustered about under the fluorescent lights holding animated discussions as roving bands of kids waged mock war around their feet. Most folks weren't even holding any merchandise. But what concerned Ethan the most was the number of people, children and adults, who weren't wearing shoes.

Ethan was turning back to follow Frank and Bobby out of the store when he noticed Garth Quattlebaum checking out two lanes over. Ethan alerted his companions and together they waited for their neighbor to swipe his card.

"Hhheeeyyyyyy kkiiidddssss," The Furry Man unholstered two finger pistols and hip-shimmied his way over to them, his belly swaying with each twist.

"I thought you went to jail," Ethan said.

"Jail?"

"Yea, for—"

"Oh, for that? No, my boy Stan the bailiff just walked me out of the courthouse."

"But we knocked on your door earlier."

"I've been here all afternoon," Garth smirked, "testing out the loudest shoes."

"The loudest shoes?" Ethan had a feeling he wouldn't like the response.

Garth reached into his bag and pulled out a pair of faux wood clogs. "It's late in the game so I'm upping the stakes. The big rattling entrance is played out. The doors close and the sound dies. I figure these clomper-stompers will cause enraging disruption all the way down the aisle."

"You're going to keep disrupting the trial?"

"Not the whole trial, just that uptight pony fucker. These bad boys have hard plastic heels that clack like a shutter in a storm. I also have a mind to tack a nickel to the soles."

"Click clack," Bobby said. "We got you a gift, man."

"Another gift? How lucky can one man get?"

"You'll like it, Garth. It's not cheese puffs. Ethan done real good."

"It's from all of us really. We saw it and thought of you," Ethan added.

Garth's eyes narrowed. "What'd you meatballs get me?"

"Man, you just gotta open it."

"Is it gonna piss me off?"

Ethan looked from Bobby to Frank, responding only after neither of them offered. "Probably, yes."

"So be it. I'd rather get bad news in my car." They followed Garth to his coupe where he sat down in the driver's seat with the door open and motioned for the plastic shopping bag holding his gift. Bobby gave him the bag but maintained close possession of the three-quarters eaten tub of animal crackers.

Garth situated the bag in his lap then closed his eyes and hovered his hands over the top, ceremoniously lowering them into it. "Hmm . . . what do we have here . . . yes . . . yes. It's very soft . . . very soft indeed. Squishy too . . . soft and squishy. And Warm. Certainly doesn't feel like something I'm gonna hate. Perhaps there is something visually appalling about the piece." He lifted the blanket from the bag and opened his eyes. His pupils darted across the blanket.

"Friends don't see your broken fences . . . friends see the extra light on your garden." He rolled the blanket over, muttering the warm words. "What the awful fuck is this?"

"We thought it might help you come up with more Platitudes with Attitude. It's basically a treasure trove of trite-isms," Ethan said.

"It certainly is that."

"We also thought it was funny, man," Bobby said.

"It can be both. I'll save the rest for later." Garth stuffed the blanket back into the bag. "What are you pussbags getting into tonight?"

"Nothing, man. We were gonna head back to the Courts," Bobby said. "Maybe pick up some Grubes and watch TV."

"No, no, that just won't do. It's Friday night. We owe it to our dear honored guest to take him out on the town. The Eagles are playing tonight. Let's take McDaniel to that."

"The Eagles are playing here?" Ethan asked.

"The Folkston High Eagles, yes. They have a home game tonight on the riverbank."

"No, Garth," Frank said. "I'm not dealing with a bunch of drunk rednecks." Ethan shared this concern.

"That won't be an issue. Remember, ever since I put their announcer on IR, I'm not technically *allowed*," Garth surrounded this word with air quotes, "in Alderman Memorial Stadium. So we can go watch, well, listen, from across the river. I used to go there in school so I could get stoned during the games without having to worry about getting expelled." This seemed like a much better practice than Bobby's habit of going deep inside his actual school to get high.

It was a nice night and, lacking any suitable alternative, everyone agreed to the plan—Ethan would've gone along with anything to get them moving from the Halyards parking lot where a new gaunter and grungier crowd was coming in with the sunset.

"What about food, man?" Bobby asked. "We still gotta eat."

"We can still eat Gruber's," Frank responded.

"No, Ethan's already had Gruber's. Give me another place."

"What about Jeanie's?" Ethan offered. Jeanie's with locals would be a good get. "I'd love to mark that off my list."

"Oh Jesus," Garth said. "You're back on that. No, Jeanie's is not an option."

"What's wrong with Jeanie's?"

Garth held up a finger. "First things first, how 'bout we call up Pizzarino's. They're quick as shit. You two," Garth pointed at Frank and Bobby, "order it to the Courts and we can stop there and catch the driver in the lot. We'll pick up my beer and whomp it all down to the river. McDaniel, you hop in with me and I'll show you what's wrong with Jeanie's. Now y'all get."

Frank and Bobby left as Ethan got in Garth's passenger seat.

"We don't have to make any additional stops. You can just tell me if it's closed."

"No, no. I'm trying to make a point. I need a visual component."

Garth took backroads, winding through the twilight such that Ethan completely lost his sense of direction. He stopped, still in the lane, next to an unilluminated sign on the right.

"Here we are, McDaniel, Jeanie's. Your boy Palwagon ate at that picnic table right there."

"Okay, I remember all that. So Jeanie's closed since Big Chuck came here." Ethan could picture the shot structure: the cameras would've been in the parking lot looking back at the table.

"No, not closed. Moved and changed names. Went back underground. It's on Main Street, now. Attached to Bogie's. And no we can't go there either. It's where all the old-timers go to eat fried chicken and slurp beans and listen to the football games on the radio. It's probably been full since four PM."

"Fine. So it's moved since Big Chuck ate here."

"No, it moved *because* Big Fuck ate here. After that episode aired, Jeanie's got overrun with starry-eyed wannabes just like you, swarming in to check another *local greaser* off their list."

"Yea, it's the Palwagon Bump. He advertises these small restaurants to help their business."

"Yea, but Jeanie didn't want to bump. She and her husband are both old and, to be honest, pretty goddam mean. The only thing on this planet they enjoy is griping and shaking their canes with their equally old and ornery regulars. They ain't equipped to wrangle with an endless stream of sheep but your shepherd guided his flock there anyway. So Jeanie decided to move the restaurant and name it after her husband."

"Well if she didn't want the press then why did she agree to be on the show?"

"You see now we're getting somewhere. You just think on that. I do have to admit I grew up adoring Palwagon. I've watched him eat at a lot of local greasers. You just ponder on how strange that particular segment is."

Ethan recalled the Folkston-Lake Marie episode's *local greaser* segment; it was indeed peculiar in three ways: it was the only local greaser at which he ate outside; it was the only time the restaurant's sign wasn't prominently featured coming in from the break; and, it was certainly the only *local greaser* segment in which the owner failed to make an appearance and receive praise and a handshake from Big Chuck. This had drawn speculation on the boards that Big Chuck hadn't actually enjoyed his fried catfish at Jeanie's.

"Shit," Ethan figured he had pieced it all together.

"Yep."

"Chuck didn't get permission to film here."

"You're mighty close, he got refused permission to eat here. He asked. They said no."

"Shit." Ethan turned back towards the window. "That's why he ate outside at the furthest table by the parking lot. That's why Jeanie doesn't make an appaerance."

"Precisely. Big Fuck pulled one over on them. Never actually showed the building. Never actually showed the sign. If you listen closely, *he* never actually says the name."

"But it probably wasn't him, personally. I mean, he has production crew and a manager that actually get all the permissions."

"That's giving the man a lot of credit, and that's fine, but he still must've wondered why he wasn't filmed ordering and why they put him outside on that particular table."

Not to mention why he didn't get to sweettalk the owner. "Yea but also he never thought about the owners getting bothered by an influx of customers. Usually people love the Palwagon Bump. It's the best thing that's ever happened to a lot of the restaurants."

"Well, you're right about that. He certainly never thought about the owners."

Chapter Seventeen

Pizzarino's was indeed quick; Garth got them home to find the delivery guy already parked and halfway to the stairs. Ethan had decided in the car that he was going to pay to express his gratitude for the locals taking him in. As soon as Garth stopped, Ethan jumped out and scampered to intercept the driver before Frank could descend from the second level.

"What do you think you're doing?" Frank asked.

"I want to pay for y'all's pizza."

"No," Garth said, catching up.

"Y'all have been great hosts. It's the least I can do."

"No," Frank said.

"What's the problem with that?"

"I don't like the look of it," Frank said. "I don't like the smell of it. It feels like charity. We don't need you to pay for our shit."

Ethan glanced at the pizza guy who seemed unmoved by the proceedings. "It's not like that. We're just friends hanging out. I haven't paid for anything. I've played your video games, rode in your cars, and drank a good deal of your booze. It's not charity. I'm only trying to keep it even, or close to it."

"So be it," Garth said.

"To be discussed," Frank said. Bobby joined him at the base of the stairs.

Ethan paid for the pizza then turned to the locals for further instruction.

"Set it on the backseat for now," Garth said. "Let's everybody put on something warm and meet back here in three minutes or less. Bobby, you help me with the booze."

Bobby made it up two steps before turning to Ethan and exclaiming, "Wait! Check this out, man!"

He leapt back down the steps, sprinted towards the office, long-jumping over both sides of the pink brick semi-circle, then launched himself up the moldy, crumbling lattice work ornamenting the office's exterior, climbing until he could swing himself over the handrail. Ethan stepped out to better observe Bobby proudly displaying his blackened hands from the second-floor walkway.

It's easy to see how this human squirrel was a star wrestler.

They reconvened and Garth drove them past the welcome sign and turned left towards the Lucas Trash and Bickerman properties.

"Noses up, boys," Garth said. "If we don't smell nothin' McDaniel can use us in his trial. Witnesses get free room and board."

Several minutes later, Garth parked the car by a black stretch of road and they all loaded out. Ethan couldn't see the stadium but a buzzy murmur suggested a crowd was very close. He helped Bobby collect the Pizzarino's bags and boxes while Frank picked up the cooler. Together, they followed Garth into the darkness, walking for maybe thirty yards before arriving at the riverbank. The bright lights of Alderman Memorial Stadium, which was really just half a stadium comprising one large slab of concrete stands, glimmered on the surface of what Ethan estimated to be McJunkin River, which he knew to drain out of Lake Marie.

This used to be Lake Marie water. I'm close.

They were eye level with the playing field such that the visiting sideline blocked their view of the action, but they could see the scoreboard and hear the announcer, which Ethan thought came through pretty clearly considering the distance. It was halfway through the first quarter and the home team was down by a field goal.

"Y'all settle on in," Garth said.

"We can't sit here," Frank said. "The ground's wet."

Ethan looked around at the sandy bank; it certainly had a wet sheen to it.

Garth toed up a clump of sand. "Shit. Reckon this didn't bother me when I was stoned."

"I don't want to get my ass wet while I'm eating."

"Alright, alright. Me neither. Let me find a log or something."

"The blanket's still in your car, Garth," Ethan said.

Garth looked blankly at Ethan.

"The platitude blanket we just got you. It's in your backseat." The stadium lights allowed Ethan to observe Garth's face transform into one of recognition and then a zestful smile.

"McDaniel, that's perfect. I'll be right back." The Furry Man bounded into the dark woods, returning moments later with the blanket bundled in his paws. With a frisbee-like flick of his wrist, he cast it wide on the sandy riverbank. "We'll give these bullshitisms the chance to actually do something useful."

Ethan set his share of the Pizzarino's load on a corner, sitting down as the announcer informed the crowd that the Eagles offense would be taking over on their own twenty-four yard line. "So you broke that guy's jaw?"

"No, like I said, the ground did. I simply arranged the meeting."

"It sounds like he made a pretty full recovery."

"Yea, fuckin' science." Garth eased himself down in stages, alternating grunts and sighs as he shifted from knee, to elbow, to butt. "It may not come through over the speakers, but he's a terrific asshole. Alright, I'm tired of just smelling this stuff. Somebody pass me one slice of pepperoni and three wings please. Y'all help yourselves to the booze. I'll save my drinking for the Courts."

They took turns requesting, passing, and consuming food and drink as, across the dark glimmering water, the Folkston Eagles methodically marched the ball down the field, the crowd roaring with each fresh set of downs.

Ethan had just finished his third slice of pizza when the crowd erupted with particular vigor and Garth's nemesis announced that Garrett Crane had just rushed for the Eagles' first touchdown.

"At a way home team!" Garth shouted. "Rule the riverbank."

Bobby poked Ethan on the shoulder. "Wait for it, man. Watch the scoreboard. This is the best part." Bobby kept his hand on Ethan's shoulder, gripping it as the home team kicked the extra point. The bulb lights on the scoreboard went dark then burst to life in the shape of a golden-yellow eagle head. "Here it comes! Here it comes!" The eagle opened its beak in semi-sync with the stadium speakers which, accompanied by joyous Folkston High fans on both sides of the McJunkin, played a piercing and powerful screech.

"The cry of the hunting eagle. So epic, man. They use to play it before the big wrestling matches, too. It always got me going. I always wrestled better in our gym." Bobby produced a pint of whiskey, took a gulp, then leaned his head back and put forth a loose, raspy, and high rendition. Bobby handed Ethan the bottle. The fiery whiskey paired nicely with the cool river air.

"You know that's not actually an eagle," Ethan said after a sip. "If I remember correctly it's a red-tailed hawk with some bass added or something."

"Of course it's an eagle, man. We're the Eagles. The Folkston Eagles."

"Yea, but so was my rival high school. We always gave them shit because they had to fake the sound of their mascot. Actual eagles sound like a songbird crossed with a sick dolphin, so whenever teams have eagles as their mascots, they almost always use red-tailed hawks with some added effects."

"No, we're the fucking Eagles. We don't need to fake any fucking hawk sounds."

"Bobs. I wouldn't get—" Garth started.

But Bobby was on his feet, kicking his way through the sand. "No! It's a fucking eagle! They play it every time an Eagle soars into the endzone." Frank turned, tight-lipped, to glare at Ethan. Bobby's arms jerked and spasmed as he paced. "That fucking sucks, man. You can't trust anything anymore. It's all just fucking bullshit."

"Take it easy, Bobs. It's just a sound they play at football games. Who cares? McDaniel's probably wrong anyway."

"Yea, I could definitely be wrong." It had been his biology teacher who had pointed out this deception, playing videos of both birds to confirm it for the class, but this seemed beside the point. Ethan was horrified to see the effect his words were having on Bobby. "It's just something we said to tease the kids at Macanaw."

"No, it's a lie. Another fucking lie. Those fucking assholes." Bobby's movements were getting faster and more violent. "I ran back to the locker room and screamed like an eagle after every match."

Frank and Garth had a wordless exchange of glances that Ethan failed to interpret. It was Frank who spoke next.

"Bobby," he spoke slowly, calmly. "They had to do it. Would you have preferred to run back to the locker room and chirp like a little songbird?"

"No, but that's not the—"

"And would you have preferred to have run out on to the mat with the gym sounding like a . . . like a garden tea party?""No but—"

"What about a dolphin? Do dolphins make intimidating noises?"

"No. That hawk screech is way cooler than a dolphin." Bobby stopped pacing to look down at Frank.

"That's right. Now, try and picture every person in Alderman Stadium chirping sweetly every time the Eagles cross the goal line."

The tension left Bobby's shoulders, a sheepish grin spread across his face. "That'd be funny, man. Wouldn't do much for the players though. They'd probably stop scoring and lose every game."

"Exactly, whatever they've done is for the best. It's a necessity."

"I guess you're right, man. It just sucks though." Bobby plopped back onto the blanket and scooped up a piece of crust off his plate. "I mean, why didn't we just call ourselves the hawks in the first place, you know?"

"I have no idea, Bobs," Garth responded. "Some bullshit probably. People are idiots."

Chapter Eighteen

A vibrating thigh pulled Ethan from darkness. He was not in his room; nor was he in a bed but, per a bleary-eyed assessment, seated upright on a couch in a dim, different, and only vaguely familiar space. He was fully dressed but for one shoe. Ethan rubbed the pillow next to him, retracing his night. They had left the riverbank, already well-lubricated, in the third quarter with the Eagles down several scores, and returned to Garth's to revisit the Stampede Collection, and begin drinking in earnest. At some point, Ethan passed out.

He fished his incessant phone from his pocket. "Ethan McDaniel."

"Hey, it's me."

Ethan blinked. "Me?"

"Yea, me. Figure it out. I got your number from your firm's website."

"..." Ethan scrunched his eyes.

"Come on, man. It's Marissa. From Sires Paulson's office. We met on the phone. And in the courtroom. You ruined my hike."

"Oh. Good morning. Is there . . . do we . . . it's Saturday." This realization brought him some relief.

"That is accurate. This is purely a social call. Or wellness check. Once more I am swooping in to rescue you from the vile clutches of Sapphire Courts."

"No need." Ethan massaged his temples and laid back down. "I'm safe." He had no interest in moving.

"Well, hear me out before you decide, because some friends and I are headed to Lake Marie if you would like to join."

Ethan whirled upright more quickly than his stomach would have preferred. "Lake . . ." he smothered an alcoholic croak in his shoulder. "Lake Marie!? What? When? Wh—" A breath. "What do you need from me?"

"Is that a yes?"

"Absolutely. I would love to. Big time yes."

"Okay. I only require that you're clothed and moderately clean."

Ethan noticed he was nodding. His mouth tasted salty and sour. "I can get there."

"Can you get there in twenty minutes? I'll pick you up."

"Twenty minutes? Of course, yes, absolutely. Although, Marissa . . ."

"Yes, Ethan."

"I did it again."

"I know, sweetheart. I'll bring coffee."

Ethan retrieved his shoe and returned to his room, brushing his teeth and holding his mouth under the faucet until he gagged. After a quick body rinse, he changed into the same, still clean, outfit he'd worn on the failed hiking excursion, all the while contemplating his various belongings around the room.

Rods. I'm going to Lake Marie but I don't have my rods. I should've brought my rods. I should always bring my rods. Like Big Chuck says, the best fishing is spontaneous—or as he says it: spon-ti-nay-yas.

Finding no solution to this problem, he went outside to wait for Marissa, his hands feeling naked and useless in his pockets.

Once more, Marissa was prompt. Ethan opened the passenger door to a large coffee steaming in the cupholder. A wax paper wrapped breakfast sandwich waited for him on the seat.

"They serve the coffee too hot so I added some milk. I also ordered you the sausage biscuit to help get you moving."

Ethan slid a hand under the warm wax paper and lugged himself into the seat. "You're a nice lady."

Marissa spurted a surprised chuckle, almost spilling her coffee. "Thank you."

She guided her pristine SUV back to sea level. "Let me know if you're gonna hurl. You seem better today, and it's a much shorter, straighter shot, but it still seems like there's a chance."

Ethan sipped his coffee. "I'm ready. I'm good."

"Where did you end up last night?"

"Watched the Folkston Eagles from across the river. Then same as last time. Watched action movies at Garth's."

"Oh yes. *The Welcome Intruder* as Sires calls him. How much are you paying him to harass Colt for making you sit in the gallery?"

"No, Garth's doing that on his own. Independently motivated. Mr. Colt did something that pissed him off."

"Well, Sires and I couldn't have planned it any better. Nothing makes a local jury hate a foreigner more than a very public spat with a local."

Marissa turned off Main Street, passing Folkston High School and its baseball fields.

"You really think it's helping y'all?" Ethan hadn't considered that Garth's shenanigans could potentially negatively impact his case, his client.

Do I owe Mr. Lucas a duty to try to get Garth to stop?

"Of course it is. At least six of the jurors had to bury their faces in their sleeves to keep from laughing last time. That jury loathes Mr. Colt." Now Ethan grew embarrassed at his failure to observe, or even consider, the jury's reaction to Garth's shenanigans.

I also missed that the jury hated Mr. Colt.

Marissa drove for several minutes before easing onto an unmarked road through the trees. The coffee cleared the beer foam plaque from his brain nooks allowing Ethan to note the turn's location on his mental map.

"Can I ask you something?" she said.

"Sure, I guess."

"Are you okay? Like, emotionally? Because passing out in strange rooms at Sapphire Courts is usually a pretty good sign of not-okay-ness."

"I think I'm fine. Proud, no. But fine. Those guys are really fun to drink with. Do any of your friends fish?"

"I was wondering when you'd ask that. Is your question really whether there will be any fishing today?"

"Yes ma'am."

"Then no. Today is strictly a leisure affair. Wine-centric. Gossip-centric. Think more like the hair salon took its row of hooded driers to the lake and set it next to some loaded coolers."

Damn.

"So we're just meeting up with some of your girlfriends?" Ethan began to feel betrayed.

"No again. People forget, but men like to gossip too. Some even relish a good chin wag more than grifting hungry fish."

Marissa turned again, this time onto what seemed to be an old horse driven cart trail: two overgrown parallel strips of brown dirt which appeared to be previously untouched by rubber tires.

"This is the way to Lake Marie?"

"One of them. The power company owns it and doesn't want to be liable for swarms of people recreating on their property. So they keep it pretty sealed off." After a slow couple of miles, Marissa pulled over, parking on the overgrown shoulder behind a row of three other cars. "Great. They're already here. It's just a short walk. Can you stand?"

By this time Ethan had consumed his entire biscuit and felt quite himself. "Yes."

"Then you can carry the cooler. They'll be upset if we neglect the box wine."

Ethan helped Marissa unload her trunk, picking up the cooler and a dark green lawn chair before following her down a root-riddled red dirt trail.

"Are you one of those tight lipped *I-don't-discuss-ongoing-trials* type attorneys?"

Ethan tried to think whether he'd discussed the case with any civilians other than his parents—Garth came to mind. "I guess I'm open to discussing the case within the parameters of my privileges and duties to my client."

"You should figure out whatever the hell that means because these guys are always interested in my cases. And it's been a long time since one went to trial. Plus the whole town is at least side-eying the Bickerman-Lucas garbage dispute."

Ethan was about to say *well Emmett Lucas certainly isn't interested* when his father's words rang in his mind *once you say something, you can't unsay it.* "They'll likely be disappointed. I honestly can't say too much, you being the enemy and all."

"Crumbs to that. I'm off duty. You're socializing with weekend Marissa. She's even more disconnected than afterhours Marissa. Anything you say out here can and will be used to tease you. But it shall not be repeated to your adversary, my weekday employer. Or repeated in a court of law."

"I don't think I can offer you the same."

"Trust me, I know. You single track hard-ons never turn it off."

A line of four lawn chairs awaited their arrival; the tips of their legs had sunk into the red clay. Marissa shouted their presence, causing the occupants, two young women and two young men, to pause their chatting and turn to raise their disposable cups at the newcomers. Marissa stopped at the far right chair to introduce her companion. Ethan only had eyes for the lake.

"Everybody, this is Ethan. Ethan this is," she pointed at the girl in the far chair, "Delia, Kyle, Emma, and, right here in front, Eric." Ethan pulled his stare from Lake Marie to return their waves and assorted greetings.

"Nice to meet y'all. Thanks for having me out." He followed suit as Marissa fought her lawn chair from its fabric sleeve and set up on the near side of the formation. Marissa opened the cooler and handed him a beer.

"Ethan is an attorney in town for that trash trial. He is also, unfortunately, a fan of a certain cloying, annoying, and not-to-be-named fishing show and yet another fanatical Lake Marie groupie."

"I can see that." This was the nearer male, an acne-scarred, gangly looking young man with flat brown hair whose name Ethan had missed in his zeal at having completed his pilgrimage. "I'll spare you the uncertainty, bud. My name is Eric. Next to me is Emma, then Kyle, and Delia."

"Eric, Emma, Kyle, Delia. Thanks." Ethan raised his beer. He recognized Eric but couldn't place him.

When would I have met anyone from here?

"While we're at it," Marissa said. "We have the local public defender, a teacher, a carpenter, and a, um, entrepreneur."

Public defender. That was it. Eric was the Caz Man's defense attorney from Monday's hearing.

"I saw your hearing on Monday afternoon," Ethan said. "I'm sorry it didn't go your way."

"Monday . . ." Eric cocked an eye. "You're talking about Mr. Mayberry?"

"Yes, I think. The twenty-eight year old who got four years. I thought you presented his addiction very well. It made him very sympathetic."

"Thanks. Unfortunately, Folkston's given me a lot of opportunities to practice that angle."

"Ethan, are you representing Mr. Bickerman as well?" Emma asked. Ethan reluctantly leaned to look past Eric.

"I'm actually on the other side. I represent Mr. Lucas and Lucas Trash."

"Well, do you though?" Marissa said.

"Yes. I do," Ethan responded, "along with Mr. Colt and Ms. Nelson."

"If you say so," she turned to her friends. "They don't even let him sit at the table. He has to sit in the gallery."

"Mr. Colt and Ms. Nelson would let me if there was room."

"Is it telling that you still refer to them as Mr. and Ms.?" Emma asked.

"Yes, it is," Marissa responded for Ethan. "I've spoken with Ethan on the phone many, many times and he knows his shit. But mommy and daddy apparently don't trust him to drive. Meanwhile, the aggrieved little guy, Mr. Bickerman, doesn't enjoy the luxury of three high falutin' city attorneys. Sires and I are the only ones standing by his side, protecting his rights, telling his story. We're the only ones brave enough to stand up for our poor would-be real estate mogul." Ethan wondered whether he should defend Ms. Nelson and say it was mostly daddy. He decided to keep quiet.

"Kurt Bickerman is an asshole and an idiot," Kyle said. "He'll be lucky to get anything. It wasn't even his—"

"Hup, hup, hup," Marissa leaned forward as if trying to block the airborne words from reaching Ethan. "Be careful! Remember, mixed company."

Kyle, a ghostly pale short and thin man with lank black hair who appeared to be outside for the first time, looked back at Marissa then glanced at Ethan. "Oh right."

"Right."

"I thought you were off duty," Ethan said.

"That may have been an exaggeration. Especially if you're not. I can't be the source of additional defense witnesses. Sires would skin me."

"Alright then," Delia said. "Ethan, are you allowed to tell us what Mr. Lucas has to say about all this? He's so no-nonsense it's hard to imagine him rolled up in all this . . . nonsense." Delia was almost an exact replica of Marissa.

"Well . . . anything Mr. Lucas and I have discussed is protected by attorney client privilege." Ethan looked down the row of staring eyes, recalling Mr. Lucas storming out of the party room. "Our team's position is that there was no, is no, and has never been any unpleasant or unnatural odor emanating from Mr. Lucas' property. Nor has he ever stored or allowed to be stored any trash on that property."

"Oh, of course. No smell from the trashcan dump. But what about the trashcans spilling onto other peoples' properties? Y'all have to admit that he was storing them elsewhere. The whole town knows that."

"That," Ethan deliberated, "is something Mr. Bickerman and his counsel must establish on the record. And even if it were to be the case, it cannot be linked or attributed to Plaintiff's land deal falling through."

"Blergh. Marissa, get this person a stronger drink."

"Gladly." Marissa pulled a bag of wine from the cooler, lifting it to pour some into a cup. "Red box wine. It's probably not what you're used to drinking down in Charleston, but it's more appropriate for your present situation."

"Thanks." Ethan, now double fisting, watched as she gave herself a spritz directly into her mouth then rigged the bag to hang from her armrest.

"So can y'all give us something, anything interesting?" Emma asked.

Marissa studied Ethan for a second, tilting her head back and forth. "Ethan's boss, the daddy, is a pretty epic asshole." Ethan glared back. "What?! That's not privileged or anything. It's, um, open and obvious or whatever. You have to admit he sucks."

"He . . . maybe . . . has been pretty shitty." Today's alcohol had met last night's alcohol in Ethan's stomach, summoning a sudden and woozy inebriation.

"Do tell," Emma said.

The group once more leaned forward to look at Ethan, who grew drunker in real time. "Well, first of all, neither of them is in any way my boss. We don't even work for the same firm. Mr. Colt and Ms. Nelson and I just happen to all represent Emmett Lucas and Lucas Trash."

"You say that like it's better that you eagerly and enthusiastically shovel shit for someone who doesn't pay you." Marissa started filling another cup of box wine.

"I was there when he was shitty to Mrs. Baldwin. He is always an asshole?" Eric asked.

"He's pretty awful." Sterling Colt had become hard to sugarcoat. "Like Marissa said, he doesn't let me sit at the table. And one day, yesterday I think, he wouldn't even let me sit in the courtroom. He also shoots down any idea or strategy that isn't his." Marissa looked at him eagerly; Ethan stopped himself before he said too much. "Ms. Nelson is nice, though. She's with a third firm. My actual boss, Mrs. Warland, is very nice as well. She's not here but I feel it's important to mention that."

"I always feel bad for Teri," Marissa said.

"Because she has to deal with Mr. Colt? It's only on this case."

"Well, that for sure. But whenever I talk to her it seems like she's just on autopilot. Like she constantly wishes she was somewhere else. But," Marissa emphasized her upcoming point by leaning forward and raising a finger, "I get the feeling she'd be much happier if she ever just let loose and called Colt a fucking dickless misogynistic asshole."

"She'll probably save that for after the trial. Attorneys can't be calling each other names during the trial. Especially their co-counsel."

Marissa returned her plastic cup to the wine nozzle. "I have zero interest in any profession that requires me to censor—", she hiccupped, "ship myself."

"The world might benefit from that," Eric said.

Marissa shrugged. "Ethan has other interesting news. He has met and befriended Bobby Canterbury. Wasn't he in your brother's class, Delia?"

The further woman, Marissa's twin, leaned forward. "Who?"

"Bobby Canterbury."

"Oh yea. I mean I guess you could say that. To whatever extent Bobby Canterbury was in a class. He barely ever went to school except on nacho day and during wrestling season when his coaches made him. How and why do you know him?"

"I'm staying at Sapphire Courts."

"Sapphire Courts!?" The group was united.

"Was there no vacancy at the jail?" Eric asked.

"I've already put him through this," Marissa said. "That's why he's here. So he doesn't have to be there."

"You might as well stay at Cochran's Mill," Delia added.

"I didn't have any say in it. Sapphire Courts is just where the decision makers put me."

"You need better decision makers," Emma said.

"Anyway, Ethan and Bobby got drunk together last week before the storm." Marissa turned to look at Ethan. "And again last night?"

"That is accurate."

"You don't do meth, do you?" Delia asked.

"Meth? No."

"I heard Bobby got caught up in that. That's why he dropped out of school. And now probably why he lives at Sapphire Courts. I hope that's not what you think all of Folkston is like."

"No, Bobby dropped out of school because . . ." Ethan didn't know how to concisely phrase this. "He was done with it, I guess. It wasn't a great decision. But it certainly wasn't because of meth. And he doesn't do meth anymore. He's been clean for a while."

"Well, he's not going to do it right in front of you," Eric said. "You're an unknown stranger choosing to stay at Sapphire Courts. You don't have the reek of desperation on you. Bobby probably thinks you're a narc. All my clients are terrified of narcs."

"I'm not a narc. I'm not even a cop."

"He doesn't know that. Meth addicts are always suspicious, always checking their corners. Meth makes you that way and, also, you have to be to live that lifestyle. Your job has *law* in the title so that's probably all he sees. So he says he's not using anymore so you won't hassle him or whatever."

"No. He's never said anything. His friends told me. They're helping—"

"His Sapphire Courts friends?"

"Yes."

"I assert the same argument. And, beyond that, almost no one *gets off* meth," Eric said. "Especially not down and out folks who've been dealt a shit hand like Bobby Canterbury."

"It's true though. He's working. He's got good friends. He's clean." Ethan took a sip. "Except for alcohol, I guess. He and a buddy are moving to Columbia in December to start anew."

"That's all well and good. But you don't live here. You don't work with these people. I see this shit all the time. He might completely mean it, but it's just talk. Every addict says the same stuff when they get busted or, by some miracle, find themselves stringing together a run of clean days and they're feeling good. But methamphetamine is the soul killer. It jumps up out of the ground and sucks people dry. At this point, the big time industrial level cooks have got it chemically engineered to be as addictive and as mentally, emotionally, physically, and even spiritually destructive as possible. Getting off it takes resources, a support system, luck, and a willing candidate. Does he even have any supportive, stable family?"

"I only know about his dad. Who apparently is actually deadbeat, absentee dad. But Bobby's got great friends." Delia made a face, shaking her head at the ground. "They're trying to be his family. That's who he's going to Columbia with. His friend is starting at USC in January."

"Bad family is a bad sign. It's not just about support. It's about holes. Meth patches over emotional holes. Family sized holes. Makes incomplete folks temporarily feel whole. Makes the weak feel invincible. The more bricks missing in a person's self-worth, the more a person's lacking, the more of a hold meth can take. The easier the wall comes down. Meth heads are insanely sensitive when they're trying to get sober. One ill-timed emotional, familial jolt and they're right back down the rabbit hole."

"Bobby's different. He's determined. He's going to make it." Ethan thought of how Frank and Garth guarded Bobby.

Could they brick over his father's absence?

"Just because you met him doesn't make him special," Eric said.

"Eric, you don't actually know Bobby Canterbury or his situation. He could be doing great." Ethan couldn't see whether this was Delia or Emma, but he was grateful nonetheless. He looked to Marissa for additional support; she sat slump-shouldered, staring at the clay around her feet, her front teeth digging into her bottom lip.

"I've represented a thousand Bobbies. The story is always the same. Meth excoriates anything unique or interesting from its users. It's the same whether they come in my office or I go see them at the jail. They swear it off and beg for a sentence involving substance abuse treatment. Then they maybe put one and a half feet in rehab. But more often than not, they're right back in two months later on some other meth induced bullshit. Even if they get clean for a second, their world's always waiting to boot them off the wagon."

"Eric—"

"I'm not being an asshole. This shit pisses me off. I genuinely feel for these people. I spend each and every day trying to help them. It's not their fault. They've been bested by economics, geography, and chemistry. It's just like catching AIDs or the plague. It's impressive really, how terminal meth is. Almost right off the bat there's a physical and emotional dependency. Being born in certain parts of Folkston is like being born in a quarantine zone, or a minefield, or the lion's den. You know it too, Marissa. How many meth heads has Sires represented and how many have actually kicked it and moved on?"

Marissa turned to Ethan, her eyes downcast, her voice soft. "It is very rare."

"See, there we have it. And nothing is going to actually change until people hear the bad news and really understand what we're dealing with."

No one spoke after this. Ethan finished his wine and refilled.

Bobby Canterbury is going to make it. He has Frank. He has Garth. He has me. I have resources. I can help.

Ethan felt restless, shifting and flexing in his seat as if he could wring out the tension in his organs.

The group had apparently not seen each other, at least as a whole, in some time and soon slipped into inaccessible reminiscing; many of their classmates had thrust themselves into strange situations that were either entirely on or off brand for their high school personas.

As Ethan finished both drinks, his thoughts flowed back to Lake Marie. The group sat facing a small, featureless, and currentless cove which bore little resemblance to the rolling green banks and reflective waters depicted on *Wettin' the Line*. The red clay under their chairs eased down to the center of a shallow spoon of water, returning up to form the far shore. Except for the gap leading to Lake Marie's main body, the cove's perimeter was a smooth oval. No rocks, no downed trees, not even any errant scraps of human debris. No features. No landmarks. No cover for the fish. Even if they had been there to fish, they would have been unlikely to see one. Ethan doubted the cove ever got more than three feet deep.

This may be Lake Marie, but it was not the place.

Ethan traced the shoreline right to where the cove joined Lake Marie's main body.

There lies the legend.

He checked left; Marissa had her whole torso turned away from him to better fill in her companions about a certain high school friend's new tattoo. His feet took him to the cove's end.

Ethan surveyed the lake, its nooks and crannies, the angle of the surrounding mountains as they dipped under the surface.

This is the place.

He contemplated his hypothetical attack plan: by boat, he would start past the cove's far corner by the downed tree, then follow the current along the shoreline to the next cove which appeared to offer significantly more water and cover; an artificial worm, perhaps chartreuse, or a crankbait would work nicely, at least at first, then he could expand to the deeper, more niche items in his arsenal.

A single jon boat, captained by a grey headed man—*a local*—puttered along the far shoreline. Ethan observed its progress, waiting for the local to stop and wet his line. It turned left into a distant cove and disappeared.

"Are we that boring?" Marissa asked. Ethan tensed—he had been too absorbed to notice her approach. "Sorry, you're very easy to sneak up on."

"Y'all were gossiping and I had to see the lake. This may be the only time I get to actually set eyes on it."

"Understandable, but still rude." She put a hand on Ethan's back, guiding him back towards the group. "Come now, have another drink before Eric thinks of something hurtful. I promise there will be no more meth or trial talk."

"Are we that boring?" Eric asked.

"I beat you to that one." She took Ethan's empty cup and held it under the plastic wine tap.

"Sorry, I just wanted to see Lake Marie. It's a really famous lake."

"We know. We know," Delia said. Eric drooped backwards in his chair so his head lolled over the chairback. "Folkston is a small town. Word gets around when a film crew starts poking around the bait shop, then pays teenagers to lug their camera and gear into the woods. It was a big to-do." Ethan wasn't sure whether this was sarcasm.

"Sorry, I just, my dad and I are big fans. I got excited to see it in person. My dad's insanely jealous."

The group resumed chatting, pausing now and then to get Ethan's unbiased input on particularly egregious developments. Eventually, the wine supply ran low and the group decided to wrap it up.

"Marissa, should we show our guest the Folkston Cavity before we go?" Kyle asked.

"Cavity?"

"It's just a cave. Or, really, a particularly deep rock overhang. It's pretty cool though. We camp there sometimes in the fall. We can work our way over there. It's kind of on the way."

The group packed up and started to leave. In case this was his last opportunity, Ethan dashed to the shore in front of him and ran his hand through Lake Marie. He knelt, watching the holy water drip from his fingers to form little dark circles in the clay.

They left on a different path, entering the woods at the tip of the spoon. After about fifty yards, just when the land really began to rise into the next mountain, there was a break in the earth where an immense granite face angled out of the ground as if to brace the mountain, leaving a deep triangle of shade and cool air.

"There you have it, Ethan. The Folkston Cavity," Kyle said proudly.

In the innermost crook of the granite, a spot where Ethan would have been much too nervous to sleep, or even sit, was a firepit and some scattered signs of recent use.

"I wonder who's been out here," Emma said. "I hope the meth heads haven't found it."

A patch of dusty soil just under the overhang caught Ethan's eye; he leaned in to inspect. The tiny tract was pocked with a system of small dimples, varying in size, but each one wide and circular at the top, funneling down to a point, like someone had pressed ice cream cones into the sand.

"What's going on here?"

"Doodlebugs," Kyle said. The entire group turned their attention to the ground.

"Doodlebugs?"

"Y'all don't have them in Charleston?" Kyle asked. "They dig these divot traps in sand and soft soil that ants and other small bugs get trapped in. The ant wanders in, starts slipping down, goes round and round, and once he gets to the bottom the doodlebug jumps out with these oversized mandibles and, you know, drinks him."

Ethan looked over the cluster of alleged bug traps. "There's a big bug hiding under each one of these just waiting for a meal to fall in?"

"A patient predator, yep," Delia said.

"Doodlebug is just the cute name," Kyle said. "Their proper name is antlion. It's actually just something else in a larval state, kinda like a caterpillar."

"A vicious caterpillar," Delia said.

"That doesn't look like it would work. Why doesn't the ant just walk the rim and leave?"

"Because antlions are wily," Eric said. "The good ones construct their slopes at the absolutely steepest possible angle, then line the slopes in extra fine sand. Even if the ant just barely steps on the rim, the very ground betrays it, taking it down until, eventually, the antlion takes another prize."

"Also, you have to look at what the ant's crossing," this was Kyle. "There's like a hundred doodlebugs. Even if it does happen to survive one encounter, it's bound to fall eventually. This time more tired and with less fight."

"That really doesn't seem fair."

"That's the way it is though," Eric said. "Once a little bug stumbles into the killing field, the prey can win a hundred times. The predator only has to win once."

Ethan inspected the divots for any potential victims, wondering how many insects had quietly lost their lives in this miniscule stretch. He found a potential victim, or survivor, to his left. The tiny black ant, little more than a speck, was about halfway down a medium-sized divot, but was facing upwards, working his way to safety. The rest of the group huddled around.

"I think this little guy's got a chance," Ethan said. "He looks determined."

"He wasn't too determined to get that deep."

"I don't know, Eric," Delia said. "He's making good progress."

"Doesn't mean shit until he's actually out."

They all leaned in to better inspect. The little ant was thorough, using his antennae to assess each potential foothold before taking the next step, still losing some ground as the infinitesimal grains gave underneath him to trickle down the slope in tiny avalanches, but systematically moving closer and closer to safety.

"Would you look at that. He's got a plan. Maybe he will make it," Kyle said.

Ethan looked up at him, nodded, then returned his attention to the crusading ant. Little by little, step by steady step, the ant fought upwards. Ethan's pulse quickened with each gain. Disaster struck three quarters up when the entire face under the ant gave out, slipping like silk towards concealed death.

"There he goes. I told y'all."

"No, no, no, no."

Ethan's breath caught as the ant braced itself, planting all six legs, sliding to face sideways until, just as he was sure the mandibles would flash, the never-say-die ant regained traction, plowing directly upwards through the sediment like a wolf through snow.

"C'mon. C'mon. C'mon. He's got it!" The ant pulled itself even with the rim.

"Yes! Would you look at that!" Ethan fist pumped and, in spite of himself, gave a little jump.

That was enough.

The vibration collapsed the rim, engulfing the ant in a fresh landslide. This time the descending madness prevented him from regaining his footing. Down he tumbled, until the mandibles flashed, lancing him on both sides before he even reached the bottom.

Ethan was still thinking about the ant on the ride home, the heroic hopelessness of its efforts. As they passed Folkston High School and prepared to re-enter town, Marissa spoke.

"Do you think that sad Teri and Captain Gargoyle are going on all these side adventures?"

"I don't know. That's hard to picture. I always pictured her as a reader. No telling what he's up to." Particularly as everyone around him validated his feelings, Ethan was growing to resent Sterling Colt and his exile in the gallery.

"It's cool that you're actually here. I mean, not just here for a trial but actually in Folkston, getting out, doing stuff."

"I am here for a trial. I'm exactly as much of an attorney as Mr. —Sterling and Teri." At this point it had been almost an hour since Ethan had had a drink and he was feeling the early, searing pangs of an impending double hangover. The sun grew brighter; words stung his ears.

"Yea but you get shitfaced and watch cheesy action movies with your neighbors and get weirdly excited about the distant prospect of fishing Lake Marie. You come out and meet people and stare at bugs. I feel confident assuming that's not how they're spending their free time. They have this preconceived notion of what it's like up here and they won't even try Folkston out. They probably only leave their hotel rooms to go to the courthouse." Ethan thought about the party room at Ristorante Rotundo—he wasn't sure what town that was. "If they think about Folkston at all it's as a jury pool or an investment property. It's just cool that you haven't gone full dead-eyed lawyer yet. Even if you're trying your damndest to get there, I'm not sure you'll ever actually make it."

"I'm already a licensed attorney. I've gone to school, graduated, and passed the bar. Once Sires rests his case I'll officially be eligible for membership in the South Caroli—"

Marissa laid her hand on Ethan's knee.

"Ethan. That's not what I'm saying. I'm talking about Bobby. You've only been here a week and you seem to really care about him. A lot of attorneys come through Folkston for trial. A lot of people come through Folkston on their way to someplace else. None of them would see Bobby Canterbury as anything other than an insect. But you, you seem to really care."

Ethan had missed Marissa's last point; the hand gently gripping his leg consumed his attention. She rolled the SUV back down to Sapphire Courts and stopped. The silence suggested it was his turn to talk.

"I . . ." He started to open the door and exit, then, remembering his manners, looked back to meet the warm eyes of the smiling driver. "Thanks for . . . lake."

Chapter Nineteen

On Sunday morning, Ethan McDaniel did a great many pushups, jumping jacks too. He'd fallen asleep in his clothes after Marissa dropped him off, waking in the night to use the bathroom and dip into his snack stores to compensate for missed meals. After which he'd returned to sleep. Now, in the cold light of day, he was awake and could recall his parting words in excruciating detail.

Thanks for . . . lake.

The words thumped his brain at the crest of each rep.

Thanks for lake.

Thanks for lake.

When his arms and legs burned with atonement, he took a cold shower and breakfasted on a protein bar and a handful of almonds.

Thanks for lake.

He tried to distract himself with his case file, stopping every few lines as his mind drifted back through the red wine haze to the sight, the feeling, of Marissa DePaul's hand on his knee.

What had she meant by that? What was she getting at? Why'd it catch me so off guard? Why can't I stop thinking about it?

For lunch, he knocked on Garth's door and asked to use his microwave to warm a lean oven burrito.

"Is that all you're eating today?"

"I goofed all day yesterday. Now it's time to pay the piper."

"Again, what would actually happen if you just sat around playing Cosmic Encounters all day? It's not like you're front and center. You don't even have a speaking role. You're barely an extra."

"You've made your point, Garth. With a pretty demonstrative assist from Mr. Colt. But I at least have to stay somewhat engaged. They, especially Teri, do sometimes use me as a source of information and springboard for ideas. They would report to Mrs. Warland that I hadn't prepared for trial. I can't say that it would impact this trial, but it would be shitty for me. You've won though. I now agree that nothing I do or don't do could cause Mr. Lucas' case to suffer. That's entirely up the attorneys seated in front of the bar."

"Emmett doesn't give a damn how this thing goes. He just wants it over. He wouldn't suffer anything additional on their account. He probably wouldn't even notice if it goes awry." Garth picked his controller back up. "The way this shit heap trash trial is sputtering along there probably won't even be court tomorrow."

Ethan's burrito was on its way to his mouth for his first bite; he stopped it midway. "Why would you even say that?"

***

Monday morning found Ethan McDaniel back in the Patricians, waiting under the parking lot tree and watching for the glass doors to open. Sterling Colt manned his post; he'd been cemented on the top step since before Ethan's arrival.

A car door opened and closed nearby; Teri Nelson approached clutching a thick packet of papers.

"You were right, Ethan."

"Ma'am?"

"About Dr. Clarkson. Our obstinate comrade up there insisted Sires would call him last. And yet . . ."

"First thing Friday or, I guess, Thursday morning. *We* were right about that. You said it too."

"And yet we both let him get his way. That can be your lesson today: first you have to learn how to be right, then you have to learn to be a big enough cocksucker for it to matter." She looked in the gargoyle's direction. He cocked his head in theirs, looking down on them like a hawk at a mole. "Nobody in school teaches you how to be the most condescending, stiff-necked asshole in the room, but that is the only person who gets their way." Ethan had never considered that she might see their efforts as equally futile. "Luckily, that lesson didn't cost us."

"Mr. Paulson handled Ms. Polly well, too. No outburst from her."

"I agree. What do you think happens next?"

"You're really asking me?"

"Why not? You generally have something approaching useful to offer and, if you don't, Colt only ever listens to himself so it doesn't really matter."

"I guess it could go several different ways."

"Try harder."

"I'd say that Sires rests his case today. Right off the bat. He only listed a couple more witnesses: Mr. Tarfman, the real estate agent, and Bickerman's business partner, Crandle, but neither of them has much to offer at this point. I bet he just waited so we wouldn't have the whole weekend to prepare."

Ms. Nelson nodded. "That's pretty good. You seem to have a knack for this." She looked up at her trial partner. "I like trying to predict trials. Such an exercise in futility. There are too many scatter-bound cats to ever be properly herded in a logical, consistent manner. And yet, it's the path we've chosen."

"Good morning adversaries!" Both turned to greet an approaching Marissa.

Thanks for lake.

Ethan wasn't quite sure how long to look at her or where to set his eyes after.

"Either of y'all have any idea what's going on?" Marissa asked.

"No. But I'm concerned that you ask," Ms. Nelson responded. "It's much too early for anything good to have happened."

"It's late actually. It's past nine and the doors are still locked. I haven't seen any signs of movement inside." Ethan checked his watch.

The doors should at least be open.

"Is this usual?" Ethan asked.

"It's not unprecedented," Marissa responded. "But last time it was a . . . well, I'd rather not say."

"Please don't." Ms. Nelson seemed to be catching on. "Nothing good ever comes from saying things out loud."

"Maybe the security guards are just late opening up," Ethan suggested.

Ms. Nelson sighed again, turning towards the courthouse. "Maybe. But it certainly doesn't feel like that."

They stood in silence. Ethan kept his eyes locked on the glass doors.

Thanks for lake.

He wondered where Marissa was looking. Several of the jurors sat down on the steps.

The doors opened in near mechanical unison, emitting a stream of matronly women, bailiffs, and meaty security guards. Mrs. Marsh brought up the rear, letting a door crash closed behind her as she scurried down the steps shouting and waving her arms.

Sirens wailed in the distance.

"Fucking cats." Ms. Nelson slammed her papers into the crab grass. The sirens grew louder until the flashing red lights stopped outside the lot. Two parallel lines of helmeted, uniformed men formed then marched to the entrance, huddled again, then fanned out around the building. "Fucking goddam cats. It's a fucking bomb threat."

"Yep." Marissa made this two syllables.

"How do y'all know?" Ethan asked.

"Because this is what they do when it's a fucking bomb threat."

"You think somebody planted a bomb in the courthouse?"

"No, I fucking wish someone planted a bomb. That would be the end of it. I think one of these . . . " Ms. Nelson fluttered her hand in the direction of the scattering jury, searching for the appropriate term of malice, "fucking nincompoop turd balls called in a bomb threat so they wouldn't have to serve today." Ethan helped her collect her case file; he had the thought that Teri Nelson and Garth Quattlebaum might be very happy together.

"Or a separate, unrelated chucklehead was up for child support payment," Marissa offered. "That's who it was last time. And the time before."

"One of my friends did that in middle school after he'd stayed up all night playing a new video game instead of studying for a test."

"It's a similar display of maturity," Ms. Nelson said.

"What does it mean for trial?"

"It's an hour delay if they clear it. All day if they hit literally any snag. We get to go home if the fucking thing actually blows up. Fucking snake bit." A single sharp pop reverberated across the lot. Ms. Nelson recoiled, dropping her papers again. "Oh Jesus."

"What was that?"

"The sound of another wasted day." Ms. Nelson rubbed her temples, her shoulders contracting into a hunch as she slumped against the tree. Ethan re-collected her papers and set them by her feet.

Several moments later, a fully outfitted and helmeted man scuttled around from the courthouse's rear to convene with one of the suits who had remained by the vehicles. The suit nodded then relayed the information to Mrs. Marsh who clamped a hand over her breast. Ethan's group watched Mrs. Marsh locate and whisk over to Mr. Colt, who now stood in the lot but not nearly far enough from the courthouse to be considered safe—Ethan pictured him cooly striding away as the courthouse exploded behind him. Whatever Mrs. Marsh said to him deepened his scowl. He jerked into his black luxury sedan and left.

"Another bad sign," Ms. Nelson said.

Mrs. Marsh used a hand to shield her eyes from the sun, rotating like a periscope to scan the waters for other interested parties, then charted a course through the growing crowd in the direction of Ethan, Marissa, and Ms. Nelson.

"And here comes confirmation," Ms. Nelson said.

When she was two car lengths away, Mrs. Marsh started shouting and waving her hands anew. "No trial today. No. Trial. Today. Some white-livered gollumpus called in a bomb threat. But that's apparently been cleared."

"Then what's the hold up?" Marissa asked.

"The bomb squad had some sort of an encounter in the basement."

"Encounter?" Ethan asked.

"They won't say. But I think we all heard the weapon discharge. Everyone's accounted for, thank goodness, but the situation now requires additional investigation which, unfortunately, requires quarantining the courthouse."

"What could there be in the basement?" Ethan asked.

"I'm just wondering which of my things they put a hole in. There's nothing down there but files and storage. But something spooked them and now I'm to send everybody home. We'll just hope to reconvene in the morning."

"Assuming the courthouse hasn't burned to the ground."

Mrs. Marsh's jaw dropped. "Ms. Nelson how could you even . . . they have cleared the bomb threat. There is no evidence of any explosive device. There has simply been some sort of incident in the basement."

"They probably just don't want their mishaps to be observed," Ms. Nelson said.

"Be that as it may . . ." Mrs. Marsh finished this sentence with her hands, shooing them away. The trio took several steps back to the sidewalk, then watched her tap on Mr. Paulson's window.

"So, what happens? What do we do today?" Ethan asked.

"Sterling is going to call me the minute he gets back to his hotel," Ms. Nelson said. "He'll want to adjust our defense strategy accordingly. Whatever that means. I'd suggest you not pick up if I call."

"I want to be there. I should be present."

"Have it your way, Ethan." Ms. Nelson returned to her vehicle.

"I can't wait to see what your esteemed defense team cooks up with its extra day," Marissa said. "I'm going to warn Sires so we can coordinate our surrender." Ethan found himself watching her walk away. He caught himself when she knocked on Sires' car window, and started walking home.

Chapter Twenty

Tuck was loading a fishing rod into his green pickup on the far side of the Sapphire Courts lot. He spotted Ethan and shouted.

"Dressed for the courtroom, I see. Damn shame, son, damn shame." Tuck spread his arms to the cloudless sky. "Today, more than most, is a terrible day to be cooped up in that musty old law barn. I choose freedom and a day on the water. Enjoy God's bounty and what not. Catch some dinner."

"Court actually just got cancelled, or postponed." It all felt the same to Ethan.

"Must've been an unusually short list of victims."

Ethan waited for his local to continue.

Could this be the moment?

Tuck looked down, mumbled to himself, then returned his eyes to Ethan. "I got an extra seat if you'd care to join. Room on the boat, too."

Ethan took several breaths, measuring his response. "Are you going out on Lake Marie?"

"That's where I fish. I have a boat stashed away up there somewhere all secrety. And a few of us," he gestured at the patch of lawn where the nightly folding chairs assembled, "have a very special piece of water nobody else knows about."

The phrase *special piece of water* shimmered in Ethan's brain.

Colt, Nelson, Lucas, bricks be damned. My local has called.

"Do I have time to change?"

"I'd very much like to watch a man fish in his fancy suit. Can't say I've ever seen such a thing before. But I reckon you're entitled to suit yourself. If you're quick about it."

Ethan started towards the stairs, and stopped. "I wasn't really planning on fishing this trip." *I never thought I'd get so lucky.* "Is there somewhere I could buy a rod?"

"I buy my fishin' beer at the fishin' shop. You can find one there. Tackle, too. You'll have to be quick about that as well."

"Absolutely. Of course."

Ethan rushed up the stairs, wrenched off his clothes, not sparing the Patricians, and tossed them all on the floor, then jumped into what passed as his most appropriate and immediately available fishing attire.

Tuck had repositioned his truck so the stairs fed directly into the open passenger door. His fingers drummed on the steering wheel as Ethan jumped in.

"Now, unless you require something else . . ." he gave Ethan the side eye.

"No, sir. I'm ready."

"Then here we go."

Ethan examined the truck's interior as it lurched over the sand embankment like an old rollercoaster. A crank, not a button, controlled the window. The green backlit dash clock read 10:13. The stereo played a song about sipping beer.

"I really can't thank you enough for bringing me along. I've dreamed, literally dreamed, of fishing Lake Marie. My dad, too. It was legendary even before Chuck Palwag—"

"Now this here trip came together pretty quick. And that's fine. I'm all for taking the day as it comes. But before we get out there, before I take you to my water, my holy place, I need to make sure we're clear on a couple essentials."

"Of course."

Let your local be your guide. Abide him and respect all local customs and etiquette.

Tuck's eyes left the road to confirm his passenger was nodding. "First, do you know what you're doing?"

"Sir?"

"Do you know how to fish? I ain't out here to babysit and I ain't out here to lead a how-to. And I'm certainly not out here to untangle your snags. I'm out here to relax, drink beer, and, God willing, catch dinner."

"Absolutely. Very experienced. You won't have to worry about me. I know what I'm doing. You certainly won't spend your morning untangling my line."

"Believe me, son, that wasn't an option." Tuck's fingers continued their dance. "And out there on the water, what I say goes. It's my boat. It's my rules. I won't have you backtalkin' me."

"Absolutely. No problem there."

"Good, good. Now, you ain't too good are ya? I've spent too much time on this water. If it had been here I would've grown up on it. So I can't have some Lowcountry city boy haulin' in some behemoth I've only ever dreamed of."

"No, s—Tuck. I'm just okay. I'm, um, right in the middle."

"That'll do fine. You just stay there. Middle ain't such a bad spot."

Tuck turned off Main Street—one turn off where Chuck Palwagon had left Main Street—then swerved to a slanted stop in front of a miniscule blue building. The faded sign above the door read *Jergen-son's.*

"You may well have gathered this on your own, but it's damn near critical so I'll say it irregardless." He pointed a weathered finger at his passenger. "This spot, the spot that I'm taking you to, is a well-kept, airtight, locked down, me-and-the-boys fucking secret. The whole damn lake used to be a secret before folks like you started popping up. This spot, my spot, is all that remains. It's pristine, fertile, hard to get to. So don't run back to Charleston and start spilling the beans to all your dandy city friends."

"Wouldn't dream of it."

"Because that's a shooting offense. I don't want to come out here one day and see a bunch of fancy high rider boats and pale kids in crisp, clean ballcaps. If I do, I'll track you down and see it through. I'm not one for computers and manhunts but if you take my fishing away I'll have plenty of time to learn."

"Got it." A day on this water was worth an eternity of looking over his shoulder.

"You sure?"

"You can blindfold me if you like."

"Now there's an idea." Tuck's smile returned. "Jergenson's has got your rod and tackle. I'm just getting a case of beer so you be quick. Time spent here is time not spent on the water."

Ethan selected the first rod he saw, thus relieving Jergenson's of its entire inventory, then cobbled together a workable assortment of line, hooks, weights, and lures from Jergenson's likewise limited selection.

Other than the stereo, which now played a song about drinking beer on the happy days and whiskey on the sad, it was a quiet ride into the mountains. Tuck hummed along to the radio, on several occasions reaching for something not present in the cupholder.

It all felt right. It all felt authentic. This was Ethan McDaniel out with his local, kneeling at his feet, learning his customs, and, soon, wettin' his line in Lake Marie. They rode for several songs before Tuck spoke.

"Okay son, here's where I'd have to blindfold you and you're lucky because the only thing I have is my fishing rag." Ethan looked around but did not observe any crossroads or signage. Without blinker or further warning, Tuck jerked the steering wheel left, launching his truck off the roadway.

Ethan yelped as they steamrolled through the underbrush filling a gap in the pines.

"YYEEEEEEHHHAAAWWWWW SON. YOU'RE DOIN' IT NOW!"

The pavement disappeared behind them. The truck bounced for an additional fifty yards before the trees stopped and the pine straw gave way to a baked red clay. Tuck parked the truck just up the bank from a rusting, trailerless jon boat.

Tuck opened his door, then paused. "Once more, this," he gestured through the windshield, "is an absolute hole-in-your-heart-don't-tell-a-fucking-soul secret."

Ethan nodded, eyes set on the water. The surrounding mountains sloped down to meet their reflections in the still shoreline. Further out, the sun sparkled off the windblown current covering the depths. It was the most beautiful thing Ethan McDaniel had ever seen.

"I wouldn't spoil this for all the world."

"That's a good lad."

The pair collected their things; Ethan followed Tuck to the boat.

"Mr. McDouglas, I'd like you to meet Boat. Boat, Mr. McDouglas may be a no good Lowcountry city boy, but, today he is our guest, and I want you to take real good care of him. Me too for that matter."

"That's her name? Boat?"

"No, that's *its* name. Boat used to be named after a woman. Then another woman. Then another. Then I lost track. *She* became *it* and *it* became Boat." He patted the aluminum rail.

"Nice to meet you, Boat." Ethan gave a wrist wave.

"Now, I should say, that its name's only Boat when it's running and putting me on fish. Otherwise, when it's acting up, it's back to being a she and we call *that* she, Bitch."

"I really hope I don't meet Bitch."

"Now my truck came later. I'd learned my lesson by then. So the truck's named Hoss." Tuck stopped loading to look Ethan in the eye. "Never name your vehicle after a woman, son. Vehicles last much too long."

When Boat was loaded, Tuck gave Ethan the order to *push 'er in*. Ethan did so. Tuck stood in the water until he judged it was deep enough, then swung himself into Boat and gestured for Ethan to do the same.

"One final rule," Tuck said. Ethan situated himself on the front bench to face his instructor. "It's terrible luck to exit the cove, or do anything really, before all aboard have cracked a beer. You may think that's just country hogwash but the fish hear about it and make themselves scarce. Ruins their appetite. No self-respecting fish wants to be reeled in by a sober angler. It also attracts Bitch."

Tuck rotated his hand at the cooler as if he was trying to coax a friendly dog to come. Ethan wriggled out the first two cans, handing one to his captain.

"Thank ya, son." Tuck slid a yellowing fingernail under the tab, cracked it open, and took a long sip without removing his other hand from the tiller. Ethan opened his, taking a deep pull as Tuck began yanking the cord for the motor.

On the first pull, the engine groaned and sputtered but failed to catch.

"Bitch."

The second pull mustered a similar, if somewhat more enthusiastic, response.

"Fuck. King. Bitch."

The third pull initiated a steady roar and churn of bubbles.

"There you are, Boat! Now, put us on some fish!"

Ethan checked Boat's aluminum sides but did not see any of the taped-on letters or numbers indicating the vessel had been properly registered. He had repeatedly viewed all four hundred fifty-seven episodes of *Wettin' the Line*, including the ones filmed before Chuck Palwagon had a deal with a programmer and filmed his excursions on his personal camcorder, and had never *ever* known Big Chuck to do something illegal. He assumed Big Chuck would approve of this even if the footage had to remain entombed in his vault.

Boat's interior matched the rust of its exterior; Ethan watched the bottom grow increasingly damp. Ethan, in the way of young men, let himself assume that Boat, and even Bitch, had returned safely from many prior outings, and would more than likely survive one more. He sipped his beer, relishing the tingle and spreading relaxation as the cold, overly carbonated liquid permeated deep into his marrow. He leaned back and breathed, taking in his 360-degree view of Lake Marie. A cloudless blue sky reflected in the slanting ripples of Boat's wake. The clean air, a pleasant mix of warm summer water and crisp autumn mountain, kissed his cheeks. The only sound came from Boat's sputtering, uneven motor as Ethan's very own local guided their vessel across the main body to track the far shore.

It was indeed a beautiful day to be outside the courtroom.

A metallic crunch signaled that Tuck had finished his second beer; Ethan supplied them both with a fresh one.

"Good lad! Keeping your captain happy, and lubricated, is the best luck of all." Tuck opened this beer in the same manner as the last, starting it off with a long sip. "A beer on the way keeps Bitch at bay. But don't forget now," Tuck tried to look serious, "that a beer on the water, keeps the sons from your daughter. And, of course everyone knows, that two beers while you're fishin' makes true what you're wishin'." He cackled after each limerick. Ethan wondered how these would look on a throw pillow.

A new sound, a dull roar, reached Ethan's ears accompanied by a steadily increasing flow out of the back of the cove.

Must be where the river comes in.

"Here we are, son. Tuck's secret spot. If you'll look forward you'll see what makes it worth keeping quiet."

Ethan looked ahead: a dark sheer rock wall, at least double the height of the surrounding trees, shot out of the red clay to form the far bank. A vertical streak of white foaming water divided the rockface, churning Lake Marie's otherwise unnaturally serene surface.

"Your own waterfall. That's amazing." *This hadn't been in the episode.*

"Indeed it is, son. Indeed it is."

"Does it have a name?"

"Best I can tell the mapmakers don't know it's here. But me and the boys got tired of describing it to each other each time we mentioned it, so we started calling it Saggy Titty Falls."

"Saggy Titty? That's the name of the waterfall?"

"Amongst the fine men who fish it."

"Why . . . that?"

"Because we're all getting older and that's the only kind we come across." Tuck cackled anew. It was a welcoming laugh and Ethan couldn't help but join him, especially having never before considered this particular drawback of advancing age. "Saggy Titty Falls. Our little haven from all the world's troubles. It's the most peaceful, and productive, fishing there is. The waterfall churns up the little bits on the bottom that keeps everything fed, and keeps the water moving and new stuff coming in. There's plenty of still water on the banks for bass and a nice deep running channel in the middle for catfish."

"Chuck Palwagon definitely didn't come here on *Wettin' the Line*."

"Because no one told Big Chuck about it and Walt Kerps, that stuck up dolt, doesn't know about it. Because Kerps only fishes Lake Thompson and everybody worth a damn would rather die than tell him about it. We only know about it because me and the boys remembered playing around the waterfall as squirts. We had a helluva time trying to retrace our steps to it once those fuckers flooded everything. Now, let's let that be the last time we mention those particular assholes."

Tuck rigged a live worm to float about three inches above a weight and tossed it into the deep water, keeping the reel open until it stopped taking line. He shut the reel, gave a couple cranks to bring the line taut, and set that rod down to rig his other rod for bass.

Ethan did the same. "Where would you like me to fish?"

"You're at the front so you fish the front. Don't worry too much about all that. I won't be polite if you get in my way."

Ethan took a moment, studying and absorbing the shoreline topography before determining where to start. This would be his first cast into Lake Marie.

After this moment, I will forever be able to say I've fished Lake Marie.

If so inclined, which he was not, he could post about it on Chuck Palwagon's *Wettin' the Online* forum. Ethan, however, was content with the envy of his father. After a deep breath, he flicked out his rubber worm to lightly splash in six or so inches from the downed tree. He let the line go slack before starting to work it along the branch. His hands conducted the rod as his eyes traced the vertical pillar of water, not much wider than those in front of the courthouse, pouring off the rocks above him.

"Pretty ain't it?" Tuck said. "Just a trickle compared to when there's been a rain."

Ethan agreed, marveling at the spectacle until his line caught, snapping his attention back to fishing. In his distraction, he had let his line venture too close to the tree.

No, not today. Not here.

He gave a soft testing flick, a branch bowed towards him.

Shit . . .

"C'mon now. You said you knew what you were doing."

"Sorry, I was looking at the waterfall."

"Well, go on 'n' cut it."

"I don't think it's caught too bad." Ethan changed the directions of his tugs, first left, then right, then up.

"Cut that before you shake up that tree and spoil the pool."

"Just a second. I won't shake a thing." Ethan opened his drag, letting out line; the limb relaxed in the water. Slowly, he reeled the line straight but not taut, then assessed the angle of the limb, slanting his rod accordingly with a series of small ticks. The angle of the line deepened, trailing the lure as it slipped the limb and sank untethered to the bottom.

"Very well done, son. If you'd shook up that tree we might as well have set the whole damn cove on fire."

"My dad taught me that. If you get caught as much as I used to, you have to learn how to get out of it."

"Well thank your daddy for me."

The pair returned to silent fishing; Ethan gave the downed limb a wider berth.

Tuck landed the first two fish, both sizable bass, singing bits of country songs as he reeled them in, humming and whistling when he couldn't remember the words.

At last, Ethan's line tugged; this time running definitively along the shore. His heart seized, remaining clenched as he guided the fish left, away from the entangling tree and towards the boat.

This was it. A fish I will remember forever.

Ethan worked cautiously; the fish dove twice, both times to the left and well away from danger, before allowing itself to be dragged in. Only when he held the fish, a moderately sized largemouth bass wholly unremarkable other than having been pulled from Lake Marie, dripping on Boat's bottom did his heart resume beating, now in triple time. The young man looked to his captain, a pink smile almost connecting his ears.

"Okay then! You're on the board."

Ethan was too happy to speak.

A Lake Marie fish. I have caught a Lake Marie Fish.

Elation flushed his cheeks, his smile stretching further as he ran his hand along the fish's brown and algae green body to its bony tail. He relished the slime collecting on his fingers.

"Go on and throw it back now. That ain't what we're out here for."

Ethan slipped the hook from the fish's lip. "Would you mind taking a picture of me and the fish? My phone's on the bench."

"You're a little old for that, son."

"Please, it's for my dad."

"If it'll get you back to work." Tuck picked up the phone, tapped a couple times, quickly pointed it at Ethan, tapped once more, then set it down without glancing at the photograph.

"Thank you," Ethan said. He raised the fish and, with great ceremony, kissed it on the top lip before releasing it back into the water. Ethan watched it disappear into the depths.

Thank you, too.

They continued to drift the cove's perimeter, each man hauling in more than his share of bass. Every now and then Tuck paused to hook a fresh worm on the catfish line.

They were back between the waterfall and the downed tree for perhaps the fifth or sixth time when Ethan's line pulled once more. He tracked it with his rod as it cruised left, away from the tree. It was not the heavy, slogging weight of a lunker, but it was vigorous and taking line. It turned back towards the tree. Ethan readied himself for a good fight, his fingers instinctively leaving the handle to tighten the drag: the knob spun lightly, without resistance, failing to engage any of the crucial gears or mechanisms underneath.

"Tighten the drag, son. It's gonna get you stuck."

Ethan flicked again and again at the knob. "There's something wrong with the reel."

"Don't blame the reel. Just do it."

Ethan flicked harder; the knob spun off, clanging off the bench and onto the aluminum bottom.

"Oh shit." Desperate, Ethan clamped the line against the rod with his finger and whipped hard away from the tree, but there was too much slack. The line surged into the tree, jerking for several seconds before going still.

"You're good 'n' caught up now."

"I might be able to . . ." Ethan gripped his rod tip and started to angle it—the knife flashed just beyond it.

"Shit!" Ethan jumped, wobbling Boat, as his line popped and sprang limp. He turned to gape at his local who was already pressing his rusty pocket knife closed against his thigh.

"I'm sorry, son. But I refuse to waste my time mucking around with other peoples' tangles. Only ever serves to let small problems grow into major pains. We haven't even caught dinner yet. And if somebody else's snag looks bound to spoil my meal, I cut the line."

His local returned to fishing. Ethan watched the floating loops of his line disappear into Lake Marie. He pictured the doomed fish pulling against its tether, a rubber worm dangling from its wide white mouth. Ethan located the plastic knob under the bench and checked over the reel: nothing appeared broken. He pinched two plastic prongs on the side, firmly pressed it onto the bolt, and twisted until it clicked. He tried it out—the knob spun with the familiar clicking resistance.

Before he could tie on a new lure, the long dormant catfish rod convulsed, doubling over, its tip stirring the surface. Tuck pounced, snatching the rod with a hoot before it could get pulled overboard.

"Hot damn, McDouglas, we're on it now."

The exhilarating whine of the powerful fish taking line set Ethan's hair on end. It shot right, toward the bank, then, perhaps sensing a lack of space, hard left back towards Lake Marie's main body.

"Here we go," Tuck said, turning to keep both line and rod on Boat's starboard side. "She's good and hooked now. Just let her do her thing. She can wear herself out."

Tuck took one hand off the rod, collected his beer, and finished it, letting the can drop to Boat's bottom. The mighty fish hauled Boat out of the cove, veered right, then left, then straight down. When the pace slackened, Tuck finally began to reel in earnest until he lifted the blunt, fat, purple fish over Boat's aluminum bottom. The wriggling fish may not have qualified as legendary, but it was certainly large enough; Ethan noted it was much more substantial than anything from Chuck Palwagon's haul.

"Clear out the cooler, son. We've got to make room for dinner."

Ethan placed the remaining four beers behind him as Tuck pulled out a previously unseen hammer and thunked the wriggling creature on the skull. There was a wretched crack and the writhing fish fell forever still. Tuck set the corpse in the cooler and closed the lid.

"Now I'd say it's a good thing we didn't go fussin' about over your little snag." He motioned at the beer and Ethan obliged.

"The best beer is the one displaced by dinner."

From the way he opened it, this beer tasted of nothing but fish.

Chapter
Twenty-One

E than endured a wordless ride back to town. The day had been exceptional, but a previously unimaginable prize rested in the sun-bleached red-body-white-top cooler squeezed between him and his local. He recalled Tuck's boasts regarding his secret catfish recipe when they met in the parking lot and spoke over this catfish's predecessor.

Have I earned it? Have I done enough? Have I earned the privilege of experiencing my local's authentic, homegrown recipe?

Even Chuck Palwagon had only ever settled for restaurants, *local greasers,* to supply his local flavor. This would be an unprecedented triumph. On the other side of the cooler, Tuck's fingers tapped loose and free on the steering wheel. For Ethan, the hush was interminable.

I followed him in custom and etiquette. I kept my captain lubricated.

One song ended and another began. Ethan dreaded their impending separation.

Did I do something wrong?

He tried to will his local to simply open his mouth and extend the offer.

Why don't you just c'mon 'n' dine with me, son?

The road straightened as they approached Folkston proper. Still, Ethan's local remained silent, clearing his throat twice as he turned back on Main Steet before swinging left down into the Sapphire Courts sand. Tuck parked, plucked the key from the ignition, and set a hand on the door handle. Ethan let his head droop and prepared to exit.

Still a great day. I shouldn't spoil it by getting greedy.

Just then, his local paused, studying Sapphire Courts' pink-bricked 'yard' section, before tilting his head at Ethan. "Alright, son. You've been good enough company. How'd you like to help me fry this sucker up?"

"Yes!" Ethan's nails dug into the vinyl. "I would love to, yes." Tuck raised his eyebrows, apparently taken aback by the enthusiasm saturating Ethan's response.

"Good then. That's good. If you'd love to join me, then, I reckon I'd love to have ya. You just meet me in the yard around six-thirty." Tuck gestured at the patch of crabgrass where the old men held court.

"I will be there," Ethan responded. "Is there anything I can bring? I know you have a special recipe but I'd love to help."

"I will obviously provide and prepare the nourishment. If you will be so kind as to provide the beer and whiskey."

"Beer. Whiskey. Absolutely. I can do that."

"Now, remember, I said *and* whiskey."

Ethan showered then made the beer and whiskey run, returning to the lot at 6:23. He retrieved a stiff, creaking folding chair from by the office and set it just inside the brick perimeter. His local's cooler rested against the strip of brick wall separating 117 from the adjacent room. It was cool but he was comfortable in his t-shirt. The orange street light buzzed on above him just when the sunset threatened to grow too dark. Ethan rubbed his hands together. It would be a fine evening for eating outdoors.

Several minutes later, a door clicked open and Tuck stepped backwards out of room 117 balancing a mound of ingredients and utensils. Ethan could discern a wooden board, a large pair of metal tongs, a clear plastic bag bulging with an off-white powder, and a jug of viscous golden-brown liquid. Ethan's local checked over his shoulder, located his guest, and called out.

"Fetch me two chairs and the hose from the side of the building, will ya? Turn it on too. Full blast. I've got to make another trip. Too much goddam shit." Ethan started towards the unlit side of the building. Tuck shouted again. "There's an aluminum burner and propane tank over there too. Fetch them as well."

Ethan did as he was told, in two trips, retaking his seat as Tuck set the wooden board on its own chair and toed open the cooler. Tuck used two hands to hoist the fish from the ice.

"Thanks again for letting me share your catfish."

"Well," Tuck lined the fish up over the board—only then did Ethan notice the prodigious nail jutting from the nearer end. His local had the fish's head hovering over the point. "You done good today." Tuck plunked the fish down; Ethan flinched as the nail punched through the fish's skull with a sequence of slurps and wet crunches. "And it's too much fish for one meal. Once you fry it as hard as I do, it don't keep for nothing." Tuck pressed the skull flush to the board. The nail sprouted out of the bulbous purple head like the spike of a nightmare unicorn. He then straightened up the tail and picked up a long thin blade. "Fouls up the whole damn apartment, too."

Ethan looked away, setting his eyes on the thick black pot resting at Tuck's feet.

"Should I clean your pot?" The pot's patchy interior demanded this question.

"Clean it?"

"Yea. It has a bit of crust on it."

"Crust?! That's flavor, son. That *crust* has taken years to develop."

"Oh, it just—"

"Don't you dare try to strip the flavor from my pot. I don't intend on living long enough to get that back." Tuck continued carving up the fish. "You can pour in the oil though. Fire up that burner, too."

Ethan leapt at the chance to participate in his local's customs, performing a brief audit of the burner, propane tank, and their attachments so he could give the appearance of experience. He secured the burner's gas hose to the propane tank on the first try, turned what appeared to be the appropriate knobs, and flicked Tuck's lighter near the eye. To his relief, it lit.

"Okay now, set the pot on the burner and pour in the oil."

Ethan followed his local's instructions; touching the pot left him with black, dirty fingers which he wiped on the nearest brick before returning to his beer. He watched Tuck finish working his knife around the fish's spine towards its tail. When the white-pink meat had been separated, he slid the knife underneath the filets to remove the skin.

Tuck then cut the meat into sizable chunks which Ethan rinsed with the hose. Tuck shook off the excess water then dropped the chunks into the bag of powder.

"Now mix that bag up good so each piece gets nice and covered. Then we just sit back, let the oil get ready."

Tuck opened a fresh beer and slid down deeper into his chair, his feet crossed on the ground as far as from his body as his legs would allow.

"So what does your daddy do?"

"He's in real estate." Ethan put the bag down. "He sells commercial real estate."

"Commercial real estate. That sounds like money."

"He's very good at it. Very respected." Ethan proudly considered his father's real estate wall which he had, brick by brick, spent his career making absolute and immaculate. "What's your trade?"

"My trade?" Tuck smirked. "You're looking at it, son."

"You're a professional chef?"

"No. I ain't a professional nothing. Never have been. Except unless maybe you want to call me a professional recreator. If you're clever, like me, there are ways to get by without breaking your back every day, groveling to some asshole who traded his nametag for a collar. So I only ever worked when I needed something, another toy in my arsenal like Boat or Hoss. But once I had enough to get what I wanted, I quit fooling with that bullshit and got back to having fun."

Ethan couldn't think of a follow-up question that wasn't overtly impolite.

To be Tuck's age, his stage of life, and have failed to assemble any professional bricks.

"You're obviously an expert angler. And know your waters very well."

"Son, I do appreciate you saying that, but I also know what you ain't saying. If folks ain't calling me a drunkard, they're calling me a bum or a deadbeat."

"I certainly wasn't—"

"But I'll tell you this. Because it's something nobody ever considers. We drove over my daddy's auto shop today. Not by or past, in Hoss. Over, in Boat. My daddy spent his first forty-five years just like you, churnin' and a-burnin' to make something of himself, teaching himself and tinkering until he knew automobile innards backwards and forwards. Big, small, new, old, American, the foreigners. And when he knew all of it, he set out figuring how to open his own shop. I was there for that. I watched him fuss over the books and pack his bags to go attend the conventions. In the early years, when Robert's Auto Shop was just getting its feet under it, I watched the furniture in our living room disappear as he tried to keep his employees paid when the shop couldn't cover the checks. Later on, when I was a teenager and daddy had just gotten approved for the loan for the tire shop, I watched the men in suits come to the door and hand him a check for the exact value of the land and building. I heard them tell him what they were doing, that they were sinking his business, his town, to make way for something elsewhere. Right when he was fixing to grow, they forced that check on him, scattered his customers, and dumped two hundred billion gallons of water on top of what he'd built. My daddy put his life into his peoples' cars. He poured his soul into that auto shop. He was a hard-worker, just like you, and a proud man before his own government clipped him. After all that, he ended up doing exactly what we're doing here." Tuck finished one beer and motioned for another one. "All that good American hard work just killed him faster."

As Ethan processed this story, his mind assessed to what extent his law practice, or his father's real estate business, could be flooded out by the government, and how the McDaniel men would outmaneuver it. "That's terrible. I'm sorry about your father."

"Me too, son. He was dead a long time before he stopped breathing. And it's been decades since he stopped that." They sat silently for several seconds. Tuck finished one beer and started another. "That's about how long it takes. Let's check the oil."

Ethan stood up to better observe. His local plucked up a scrap of fish skin and dropped it in the oil—it popped and sizzled, leaving a bubbly wake as it circled and twisted around the surface.

"And ready we are. Grab the bag, will ya." Tuck waited for Ethan before continuing. "Now, one by one, start placing, *placing*, the fish in the oil." Tuck sat down and checked his watch. "Don't burn yourself. Be sure to lay it away from you. That splatter'll set your socks on fire."

Ethan opened the bag and, with one final glance at Tuck, whose eyes remained firmly on his watch, used the tongs to place in the prodigious chunks.

"Quickly now. The goal's to cook 'em even. Don't want one going dark while you're fussing with its buddy."

Ethan sped up, stifling a fresh yelp when a splash of oil lighted on his wrist. When he had finished, he tapped the bag to indicate such, and set it down.

"Give 'em a quick turn. We don't want 'em sticking to each other. Good even cookin'. Worked too hard to spoil it now." When this task was done, Ethan rinsed his hands, once more wiping them on the brick.

The pot popped and sputtered as the growing aroma of salt, spices, and fried fats roused hungry currents in Ethan's stomach. He had barely eaten that day. In all the local and Lake Marie excitement, he'd never even thought about it.

"Alright kill the gas and ready the plates. I'll pluck 'em out. Don't want you knockin' all the crisp off. Hold the plates near so I can serve us."

Tuck plucked the chunks, now round, ridged, and deep brown, from the pot, shaking each piece free of excess oil and alternating placement on the two plates. Ethan's eyes twitched to capture every subtlety of his technique. This was true authentic, local flavor.

He would have something on the great Chuck Palwagon himself.

Tuck selected the plate with the darker, crispier pieces, then sat down. Ethan followed suit, examining his bounty in the orange street light. The chunks were much too large to be popable; rather, their girth would generally necessitate the use of utensils, which Ethan did not have. He turned to Tuck for guidance and found him pinching his first piece apart and placing a steaming half, still an ambitious mouthful, into a wide-open maw. Ethan attempted the same and, despite scorching his fingertips, opened the crust enough to blow on the moist, dense magma before bringing it to his tongue.

The first bite was a delicacy—a satisfying salty and peppery crunch gave way to a juicy warm interior. The necessary chewing forced him to savor the batter's heavy notes. The second bite was a chore. The notes, most notably the salt, did not ebb and flow with each swallow, but accumulated like snow in a blizzard.

This must be an acquired taste, like scotch or a cigar—Ethan had thrown up halfway through his first cigar—*that I will come to appreciate if blessed with enough opportunities. I'm not a true local so I can't truly appreciate the cuisine.*

By the third bite, the salt burned Ethan's tongue and gums. His aching jaw mashed double time, grinding its way through the batter shell and rubbery meat. A slug of beer, Ethan would have preferred water, followed each successful swallow, greasing the works just enough for continued operation. Ethan never stopped; although his bites grew smaller and smaller, and required more and more beer. Tuck cleaned his plate and licked his fingers, emitting the standard *mm oh yea* noises associated with a well enjoyed meal of one's own making.

"That's how it's done, son. That is how it's done. They ain't gonna give you that in the city. I don't care what restaurant. I caught it. I cooked it. I whomped up the batter. Ain't even a Folkston meal. That's just the Tuck Special."

Ethan tongued a lump of gunk off his front teeth in preparation for the final morsel, which had chilled and congealed in the night air. It was almost beyond his ability to eat.

"That was really good. Thank you." The batter was an insatiable sponge in Ethan's stomach.

"Don't I know it." Tuck's chair balanced on two legs as its occupant leaned forward to set the cardboard beer box in the cinderblock fire ring. He set it aflame, sending its other worldly blue and green flame dancing through the ensuing blankets of pine straw and incrementally bigger twigs. When he had some decently sized timber burning, he returned the back two chair legs to the soft dust. "Whiskey, please."

Ethan produced the bottle from under his chair as Tuck gulped down the last of another beer, turned it over, and shook the remnants onto the grass. He accepted the whiskey bottle and poured in a touch of whiskey, sloshed it, drank that, and gave himself a more considerable amount.

"I can get some cups from my room."

"No sir, no need. This is just how I like it." He handed the bottle back to Ethan who re-wetted the bottom of his own empty beer can and shot it down in the manner of his local, scalding the unwetted lining of his stomach. Under the pretense of using the facilities, Ethan dashed upstairs where he filled and emptied two discarded sports drink bottles worth of water; both dissipated into the desert sand lining his stomach. When he returned, Tuck had sunk even deeper into his chair. His outstretched legs rested on one of the perimeter bricks.

"Well son, you have just been lucky enough to experience one of my favorite days. Nothing, I mean absolutely nothing, beats a successful afternoon on the water followed by a fried catfish dinner. The goddam Tuck Special."

The salt persisted on Ethan's tongue. "It was a good day. And a great meal. Thank you."

"Much better than being cooped up in the law barn."

"It's hard to argue with that. My dad will be really jealous I got to fish Lake Marie. Especially with a local. And *especially* especially a local who cooked our catch in his own homemade batter."

Tuck emitted some sort of grunt, perhaps a burp. "The goddam Tuck Special." The booze had loosened the local's movements; his square head rolled from shoulder to shoulder as he inspected his fire. His lips pulled back in an amplified grimace. "Was not my intention to put your daddy out . . ."

"He'll be happy. Just jealous I got to do something he wants. Like you said, much better than being in the courtroom."

"Don't I know it." Tuck peered over Ethan's shoulder at the parking lot's outlet. "Now who we got here?"

Ethan turned to see two figures drifting in over the sands. One tapped the other and pointed at Ethan and Tuck. After some discussion, the first one began moving in Ethan and Tuck's direction. The other followed. It took until the pair reached the glow from the streetlight for Ethan to recognize Bobby and Frank.

"Evenin' son, Mr. Frank," Tuck bellowed. "I'm afraid we don't have nothing set aside for y'all. Weren't expecting latecomers."

Ethan smiled and waved at his friends.

"Nah, nah we ate," Bobby answered as if the words were an afterthought. For the first time Ethan could remember, Bobby Canterbury wasn't bouncing and beaming; he appeared afraid or confused, indecisive eyes flicked from Ethan to Tuck to pot to booze to Ethan to Tuck. "You take Boat out today?"

"*We* did, indeed. Some folks find the time to go fishing with ol' Tuck. So we had ourselves a time out on the water. And have just finished enjoying the spoils of our leisures."

Bobby's eyes stilled on Ethan. "You blew off court?"

"It was cancelled because some idiot called in a bomb threat. I saw Mr. . . ." Ethan realized he didn't know his local's last name, "Tuck in the lot and he agreed to take me out on Lake Marie." The corners of Ethan's lips twitched skyward when he said the name.

"That's cool, man," Bobby said to his chest. He remained on the cracked asphalt, the toe of his boot worked one of the oversized bricks separating him from Tuck and Ethan. Frank stood silently several yards behind him. "So the two of y'all went fishing together?"

"That's what he just said, son. McDouglas had never been on Lake Marie, so we joined forces to enjoy the afternoon and catch ourselves some dinner."

"McDaniel," Bobby said without lifting his eyes.

"It's great country up here," Ethan said. "Beautiful. And the fishing was incredible. I'm already planning to come back up with my dad."

"With your dad, yea."

"You boys have work in the morning?" Tuck lifted the whiskey bottle.

"Yea . . ." Bobby threw a barrage of quick glances at Ethan as if fighting a compulsion to stare. He had rocked the brick from the dirt and flipped it on its side.

"Well, I'd offer y'all some fish and whiskey but, like I said, the fish is gone and I imagine Papa Frank back there won't let you imbibe on a school night." Bobby turned back towards Frank who had still not fully approached. "You boys go on, hurry up to your rooms, and get yourselves ready for bed."

Bobby looked back at Frank, who inclined his head towards the stairs, then threw a final glance at Ethan. "Yea, good night, Ethan. Tuck."

"Always nice seeing you, son. Don't forget to brush your teeth now."

Tuck laughed to himself as the two young men disappeared up the stairs. Ethan checked his watch.

"Unfortunately, I think it's time for me to head up as well. Although I really hate for this night to end."

"Right, right. Back to it. Law barn in the morning."

"Yes sir, Tuck. It doesn't appear the law barn actually blew up."

"That is unfortunate." Tuck craned backwards to look up into the streetlight. "Well, son. I must say I'm a little disappointed. I was hoping that I'd showed you the folly in all that fussin' about."

"You made a very persuasive argument."

"You can always go fishing if you don't let silly shit tie you up."

Ethan nodded; this bore a striking resemblance to Chuck Palwagon's *Wet the line, anytime,* motto. "Good night, Tuck. Thanks for a great day on the water. I guarantee I'll never forget it."

"Go on get to bed, son. This one's over."

Ethan left the drunk old man sitting alone in the dark.

Chapter Twenty-Two

Ethan woke up before his alarm, savoring his fresh Lake Marie memories in the quiet darkness for several seconds before realizing what he had to do.

"Ethan? It's so early. Is everything al—"

"Dad! Are you ready to hear something incredible?"

"Something incredible . . ."

Ethan couldn't wait, jumping back in before his father could finish. "I fished it. I fished Lake Marie."

"You fished . . . REALLY?! OH MY GOODNESS!! THAT'S GREAT! How? When?"

His dad's shout must have caught his mom's attention; Ethan heard the pitter patter rumble of her charging in from the master bath *WHAT HAPPENED?! WHAT HAPPENED?! DID ETHAN WIN HIS TRIAL???*

A soft thump as Mr. McDaniel clasped his palm over the speaker; Ethan nevertheless heard him whisper *he went fishing*. There was nothing further from Mrs. McDaniel.

"Ethan, my son, tell me everything."

"Yesterday morning I saw my neighbor, Tuck, loading fishing gear into his truck. We've chatted before, talked fishing, and he's offered to take me out but, obviously, I never could because of the trial but yesterday—"

"Wait, you fished Lake Marie and found your local?"

"It's better than you could ever imagine, Dad. My local, Tuck, has been fishing Lake Marie for years, decades, for as long as it's been a lake. He even stashes his boat in a hidden spot along the shore."

"Oh my goodness."

"We had to pull off the road and tramp through the woods just to get to it."

"Oh my goodness."

"We fished at his secret spot by a waterfall that doesn't even have a name." Even as he approached thirty, Ethan was reluctant to relay, and explain, Tuck's informal appellation for the falls to his father.

"Oh my goodness."

"It was incredible, Dad. That lake is perfect. Beautiful, remote, serene, and perfect. Just like on *Wettin' the Line*."

"My ass. Big Chuck never wet his line anywhere near this gentleman's secret waterfall. Tell me though, were they biting?" This was the preferred phrasing among the McDaniel men as it placed the blame on the fish and prevented the responding party from having to ever plainly admit he'd failed in his attempt to catch fish.

"The bite was on. Pulled in a good many sizable bass. And a catfish. And . . ."

"And what?"

"Guess what I had for dinner last night."

This time Ethan let the silence linger, building the suspense. He well knew his father would be ecstatic about this final piece of information.

"I want to hear you say it."

"I supped on genuine, authentic, fresh-from-the-lake fried Lake Marie catfish."

"Oh, of course you did. At a little hole-in-the-wall local restaurant?" Mr. McDaniel's voice bounced with enthusiasm. On every road trip and vacation, fishing and non, the elder McDaniel was interminably questing for the idyllic unknown roadside local establishment, often over the strenuous objections of his tired, hungry, and bathroom needy family.

"Better. I supped on our own catch. Tuck, my local, pulled in a channel cat, cleaned it, tossed it in his own personal, secret recipe batter and fried it up in a cast iron pot. We ate it in folding chairs on the motel lawn."

"My boy, my boy!" His father sounded far from the phone; Ethan pictured his head lolling back to bask in the glory of his firstborn's achievements. "Tell me, please. Was it incredible? Absolutely perfect? Actually, don't bother. I know how it was. I can picture it. I can taste it."

"That last part will be particularly hard to recreate."

"That's what makes it so special, son. A truly singular, unique, and, most importantly, authentic experience never to be recreated." Devoted fans of *Wettin' the Line* would recognize this as a frequent Chuck Palwagon line. "I'm proud of you. And deathly jealous."

"Thanks, Dad. I'm pretty proud of me too. I'll keep an eye out for rentals closer to the lake. I don't think you'll want to stay at Sapphire Courts. Even if it is where my local resides."

"No, I'm quite certain I would not. Wait, yesterday was only Monday. How did you get to go fishing?"

"Court was cancelled. Someone called in a bomb threat."

"A BOMB THREAT?!"

Fresh rumbling announced the return of Mrs. McDaniel. *IS HE OKAY? IS HE OKAY?*

"Tell Mom I'm fine. I hadn't even entered the building yet. And it was a false alarm. Possibly just a deadbeat calling it in to get out of jury duty or child support."

Another clasping of the speaker. *He's fine. False alarm.*

"So other than bomb threats and catfish, how are things going?"

"Good. Great even. I've made some friends here. Two young guys and an ex-cop who lives next to me."

"Friends? In that fleapit motel?"

"Yea."

"Ethan . . ."

"They're not permanent residents. They're only living here for a little bit longer. The two young guys, Bobby and Frank, are moving to Columbia in a couple months so Frank can finish his undergrad at USC. I've been thinking I could help them out with housing. Maybe even get them jobs. I still know some folks there."

"That would be very decent of you. It's always good to help the less fortunate. Especially with their education."

"One of them, Frank, is actually going to law school, too. I figure by the time he graduates I'll have built up some sway at the firm. Maybe I could help him get signed on as an associate."

"Yet another reason to keep stacking your bricks."

"That's what I'm doing here."

"Although you do need to be careful. Make damn sure he's decent. You don't want to stick your neck out and have them bring on some no-account rural scoundrel. That would reflect poorly on you."

"Dad, Frank's not—"

"I'm not arguing it's fair. It's just the people at your firm think highly of you. And rightly so. You've built that. You've worked too hard to risk it on someone who's just going to topple everything, demolish your reputation."

"I really doubt—"

"I'm not going to argue with you about it. Just know that I'm your father, it's my job to worry and warn you about these things. But what happens now with the trial? Is court back on today?"

"Barring another setback."

"Great. It's time for me to get dressed. Let me know how it goes."

The male McDaniels exchanged goodbyes and well wishes. Ethan commenced his own preparations for the day.

Back in the courtroom, Ethan assumed his seat several rows deep in the gallery. Marissa occupied the first row directly behind Mr. Paulson. As far as Ethan could tell, Marissa hadn't noticed his entrance; he attempted to review his deposition summaries for the first two defense witnesses, throwing frequent, involuntary glances at her over the page. Finally, she looked over and, to his enchantment, smiled and started towards him.

"We actually made it in today," he said.

"Indeed." She sat down on the pew next to Ethan. He had to scoot to make room for her between himself and the armrest. She leaned in close, her eyes gleaming with excitement. "Do you want to know something amazing?"

"Yea . . . yea of course."

"It's absolutely incredible. And also explains why court was canceled yesterday." Ethan waited for Marissa to continue. The large, predominantly empty courtroom emphasized her closeness. "So yesterday, while the bomb squad was sweeping the courthouse we heard that pop, right?"

"Right."

"And we figured it was a gunshot, right?"

"Right."

"Well, it was so . . ." Marissa smothered a giggle in her shoulder, coming back up with cherry red cheeks and watering eyes. "What happened was . . . every year Mrs. Marsh puts on a haunted house in the courthouse basement for the Folkston kids. She's done it forever. Since way before me. And every year the centerpiece is this motion-activated witch named Gladys who jumps out at you from behind some curtains or something when you cross a certain point. She screams too. Something basic like *I'll get you my pretty*. But she, Gladys, is an absolute legend. Every kid in Folkston has their Gladys story." Her voice grew shrill, almost squeaky as she fought down laughter. Ethan, despite not seeing the humor in the situation, ached to join in Marissa's laughter, but couldn't determine the appropriate time to start. "And . . . I guess . . . Mrs. Marsh must've started putting it all out because yesterday when they were sweeping the building they set Gladys off and she . . . popped out and they . . . they shot . . . right between . . ." Marissa was overcome.

"We lost yesterday because of a Halloween decoration?" This was said by a man without humor. Ethan looked up to where Mr. Colt and Ms. Nelson had turned to listen to the story of yesterday's demise. He scooched another inch, embarrassed for them to see him and Marissa sitting so close, and hoped his cheeks were not as red as they felt.

"I'm sorry," Marissa said, wiping her eyes with her blouse. "I'm sorry . . . it's just . . . poor Gladys."

The bailiff stood and announced, "All rise for the Honorable Eustus Grimmaly." Marissa collected herself with a long exhale and re-crossed the aisle. The defense team swiveled back to face the front of the courtroom, but not before Ms. Nelson smiled and raised her eyebrows at Ethan, who instinctively shook his head.

Mr. Paulson stood and promptly rested Plaintiff's case. Mr. Colt started the defense's case with two witnesses so preliminary that Mr. Paulson's brief cross-examination only served to prevent his rival from having the final word. Together, they took under half an hour.

After the debacle in the *stanza de festa*, Ms. Nelson was tabbed to handle the direct examination of Mr. Lucas. It was not brief. She began at the very beginning, inquiring about her client's familial history in Folkston, his parents, growing up in Folkston, and the details of his successful tenure as Folkston High quarterback, before finally moving into the early days of Lucas Trash. Mr. Colt, in the unusual situation of having been relegated to the bench, made a show of taking vigorous notes, occasionally nodding as if to illustrate to the jury that he approved of his colleague's questions and phrasings. Ethan, now accustomed to the cheap seats, observed and listened intently.

Around noon, Emmett Lucas admitted to several trash cans *finding their way* onto the neighboring properties but, as expected, denied ever storing or allowing trash to be stored in the trash cans or on his property. Mr. Lucas admitted to sloppiness on his part as different workers didn't always set things where they'd been instructed. Ms. Nelson buried the admission in another hour of testimony.

At one-thirty, Ms. Nelson knelt next to Mr. Colt, whispered, nodded, then stood, thanked Mr. Lucas, and sat down. Judge Grimmaly checked the clock behind him then inspected the jury. "We've been at it for a while now. Given the time, I think it's best we recess for lunch. We can proceed with any cross-examination Mr. Paulson may have at half past two."

Mr. Colt and Ms. Nelson both shot to their feet to almost shout. "Your Honor!" They glanced at each other.

"Assuming you two have the same objection," Judge Grimmaly said, "I'd rather hear it from Ms. Nelson."

"Your Honor," Ms. Nelson took charge, "we respectfully object to Mr. Paulson being given additional time to prepare his cross-examination of this case's primary and named defendant after being able to hear the entirety of his testimony."

Judge Grimmaly scratched his chin and rolled his head in the direction of Mr. Paulson, who remained seated, then rolled it back to Ms. Nelson. "Ms. Nelson, while I understand your concern, the breaks in a trial simply must land somewhere. Whether they appear to be of some benefit to one side is not something the Court can always control. Let me assure you that, based on my experience presiding over Mr. Paulson, he'll almost certainly squander any opportunity or advantage this may present. I'm confident an additional hour will do him no discernable good." Judge Grimmaly turned and smiled at the jury in a show of jest. "If there's nothing further, we will reconvene at two-thirty sh—."

"Your Honor!" Mr. Colt was back on his feet, leaning forward to pillar a finger on his desk. "Your Honor, quips aside, Plaintiff cannot be given such an undue advantage. He has heard our client's testimony in full and—"

"I've ruled on the matter, Mr. Colt. Your objection is preserved for the record. Please take your seat."

Mr. Colt remained standing. "Your Honor, I must strenuously object to Plaintiff being given such an undue advantage at this stage of trial."

"Go to lunch, Mr. Colt."

"Your Honor" Mr. Colt slapped the defense table. Ms. Nelson jumped. Mr. Lucas leaned forward. "I strenuously object to—"

Judge Grimmaly half rose from the bench, planting both hands on his desk. "Okay, Sterling. Is your *strenuous objection* on the same grounds as Ms. Nelson's ordinary and I suppose more facile objection?"

"I strenuously object to Plaintiff being permitted additional time to prepare his cross-examination after hearing the primary defendant's testimony."

"Strenuously object . . ." Judge Grimmaly slid back into his seat. "Mr. Colt, I'll allow you this because I must admit to being unfamiliar with the standard for *strenuous objections*. So, you return at two-thirty with a memorandum citing authority for the elevated weight given to one party's *strenuous objection* and," Judge Grimmaly raised a finger, "and this is equally important, how this precedent requires a ruling in your favor. If you do that, I will gladly reconsider."

"Your Hon—"

"We are in recess, Mr. Colt." Judge Grimmaly waved out the jury. Strenuous or not, Ethan wondered whether it might have behooved Ms. Nelson and Mr. Colt to wait for the jury to exit before lodging their objection. He approached the defense table before taking his leave.

"Mr. McDaniel, do you have your laptop with you?"

"Yes sir."

"Great. Find me authority on—"

"Sterling!" Ms. Nelson mangled a manilla folder into her case. "What are you not understanding about that? There's no such thing as a strenuous objection. If you give the judge a memo, even if Ethan conjures up some bullshit about strenuous objections, it's just going to piss him off for the entirety of our defense."

"I am not taking this lying down. I'm going to beat him at his—"

"This is not something you can win. He's not going to read any half-cocked bullshit you make Ethan dig up. If it's so damn important to you, do it yourself. Don't drag Ethan down with you." She shoved something else into the margins of her briefcase and marched away. Ethan remained at attention, watching Mr. Colt pack his things for several seconds before realizing that he too had been dismissed.

Trial resumed at two-thirty without mention of strenuous objections.

Mr. Paulson took a friendly, ambling course in his cross-examination, congratulating Mr. Lucas on his football career and listing some previously unmentioned civic duties Emmett Lucas had performed for the people of Folkston over the years. This course of questioning made Ethan uneasy—he'd heard of experts in cross examination building up a witness' reputation then turning it against itself, coaxing a credible witness to provide credible testimony which ultimately undermined their own credibility. It was twenty minutes before Mr. Paulson even mentioned *trash*. Sometime after that, Emmett Lucas provided an opening.

"Mr. Lucas, did I hear you testify that you use Lucas Trash to service your own home?"

"Yes you did."

"And Lucas Trash supplied your home with a trash can."

"Objection, Your Honor," Mr. Colt stood. Ms. Nelson's hands spread in disbelief. "As Mr. Paulson is not testify—"

"You did not question this witness, Mr. Colt," Mr. Paulson addressed the opposing attorney rather than the judge. "This is not your objection to make."

"Please direct your comments to me, counsel," Judge Grimmaly said. He looked from Mr. Colt to Ms. Nelson, and sighed. "As long as it's only you from here on out, I'll allow it."

"Thank you, your Honor," Mr. Colt said. "I simply request that, as Mr. Paulson is not the witness testifying at this time, he rephrase his comment as a question for the witness to answer."

Judge Grimmaly scratched the bridge of his nose, his thick glasses bouncing up and down against his fingers. "Rephrase it as a question, Mr. Paulson."

"Did Lucas Trash supply your home with a trash can?"

"That's right."

"Can you tell me about that trash can?"

"Well, it's a big plastic bin with wheels. Elk Tongue Brown, the manufacturer calls the color. Mine's the same as all the rest of 'em. Ain't nothin' special about it."

"Okay, and am I correct that you use those wheels to roll it to and from the street?"

"Roll it on the wheels, yes."

"And do you personally roll your trash can to and from the street?"

"No, not usually. That's my son Jakob's job. His family lives on the property too."

"Your son Jakob handles the trash in both your households."

"Objection, your Honor, would—"

Sires Paulson didn't miss a beat. "Does your son Jakob handle all the duties associated with the trash cans on your property?"

"Yes, he does."

"And does that entail anything other than taking the can to and from the street?"

"No sir, it don't."

"Okay, and—"

"Well let me take that back." Silence gripped the courtroom. Mr. Colt and Ms. Nelson both shifted. Ethan held his breath—every trial horror story ever shared by any professor or partner started with the storyteller's primary witness walking back an answer unprompted. It wasn't so much an adventure into the unknown as a sudden sinkhole to hell. "I do occasionally have Jake run it over with the hose. So it would entail that too."

"And when you say run it over with the hose, what does that mean?"

"I mean run it over with the hose. Turn the hose on, point it at the can."

"Spray the can with water from the hose."

"Objection—"

"Does your son spray your trash can with water from the hose?"

"Yes."

"And can you tell us the purpose of spraying your trash can with water from the hose?"

"To get out the gunk. Jake sprays both cans inside and out then turns them over to dump the gunk. Let's 'em dry like that."

"Well, if the trash can is only getting used for trash, then why bother getting out the gunk?"

"Because it gets hot in Folkston, if you let that gunk sit there it will get a stink on."

Oh no, Ethan thought. Ms. Nelson's shoulders drooped.

"So is the purpose of spraying the trash can with the hose and removing the gunk to prevent it from smelling?"

"That is correct."

"Okay, let's change course. The trash cans you kept on and near your business' property, at Lucas Trash, they were old residential cans, correct?"

"Yes sir, we collected 'em from clients when we got the new ones in."

"You collected them from homes."

"Object—"

"Did Lucas Trash collect those cans from peoples' private residences?"

"Yes."

"Why?"

"They were old, worn out. Had been out there for a few years. Distributor sent a fresh batch. So we collected the old ones and put out the new ones."

"What was your process for collecting the old trash cans?"

"Nothing to it. Just sent out two trucks on a couple routes. One picked up the cans and the other picked up the trash."

"Did you give your customers notice that you were doing this?"

"Didn't see any reason to. Never thought anyone would complain about a new trash can. If they noticed at all."

"So, is it fair to say you didn't ask the customers to handle or prepare the trash cans for collection?"

"Didn't talk to 'em about it at all."

"How many trash cans did you collect?"

"At that time? Would've been about three hundred. Probably a little over."

"And after you collected the trash cans what did you do with them?"

"Put them in the yard at the shop."

"You didn't . . . is it fair to say you didn't process them in any way?"

"That is correct."

"Did you or one of your employees clean them in any way?"

"No sir, we did not."

"You didn't run them over with the hose." Sires glanced at Mr. Colt who remained seated and silent.

"Not that I recall."

"Is it fair to say that you would remember spending a day hosing off over three hundred old, worn out trash cans?"

"That would've been a particularly nasty day, yes."

"In your experience in waste collection, is this gunk that collected on your personal trash can unique to your personal receptacles or does that gunk collect on everyone's trash cans?"

"Any place you're putting trash, if you ain't cleaning it, you're gonna get gunk."

Sires Paulson scanned the jury before returning to his table, spending several seconds looking over a document before speaking. "Thank you, Mr. Lucas. As always, it was a pleasure speaking with you. That will be all."

Ethan watched the jurors nod to each other, some jotting down notes as Ms. Nelson stood. She questioned Mr. Lucas for an additional five minutes, mostly recapping his prior testimony, highlighting points made on direct, before thanking him and requesting that he be excused. Mr. Colt tracked her return, his grey head turning like an anti-aircraft gun firing upon an approaching bomber.

Mr. Colt waited for the judge, jury, and opposition to exit for a brief recess before turning on his trial partner. Ethan had approached to offer aid and was given a front row seat.

"What the fuck was that? A couple of fumbling questions you've already asked after that admission? You've left it wide open for Sires to take this thing home."

"How would you have me fix that, Sterling? When he," she gestured at Mr. Lucas, "all but admits that he stored three hundred plastic boxes of stinking gunk on his property, what am I supposed to do? I didn't know what else he'd say so I tried to soften the blow and get out of there without him sinking our case again." Ms. Nelson turned to her client. "No offense."

"Your opinion don't matter to me."

"You could've—" Mr. Colt started.

"Don't give me your condescending bullshit. Sires outmaneuvered us. Outmaneuvered you. It's just damage control right now. You need to figure that out before you blow up the award."

After the recess, Mr. Colt stood and, with what Ethan thought was a desperate attempt at coolness, called Dr. Singleton, the defense's expert, to the stand. All heads turned to the rear door as the bailiff opened it and Dr. Singleton entered. The assembled eyes remained on the backdoor as the doctor moved through the well and assumed the stand. Ethan knew everyone was wondering the same thing. He wondered it too.

Would the Furry Man make another appearance?

Mr. Colt monitored the door even as he greeted his witness. "Good afternoon. Would you please state your full name for the record?"

"Dr. Joseph Almoral Singleton."

Mr. Colt turned to halfway face the doctor. "What is your profession, Dr. Singleton?"

"I am the Head Research Chair with the National Lung Association specializing in volatile organic compounds."

Mr. Colt risked a final backwards glance, then turned to fully face the witness. His shoulders relaxed. "And what is—"

The doors slammed open in two close but separate metallic thunderclaps. The Furry Man entered, strutting in as the doors slammed off their respective stops. Today's shirt was an ill-fitting, eye-splitting neon green tie-dye with an inexplicable picture of a cat in sunglasses; but it was Garth's plastic imitation clogs that stole the show, clip-clopping down the aisle long after the doors came to rest. In the well, Mr. Colt had ducked at the disturbance, stepping forward and raising an arm to shield his head. Now he straightened and turned, crimson and snorting, as his unlikely and wholly unnecessary nemesis found his seat, the echoes of his grand entry fading to silence. Mr. Colt opened his mouth to berate the Furry Man then thought better of it and looked up at the judge. Eustus Grimmaly tilted his head forward to stare back at Mr. Colt over his glasses. There was a long silence.

Then Ethan swore he saw the judge start to smile.

"Your witness, Mr. Colt." He raised an upturned hand.

Mr. Colt whipped back to the Furry Man, chest heaving, his body angle stiffening such that he leaned slightly forward like a petulant child. His face flickered purple; his lips curled back and up like a hound before the sneeze. The room watched, mystified, as the suited grey-haired man locked his arms, balled his fist . . . and shrieked.

It was the high, desperate, impotent tone of a child in tantrum; the wall panels and thin carpet quickly dispensed of it. The damage, however, was permanent. Every professional jaw in the room, Judge Grimmaly's included, dropped in a mixture of wonder, amusement, and concern. The jurors were less composed; several of the women placed a concerned hand on their breast; every man open mouth grinned. Ethan watched the color drain from Sterling Colt's face, leaving him looking old, frail, and exposed. He shifted, studying the room as if to confirm everyone present had seen, and heard, then stood facing no one in particular, fingers clasping and unclasping at his hips. The thought struck Ethan that if Sterling Colt ever found himself the mascot of a sports team, the team would surely have to look elsewhere for its stadium sounds.

Everyone blinked and started when Judge Grimmaly finally broke the silence. "On second thought, it's late in the day. We've been at it a while and have covered a lot of ground. I think it might be beneficial if we simply adjourn for the evening." He gestured for the bailiff to guide the jury out. The Furry Man was gone as quickly as he appeared, slipping out at the same time as the jury. Everyone else, courthouse employees and litigants remained still. Mr. Colt stood like a statue in a park, finally stepping to his chair, snapping his brief case shut, and pacing out, leaving the majority of his case file on the table.

When the doors closed behind him, Mrs. Marsh stood up. "Would Mr. Colt like to rephrase *that* as a question?"

Chapter Twenty-Three

"**A**h-Haha! Did you see that shit!? Did you *hear* that shit?!"

Ethan had gone directly to Garth's apartment from the courtroom. The Furry Man held a glass in which he'd already plopped two celebratory ice cubes. "Game, Quattlebaum! Here you take this one. I take my victory bourbon neat."

"You know I can't."

"Why the hell not? You worried you might scream something weird in front of the jury?" Garth turned back to the bourbon shelf, stopped, and returned his gleeful gaze to Ethan. "Aggghhhhhhhh-hhhh." It didn't nearly match the desperation of Mr. Colt's bleak performance—it contained far too much mirth—but if art is for the performer, it was well received. "Are you seeing him tonight? Please tell me yes. I want to relish this for as long as possible. I need more content."

"They usually let me know. They haven't said anything yet. They're probably regrouping after the . . . incident." Ethan was somewhat surprised Ms. Nelson hadn't at least reached out. He set his phone on his knee for easier access, wondering to what extent settlement was now a possibility. The defense's case, which had been rolling along according to plan, had unraveled almost instantaneously with the double whammy of Emmett Lucas' gunk admission and Sterling Colt's . . . break in decorum. "On second thought, I will take that bourbon."

"That's my boy." He screamed again as the brown liquor sloshed into Ethan's glass. "What do you think? I mean, seriously, is that the worst display of lawyering in the long history of professional douchebags?"

Ethan searched his memory, the tales told by professors and older partners—nothing quite equaled this. "It was a pretty significant . . ." Ethan rubbed his temple with his hand. "It wasn't great."

Is my first trial going to be a loss? Is that still a brick?

"Ha! Those rural jurors hated that pompous old fuck from day one. Emmett would've been better served if ponyboy hadn't shown up at all. You could've done better than him."

"There's an idea."

"Isn't there a contingency when one attorney makes an ass of himself? Like a, uh, an emergency eject button. Or self-destruct code."

"It would have to settle, I guess. An attorney doing something . . . like that certainly doesn't just end the trial."

What if Colt's incident gets out, becomes infamous? Could I still put this trial on my resume? Or discuss it at interviews? Would I be stained by association?

"Right. But when the wieners holding the purse strings hear about this they're gonna have to bail, right? The jury already hates y'all."

"It was a pretty bad day all around. Even before the Furry Man clomped in." Ethan peeked at his phone. "But, for now, it's still on."

"Well shit, it may still be on but it's certainly different." The Furry Man still seemed disappointed.

"I have to agree. In addition to your shenanigans, Mr. Lucas' testimony was not great for us."

"What'd he do?"

"He admitted to cleaning his personal trash can so it wouldn't smell but that he didn't do the same for the cans collecting on the Lucas Trash property."

"And thusly opening the possibility of smell protruding from the property?"

"Something like that."

"Well shit. In any event, either put on a smile or go home. I can't have you sour and sober spoiling my celebration. The Furry Man's gonna soak in his victory." Ethan took a big sip of his bourbon. *Is all this for nothing?* He finished the glass and held it up for Garth to refill. "There you go. Take a seat and assume the sticks. Play all you want."

Ethan had just completed his sixth, maybe his seventh, round of multi-player when Garth's own door crashed open—Ethan half expected a vengeful Sterling Colt to barge in, but it was Frank Besch, still in his foundry coveralls. His red-rimmed eyes homed in on Ethan.

"Where the fuck is Bobby?"

"Bobby? I haven't seen him," Ethan said. He met Frank's searing glare for a moment but couldn't hold it.

"We've been attending to other business, Frank," Garth said. "Don't you drive him to and from work?"

"He no-showed. He meets me in the parking lot every morning but I had to leave alone today because he never came out. He's not in his room. He hasn't answered his phone all day."

"Shit."

"I called and called. Every break. It's not good Garth. I even checked his room again when I got home. No sign of him. Which means . . ."

"Shit." Garth set his victory bourbon on the table. "Did anything happen? Did something set him off?"

"Yea, something set him off. Bobby went haywire when he caught dick shit here having a fucking father-son bonding love session with his dad." Ethan had to trace the path of Frank's long finger to the middle of his chest. His hand lifted to shield the point of impact.

"Me?"

"Yea, you. Fucking asshole."

"I didn't . . . you mean . . . ,"

"That fucking weasel Tuck Canterbury is Bobby's piece-of-shit father."

Ethan froze.

"I hope you enjoyed your fairy tale fucking fishing expedition you fucking tourist. You've absolutely fucked Bobby." Each of Frank's extremities vibrated at a different frequency. He still hadn't moved from the doorway. "God damn you. God damn you."

"Jesus, McDaniel. What were you doing fishing with Tuck?"

"I . . . I didn't know."

"They didn't just fish. They whipped up a fish fry for themselves right in the yard. Bobby and I caught them on the way back from Gruber's. Old fucker really made sure to rub it in. I tried to calm Bobby down but he shut his door on me. I could hear him pacing and muttering most of the night. I thought he chilled out and went to sleep when it got quiet but he must've slipped out."

"He never mentioned—"

"Of course that lousy shit didn't mention the son he abandoned. They never goddam do. You would know that if—"

"Frank, where would Bobby have gone to get his fix?"

"I don't know. With McCann out and Caz Man locked up, there's no telling. It could be anyone at Cochran's."

"Fuck."

"I've already checked the usual places and dirtbags. No one has seen him. Or so they say. So I . . . I . . . ," Frank's voice lost its edge. He slumped against the doorframe.

"Take a breath, man. I'll call into the station. See if he's been picked up already. Depending what got him arrested, this might not be the worst outcome."

Frank finally fully entered the apartment; his eyes flitted to the empty bean bag, then to Ethan, then to a spot on the coffee table, remaining there while Garth stepped onto the walkway to make his call.

"I really hope he's okay," Ethan said. This induced some sort of lip contraction and a series of heavier breaths. He decided against trying this path again. His mind ran through the list of places Bobby had shown him that afternoon. "Have you checked—"

"Where? The water pit? The school? The church where he used to buy and shoot up? Behind Grubers where he used to stash and read comic books?" Frank said this without lifting his eyes from the table. "You've been here a week. Do you really think he showed you some special place that he hasn't shown me a thousand times? You're the cause of this. Not the solution."

Ethan sat quietly, shaking; he very much wanted Garth to return to the room, hoping his presence and a positive report would release the accumulating tension in Frank's neck.

After an interminable silence, Garth did return, shaking his shaggy head and flipping his phone onto the counter.

Frank slapped the wall. "Fuck!"

"Yep." Garth dumped his bourbon into the sink, cocking his arm as if he wanted to smash the glass; he settled for setting it on the counter.

"What makes you so sure Bobby's out there shooting up?" Ethan asked. "I mean, maybe he's just gone for a walk. He walked it off last time."

"You don't ditch work to go on a fucking twenty-four hour walk. This is the script. Whenever he goes off the rails he goes to Cochran's, shoots up, and gets in trouble. Only twist is Caz Man, his usual source, being in prison."

"What can I do? How can I help?"

"If I knew what to do, I'd be doing it myself," Garth said. He sank onto his side of the couch. "It is unfortunately quite clear Bobby had, and has, a mind not to be located." They were silent for a long time. The light in the window began to fade. On screen, the dreaded kill sergeant lounged in a lawn chair, sipping a cocktail with a little umbrella. Ethan briefly wondered how much time the game designers had spent on this sequence.

"It could still be fixable. A bender on its own is not so bad," Garth said finally. "Bobs can get high and clean back up like it never happened. It's even preferable to him getting picked up early in some ways. The backslide sucks. The missed work sucks, too. But even if Mr. Howard fires him, y'all are leaving anyway. We'll just have to keep him fed and occupied for a couple months. Right now, as far as we know, we're still good."

"Unless he does something stupid."

"But it doesn't appear that's happened yet. As far as we know, he's strung out in a Cochran's Mill basement. That's fine. When whatever dealer he's met up with runs dry, Bobby will sober up and come home repentant. Tuck will still be here but Ethan will be gone soon. We can keep a closer watch until y'all go down to Columbia."

"Until he does something stupid." Ethan cringed at the certainty with which Frank deployed *until*.

"In which case we will be left to deal with that."

"You know better than to believe any different."

"You're probably right!" Garth shouted. "We both know that. I've seen enough to know how this will go. But Bobs is due for a break. Maybe the world's finally tired of shitting on him. The meth can lead him anywhere; maybe, it will just lead him back here. If he breaks something here, that's . . . potentially manageable." Garth turned to Ethan. "Go back to your room. There's no sense in you being here. Go get rested for trial and whatnot."

"I want to help. Or at least be here for him when he returns."

"You can't help. And, if he does come home, it would be better if you're not here. It's really the only chance we have of calming him down. Honestly, it would be best if Bobby Canterbury doesn't see you again."

The words stunned Ethan.

Garth checked his watch. "We've also turned an unfortunate corner. Methamphetamine binges only ever die in the daylight. Once that sun started setting, unless something truly awful happens, we're unlikely to see Bobby before the morning. Hopefully whoever he fell in with doesn't have a large stash and he'll slink back first thing tomorrow."

"Please, I need to fix this. I can help," Ethan said. "Maybe if he can just scream at me, or punch me or something, rather than continuing to go off the handle. Maybe that will cool him off."

"Trust me, we won't hesitate to wake you up if that looks like an option. You go back to your room too, Frank. He may look for you there and it's best if you're home."

Frank sent Ethan a final, withering glare but left without further argument.

"I promise I had no idea. I never would've gone if—"

"Just go to bed, Ethan. It really doesn't matter."

Ethan left Garth seated on his couch, staring blankly at the television. Down the walkway, Frank's feet caught the furthest reaching glimmers of orange streetlight. Ethan closed his door, locked it, and began to undress, finally peeling out of the darker of his two blue suits.

It was still light out, much too early for sleep even on a calm day. Ethan's stomach was too agitated for real food but he forced down a granola bar then sat down at the desk with a mind to distract himself with the case file.

You've still got a trial, McDaniel. You still need to be prepared for that. Remember your bricks. You're still piecing together bricks . . . What do we need to get from Dr. Singleton? What is the most convincing way to do that? How can we recover from Mr. Lucas' unfortunate admission? Or Mr. Colt's vocal emission?

He read and wrote words but his thoughts wouldn't stay put, wandering back to the evening's events, returning always to meth and fried catfish. To his local. To Tuck. To Bobby Canterbury, his new friend.

He clung to hope that Frank had misinterpreted the situation and that Bobby Canterbury would come ambling back through the sand, sober and happy.

Frank's been wrong before. Maybe Bobby's sick and overslept, slept hard through the day. Ethan had taken cold medicine one time that had put him under for eighteen hours.

Maybe he's very sick and spent the day at the doctor. Didn't have the presence of mind to take his phone. Ethan liked this one; it was both palatable and somewhat conceivable, even if it required illness on Bobby's part.

Bobby being sick is better than Bobby backsliding into addiction and legal trouble. Especially because of me.

The room finally fell dark. Rather than flipping on the desk lamp, Ethan abandoned the pretense of working and slid into his sleeping bag, only then noticing that he was still wearing the Patricians, having overlooked them when first stripping down.

What does it matter at this point?

The erratic streetlight whirred to life. Orange replaced back.

Ethan pictured the yard below, now well lit. He and Tuck had just sat there last night frying their Lake Marie catch. Everything had been perfect. Everything had been a dream.

Maybe Bobby just went down to talk to Tuck. Maybe that's where he is. Maybe they went fishing all day and that's why Bobby hasn't been answering his phone. Maybe father and son have reconnected.

Maybe I've helped.

Ethan sold himself on this thought.

Everything usually works out. Fathers and sons have a bond that nothing can break and Bobby didn't seem erratic last night, just hurt. He's been doing better. Making smarter, healthier decisions. Even Frank has to admit that. Who's to say that Bobby didn't do the responsible thing and just go talk to his father?

Ethan pulled out of the sleeping bag and removed the Patricians. He washed them and hung them to dry.

He slid back into the bag and zipped it tight. He had almost soothed himself to sleep when he became aware of a metallic rattling, steady and growing nearer until it culminated in a brief moment silence, then a heavy padded thump like a sack of dirty laundry being plopped outside his door. Ethan rolled towards the curtains as a silhouetted figure stopped outside his window.

He had just started to sit up when the glass roared towards him. The curtains were torn from the rod. One big sudden boom devolved into an infinite clattering cascade. The glass shards dispersed swirling fragments of orange light across the walls, creating a brief and dismal disco ball effect, before skittering across the desk and end tables. Ethan lunged off the far side of the bed, taking most of the sleeping bag and covers with him, banking off the bathroom wall before thudding to the floor, his hands clasped tightly over his head. In the middle of all this, something heavy had chunked off the far side of the bed's wooden frame.

Then there was silence.

Ethan remained pressed against the bedframe, motionless, fetal, and small, hoping to go unnoticed and unmolested in the ensuing break-in. He ran a quick mental inventory of the items he had in the room—he'd read that break-ins usually turn violent when there was nothing of value to be stolen: *firm issued laptop, suits, wingtips, the Patricians.* When no sounds of entry came, he peeked over the bare mattress at the shattered scene.

The room was empty.

Then came the shrieking; not from directly outside his room—as Ethan feared—but from a distance, down the walkway, or down in the lot, echoing up off the brick and cracked cement.

"I DID THIS!"

"I DID THIS!"

"I DID THIS! WOOOO!"

The cries were shrill and piercing. Ethan, still crouched behind the bed, recognized the voice but didn't want to believe it.

It's a shriek. It could be anyone. Everyone sounds the same at this pitch.

A substantial part of Ethan was simply relieved the storm had passed beyond his room.

Another familiar voice came through the darkness, this one closer to the window, but soft and without malice. "Ethan? Ethan?" A shaggy head leaned through the window hole. "McDaniel, you alive in there?"

"I'm here."

"Hey bud. You okay?"

"I think so." Ethan unraveled from the sleeping bag and stood up, checking his body for any previously unobserved injuries. He'd seen enough action movies to know that, in all the excitement, grievous wounds could go unnoticed. He passed this inspection and surveyed the war-torn room. The curtains lay splayed out across the window-side of the bed. Glass covered everything. Garth, silhouetted by the streetlight, still spoke to him through the television sized hole in the glass. "Yes. Yes, I'm fine. What happened?"

"Bobs came home." Garth gave a long look over his shoulder then turned back. "You got shoes back there? You'll need 'em."

Ethan slipped his bare feet into the wingtips and crunched through the field of broken glass to unlatch the door, smothering the impulse to identify which specific movie this called to mind. Resting on the carpet next to a beige flower blossom of shattered bedframe was a large, dull pink brick. Black fingerprints stained the top.

The shrieking continued as Ethan emerged on the walkway next to Garth; Bobby, naked but for denim cargo shorts, prowled the parking lot below.

"I DID THIS!"

Bobby's movements were jagged and grotesque. He stomp-marched through the sand in short arhythmic steps. With each fresh shriek, his arms surged skyward in triumph; sometimes jolting to a stop at his ears; other times blasting forward in a torrent of punches ending with a full backwards retreat to pound his fists against his serrated rib cage.

"I DID THIS!" He flexed and pounded his chest.

"I DID THIS!" He flexed and punched the air.

"I DID THIS! WOOOO!" He flexed and flexed again.

"I AM THE ONE WHO DID THE THING! I—" upper-cut, "AM THE ONE WHO DID THE MOTHERFUCKING THING!"

Garth gently pulled Ethan back from the rail. "Don't engage. Don't let him see you."

"Did he break anything else?"

"Just you man." Garth's voice was flat, lacking any of its usual fervent sarcasm. His neck sagged into his shoulders; his chin dangled against his chest. Ethan looked down the at the line of closed doors and unlit windows. Even the curtains and blankets were still.

They all must've heard . . .

Far down by the stairs, Frank stooped over the rail, watching as his friend and ward dissipated into the sand.

"I DID THIS!"

"I DID THIS!"

At last, Bobby grew quiet, halting his manic pacing to scrutinize his feet and rub his arms. He appeared briefly reflective, as if considering his situation and, perhaps, the proper course of action upward from this low point.

We're okay. He's cooling down.

Frank used this calm to descend from his perch. Garth and Ethan stepped forward again to watch him approach.

"Frank should be able to calm him down, right?" Ethan thought about Bobby's fit on the riverbank.

"We can hope."

A door opened underneath them. Ethan jumped back as Bobby shot around, peering first at the door, then at the approaching Frank.

A voice shouted from underneath them. "What did he do, Frank? He's not sayin' any—"

"Shut up, Deborah."

"But what did he do Frank? I heard a—" This reignited the shrieking.

"I DID THIS!" Bobby's voice was a shrill, strained growl. He slapped his chest.

"Shut the fuck up, Deborah. Get back inside."

The door closed.

"I . . . DID . . . THIS!" He spread his arms high at the night.

Bobby resumed his stop-and-go stalking, his body sputtering and straining like an overburdened engine. Frank fell in with Bobby's manic footfall, hands out, palms facing the ground.

"Bobby."

"I DID THIS!"

"Bobby, please. It's Frank."

"I AM THE ONE!"

"You gotta chill out, man. Listen to me. Bobby man, take a breath. Let's take a breath and go somewhere else. Let's go hang out, man. Watch a movie or something." Frank fought to sound calm but couldn't keep his panic from dominating his voice. "Let's get out into the woods or somewhere where you can get this shit out of your system. Or go to the water pit. I'll get you Gruber's."

When this failed Frank stopped his feet, watching Bobby circle the lot, waiting for him to come back around. When Bobby did, Frank placed a hand on his shoulder. Bobby became a blur, whirling at the hips, catapulting his open hand at full extension.

"KEEEEEEYYYYAAAAAHHHHHH!!!"

The slap echoed off the brick and sent Frank two steps to his right before he straightened; Frank didn't stop, firing a scowl at Ethan as he retreated towards the stairs.

"Fuck." Garth fell back against the bricks. Ethan watched for another second, enough to see Bobby crow hop into a knock out air punch, then followed. Frank walked to them and leaned next to Garth, facing the night.

"Someone's called the cops by now," Frank said. "They're gonna have a time with him."

"Yep." Garth inclined his head towards Ethan. "*That* is meth."

"High voltage, crystallized fucking douchebag." Frank massaged his jaw. He sounded tired. "This ought to do it right?" He gestured at the ruined piece of property next to him.

"That should do it."

The fussy wail of approaching sirens reached Sapphire Courts. "Welp, that's it for me." Garth straightened and reached for his doorknob. "Good night, gentlemen."

"You're not staying?" Ethan asked.

"Nothing to be done now."

"But we can't just leave him out here."

"Okay, you go on down there and wrangle him in. Maybe you can get him charged with assault, or hell, even murder. We can't do shit now except escalate his charges. And if the cops see me seeing all this then they'll see to it that I say what I've seen." Garth's eyes lingered on Bobby flexing and spasming in and out of the street light. "Not that it matters though. I have to imagine that between all this," he swept his arm from streetlamp, to lot scene, to Ethan's shattered window, "they'll have all they need. Not to mention your statement."

"My statement?"

"Yea the cops are going to get a statement from you. You're welcome to return to your room but they'll find you. Once they see the broken glass, they'll have to make sure he didn't kill you. Then they'll get your statement. Best just stay out here and answer the nice deputy's questions."

"But what should I say to them."

"You know," Garth's gaze drifted from the streetlight back down into the lot. "It really doesn't fucking matter."

Garth closed his door; his window joined the others in darkness. Frank slipped down the hall to his own quarters. Ethan watched him go. His door closed as the blue and red lights began to spread over the sand.

The cruiser parked at the base of the slope. The first officer exited and approached Bobby, speaking so softly that Ethan couldn't make out the exact words. His partner exited the passenger side to follow several steps behind. Bobby turned to face them, his eyes wide, his chest tremoring. The officer's hands were set waist high, palms down, very similar to Frank's rendition of the universal hand signal for *let's everybody just cool off*. He took small, soft steps in Bobby's direction. Bobby gaped uncertainly at the man, looking like an abused dog cornered by an unknown, desperate to avoid another bout of cruelty. The officer took another step forward; Bobby tensed. Ethan could hear him now.

"There's nothing to worry about. We're just here to help you calm down. We just want to help you calm down and make sure you're okay." He took several slow steps forward. Bobby flinched at every movement. When the officer was in striking distance, Bobby blurred again, this time towards the officer. The officer had been braced for a strike, but not this spasmodic surge; he ducked backwards from his assailant but his dodge did not appear entirely successful. Ethan couldn't discern to what extent Bobby's blow landed, but the man stumbled backwards twisting to land face first in the sand.

The beast that was Bobby Canterbury heaved up to his feet, tensed and hunched into something resembling a wrestler's stance.

The second officer cursed and levelled his taser. The beast that was Bobby Canterbury turned on him in a stalking offensive. The second officer gave ground, commanding, shouting, then pleading, for the beast to stop. The beast that was Bobby kept coming. With one final plea, the officer fired his taser.

Nothing happened; the beast that was Bobby ripped something out of his side, pounded his chest, and proceeded.

"I DID THIS!" This was a roar.

The second officer now reached down to his other hip, for his pistol. The beast that was Bobby's cry crescendoed and cracked as he coiled back on his knees, a lion preparing to pounce. The officer's pistol was out and on its way up.

"NNNNOOOOOOOOOOO!"

The beast's head jerked towards Ethan, who wouldn't realize until much later that it was he who'd screamed. For a moment, they locked eyes; Bobby Canterbury's desperation and hatred flooded into Ethan who, for the first time in his life, felt true guilt and helplessness. There was a soft electronic thump, much quieter than a gunshot. The beast broke eye contact and went silent, his thin frame jerked and stiffened to career left-backwards as two super-charged mandibles dragged him down, away from where the first officer, still seated, had recovered enough to discharge his taser. The two officers sprang on the opportunity, cuffing the beast's hands and ankles, linking the chain and folding its lanky frame into a squirming basket, and pulling the restraints tight enough that it could shake hands with its feet. Together, the officers lifted and tossed the beast that was Bobby Canterbury, now shrieking anew, face down on the backseat.

"I DID THE THING!"

"I DID THE THING!"

The officers stood by the closed door for a second, catching their breath and checking each other over. In the relative quiet, the officers turned their attention to Ethan on the balcony and the shattered window behind him. They made eye contact, held up a finger, and advanced. Ethan watched them grow out of the stairwell.

"Good evening, sir. I'm Deputy Culkin. That's Deputy O'Shaughnessy. Are you okay?"

"I'm fine."

"Are you in need of medical assistance?"

"No, I'm . . . I'm fine."

"Okay, good. That's good to hear. Do you mind telling us what happened here tonight?" Deputy Culkin's forehead was cut. His cheek had started to swell.

"I, um, I guess I only saw part of it."

The deputy tapped several of his legion pockets before locating and removing a yellow note pad. When Ethan didn't continue, he lifted his eyes towards him.

"What's your name, sir?"

"Ethan McDaniel."

"And do you live here in Sapphire Courts, Mr. McDaniel?"

Ethan checked himself before answering; he was naked but for boxers and the gleaming leather wingtips. He diligently filled Deputy Culkin in on his purpose for being in Folkston, highlighting his shoes when he mentioned the trial. Deputy O'Shaughnessy started taking pictures of the window and interior, crouching, leaning, and stretching to get specific angles without disturbing the wreckage.

"So, you're an attorney from Charleston?"

"Yes, sir, officer."

"Deputy. And you're involved in that trash trial?"

"That is correct, sir."

"But you're staying at Sapphire Courts . . ."

"That is correct. I didn't get to pick my, um, accommodations. Emmett Lucas can vouch for me if you'd like."

"That's fine. And did you witness what happened tonight, Mr. McDaniel?"

Ethan paused, then tried to force himself to continue speaking before it became obvious he was piecing together a fabrication. "I . . . I was asleep in my room, this room. I came outside when I heard the shouting."

"When you heard the shouting?"

"Yes. As you saw, Bobby was shouting, shrieking in the lot."

"Was that before or after your window was broken?"

"What do you mean?"

"Were you in there sleeping with a broken window?"

The window . . . Ethan wished he had taken more time developing his story. He stalled, watching Deputy O'Shaughnessy finish his first round of photographs and begin setting up tiny numbered yellow placards by various bits of rural shrapnel.

"Mr. McDaniel?"

"Oh, the window. Bobby had nothing to do with that." Ethan realized he wasn't great at this. "That is, um, as far as I know, unrelated . . ."

"Okay. Do you mind telling me when and how the window came to be broken?"

"Oh earlier. Much earlier. I'm not sure how that happened."

"But you observed the broken window, and after that you not only re-entered the room but actually slept in the bed?"

"..."

The deputy closed his eyes and sucked his lips under his teeth. Bobby's incessant *I DID THIS! I DID THIS! I DID THIS!* filled the silence. Ethan's peripherals told him that the squad car was rocking back and forth.

Deputy Culkin pivoted to address his partner. "Hey Hank? Can you remind me what the consequences are for knowingly providing false information to an officer in the course of investigating a crime?"

"That depends on the subject crime, Markus. It's a misdemeanor for misdemeanors and a felony for felonies."

Deputy Culkin worked his lips back out, examining with interest something by the bulb on the streetlight. Ethan's stomach dropped—he had not fully considered the ramifications of lying to investigating officers.

What am I willing to do to help, Bobby?

Deputy Culkin stepped back to face Ethan, giving him a long look before continuing his questioning.

"So, do you know the man down there?"

"Do I know . . ."

"You said his name earlier: Bobby."

"I, uh, we've met. Only briefly during the day though."

"Today?"

"No. A different day. He was very kind."

"Kind? How so?"

"He showed me around town. Took me to Grubers. Showed me his water pit."

"On the first and only occasion you met, he very briefly took you to Gruber's and the water pit?"

"I guess it wasn't that brief."

"Right. And how did a brick come to pass through your window."

"Oh he . . ." Ethan paused, wondering if this had been some kind of lazy ruse. "Well, like I said, that's a, um, separate incident." He pointed at the window. "I don't know who did this."

"I DID THIS!"

"Was it broken last night?"

"No."

"Was it broken this morning?"

"No. It was fine when I went to court."

"When did you first notice it was broken?"

"Oh," Ethan was desperate to avoid another long pause. "It was broken when I got back from court. Just after five."

"And are you aware of any reason why someone would've smashed this window, your window, today while you were at court?"

"I am not. I've only been in town a few days. Anything I said would just be a guess."

"Well, sir, let's start there. Can you give me your best guess as to how that brick came to be thrown through your room window?"

"I . . ." Ethan inspected the scene, scrambling for a reasonable explanation for the shattered window and exploded bedframe that didn't include the nonsensical screaming in the squad car. "I . . . don't have to."

"Sir?"

"I have rights. Especially when it comes to self-incrimination."

"Self-incrimination?"

"Yes. I would like to invoke those rights now."

Deputy Culkin's lips now disappeared entirely. He shifted his pen and pad, freeing a hand to rub his bald head. "You must be some attorney."

"I'm learning every day."

"Okay and after you woke up atop the broken glass in the room with the shattered window. You heard the shouting, and came outside, what did you see?"

"I saw what you saw. Bobby shouting and walking around the lot."

"Anything else?"

"No. Y'all arrived soon after that."

"Did you ever see Bobby—do you know his last name?"

"Canterbury, I believe."

"Did you ever see Bobby Canterbury on the second floor?"

Ethan thought for a second. "Not tonight. No, sir. Just in the lot."

The deputy scanned the carnage and sighed again. "Did anyone else join you out here tonight, Mr. McDaniel?"

"No, sir."

"No other residents came outside to see the commotion?"

Ethan shook his head; when he spoke, only dumb things came out.

"Has anyone coerced you tonight? Threatened you to prevent you from cooperating with this investigation?"

Ethan shook his head again.

"Are you in any trouble? Are you safe?"

"Safe? Yes."

"Because you don't have to stay here tonight or any other night. If you feel like you're in danger, we can take you somewhere safe."

"No sir. Nothing like that."

"Do you have somewhere else to stay?"

"I have a car. I will go to a different hotel I guess."

"Right. That's fine. Anything else you'd like to tell us about what happened here tonight?"

"No. Not that I can think of."

"Well then. If there's nothing else you'd like to add, Deputy O'Shaughnessy and I are going to leave now. This is my card. I want you to know that I don't believe you. Although I am going to call Earl Macadoo and inform him that the window to your room has been smashed in and that you're not cooperating. That you've claimed your rights against self-incrimination. We'll see how he wants to proceed."

"I understand. Thank you."

Deputy Culkin nodded, smiling one of those smiles that only convey aggravation. Behind him, Deputy O'Shaughnessy collected his yellow placards. "Good night, Mr. McDaniel."

"Good night, officers."

Bobby's squeals grew faint as the squad car crawled up out of the sand and onto Main Street. Ethan gave the scene his first calm and deliberate inspection. The door to his room was open and, with the curtains and window removed, he had a full view of its diminutive and dreary state. It looked like a piece of cheap stage design. Tiny fragments of glass glittered like stars and rippling water.

I did this . . . I did this.

Garth's door cracked. "Is the fuzz gone?"

"Yea." Ethan studied the sandy slope leading out and away from Sapphire Courts.

"They hate being here at night. They take Bobby with them?"

"Yea."

"Figured."

"Bobby hit the cop in the face."

"Fuck me. He catch him with a punch or a slap?"

"Hard to say. The cop kinda dodged it. I think he got him pretty good though."

"Which deputy did he get?"

"That would've been Deputy Culkin. He was cut and swelling up when I spoke to him."

"Hmm. He could've picked worse."

"Deputy O'Shaughnessy was with him. He took pictures."

"That's the nightshift. What'd you tell 'em?"

"I think I helped Bobby out. At least on the property damage and enhancement. I didn't tell them that Bobby did it. Although, I may have accidentally implied that I did it."

"You lied to the cops?"

"Yea. Of course. I had to help Bobby."

"Jesus, that was fucking stupid." Garth opened the door to accommodate his girth. "Take a look behind you, right at the top of the light pole. Tell me what you see."

Ethan turned as instructed—there, at the top of the pole, right where the arm branched off, were three cameras—one pointed almost directly at Ethan's window. "Oh . . . sometimes those are just for—"

"They're real and they work. For as often as the cops get called out here they might as well be a live feed into the station. You could've at least given 'em a viable story, then *maybe* they wouldn't have pulled the footage."

"What if I pay to get the window fixed, or replaced? I'll start calling tomorrow. Faster the better, right?"

"Faster the better, indeed. Pump the bad water under the bridge. Hard to stay mad over something that's fixed. Especially if you never saw it broke." Garth gave Ethan a weary smile. Some of the weight and tension left Ethan's chest. Then Garth continued, "I can help you there but, overall, for Bobby, it ain't gonna help shit. The first thing Bobby's gonna do when he sobers up is devour his complimentary sausage biscuit, and get to chattin'. They'll be nice to him. He'll be nice back and give them everything they need."

Ethan recalled the local lad who'd been more than happy to return to the store that had banned him for frequent shoplifting and had proudly showed Ethan where he used to get high in the school from which he had dropped out.

"Even if he doesn't," Garth continued, "at this point they're prosecuting his record more than the crime. A lifetime achievement award rather than anything specific he did tonight. And we can't forget that he bitch-slapped a sheriff's deputy. Even if it is Deputy Culkin. They really hate that." Ethan's chest seized anew as this realization settled in. "Now, there's nothing to be done tonight, and your room ain't fit for sleepin', so there's a spot on the couch if you're interested."

"You mean, sleep at your place?"

"Again, yea. Unless you want to sleep on the glass."

"What about Bobby? Shouldn't we go to the jail?"

"You can put down a blanket in their parking lot if you want. But he's in at least until morning. Almost certainly more. They'll process him. Put him in a room alone while he dries out. When he does so, all the way, he'll be back to his wonderful sober self. He's actually a wonderful fuckin' inmate. Friendly, obedient, weirdly neat. They love housing him."

Ethan looked at the jagged rectangle that was his window. "And what about this?"

"What about it?"

"Don't you have a tarp? Or a trash bag or something? We should cover it. My stuff's in there."

"You really think a tarp will keep the junkies out?"

"It'll make me feel better. I don't like looking at it."

"If it helps you, man."

After some searching, they located the old cardboard box for Garth's TV, stomped it flat, and taped it over the hole. When it was done, Garth stepped back and examined their handiwork.

"Feel better?"

"I guess."

"Some fuckin' night."

Garth led Ethan back into his apartment where the Furry Man slumped into Frank's chair, sharing a sigh with the cushion, what had been the bottle of celebratory bourbon tilted in his lap. Ethan pieced himself onto the couch, remaining upright, not sure whether the conversation would continue.

After a moment, Garth spoke. "Lay down."

"What?"

"Lay your dumb ass weary head down."

Ethan obliged, resting his head on the throw pillow, waiting, hoping for Garth to provide some comforting words, or go to bed. Garth surprised him by sitting in silence. Ethan could hear his fingers wringing at the glass bottle.

Does he blame me for this? Can he? All I did was go fishing. There was no way for me to know it would lead to this.

Ethan spoke. "I did this, right? I mean, Bobby almost certainly would not have flown off the handle tonight but for me fishing with his dad."

"That's about how Frank sees it."

This wasn't the response Ethan wanted. "But, you have to understand that all I did was accept an offer to go fishing. There was no way I could have known that it would have this effect on Bobby. I certainly didn't intend to hurt Bobby's feelings."

"That's not how Frank sees it."

"You have to agree though. It can't be my fault. There's no way I could've foreseen that going fishing with Tuck would have caused Bobby to do this. I didn't even know Tuck was his dad. So I can't be held li—it's really not my fault."

The liquor sloshed beyond Ethan's head. When it stopped, Garth spoke again. "Understand Frank's frustration at this. And mine. This type of shit happens all the time. You, a big city boy, strolled into Folkston last week and what did you know about his town?" This was apparently rhetorical because Garth kept on. "You knew it had good fishing and possibly smelled like trash. So you came to town all geared up for your big important trash trial, locked and loaded to further your career, hoping to maybe wet a line and pick up a story for the folks back home. You were juiced up at the prospect of both padding your resume and stumbling upon a bona fide Folkston local to take you under his wing and show you all the little quaint secret spots most tourists don't experience. That authentic bullshit. As I see it, your only goal was to use Folkston, its problems, and its people to forge another brick in your precious career. And, as it always does, shit worked out for you: you've got your trial; you've found your stupid local; and, you've done your fishing. And we've certainly provided you with fodder for your next set of cocktail parties. So everything came up roses for Ethan McDaniel, Charleston attorney-at-law."

A portion of Ethan's brain remembered its legal training, assembling arguments in support of his innocence; the rest of Ethan McDaniel sat silent, mentally and emotionally flat-footed, as Garth, increasingly red-faced, continued.

"You sauntered into our home, only seeing what you wanted to see, only looking for what suited you, fiddling with knobs and pressing buttons, only ever set on getting yours, and you fucked with shit you didn't understand, and now one of us, someone who was on his last fucking chance," Garth was now yelling, "pays the price while you waltz away like a fucking prince."

Garth caught his breath; lawyer Ethan made his move. "You could have warned me. You could have just told me Tuck was his father."

"Frank and I spend our days trying to erase that fact. Trying to cover and repair all the damage that fucker's done. Why would we ever even think to let you in on that?"

"You knew I liked fishing. It wasn't impossible we'd end up going out."

"That's bullshit. Don't you dare put that on me. Almost everything I do is in some way geared towards protecting Bobby Canterbury, walling him up from meth heads and asshole dads. It's a big goddam world to protect him from. Don't tell me I had to predict some city lawyer slipping in to fuck it all up."

"But that's my point. How can you blame me for going fishing with Tuck when you didn't even think to warn me not to?"

"Listen, when you got here Bobby Canterbury was an honest working man about to put this town, this way of life, and that colossal fuck downstairs in the rearview mirror."

"That's not fair though." It took Ethan several seconds to piece together his next words. "Remember he threw the brick at me. I'm the victim."

The liquor bottle exploded against the door.

For the second time that night, Ethan showered in shattered glass. He lurched his head away from the door, ending up crouched on the far side of the couch in time to watch the shards bounce across the coffee table.

"The victim?" Garth was standing. "You have the nerve to call yourself the fucking victim? For one almost bad night? Do you know what kind of home Bobby was born into? You were born on solid ground with the foundation for your life anchored in fucking stone. All you had to do was start blindly laying your precious bricks and you could rest assured that everything would end up goddam hunky-dory. Bobby Canterbury was dropped into quicksand, quicksand infested with fucking buried monsters. Monsters masquerading as friends and parents. He may not have always helped himself but every step he's taken has been blind and every step could've gotten him fucking devoured. Can you even imagine that? I mean, who did I hear you call this morning?"

Ethan, too frightened to continue his argument, tried to think back that far; it seemed so long ago. "I . . . I called my dad."

"Your loving father. And you two enjoyed a lively, lovely, and loud conversation. Do you think Bobs has ever gotten to make that call?" Ethan crept his feet back to the floor as the furious, bloodthirsty red drained from Garth's face. "Understand this. Not only do you have your own banner father, you've now got as many happy memories with Tuck Canterbury as Bobby does. Tuck only ever showed his son affection to throw it in his mom's face. He probably only spent time with you to throw it in Bobby's face."

"No . . ." Ethan stumbled for words. "We . . ."

"Tuck Canterbury's lazy good-for-nothing ass fishes just about every damn day. Usually catches a catfish too. Before last night, did you ever see him cooking or eating in the yard?"

No . . . Could I have simply been a pawn in Tuck Canterbury's manipulations to hurt his son? Was my time with my authentic local on Lake Marie a lie?

"Bobby's father was probably thrilled to see his boy make an ass of himself. Can you imagine that? I mean, fuck, you didn't see his damn door open, did you?" Ethan didn't think Garth was looking for an answer, but his head shook anyway. "Exactly. Fuck fair. Fuck you for saying you've ever experienced unfair. To me, to Frank, you're nothing but a fucking vulture picking at the carcass of whatever inspiration this town still musters. You and your other goddam suits are just gnats racing in to suck the blood out of Folkston's scraped knee. It's not fucking fair that you're here to feast on this town's failed ventures while we suffer through them. You were never at risk here. You don't even have any skin in that stupid fucking trial. You'll be gone tomorrow or thereabouts. But you came here, stirred shit up, and Bobby got fucked."

Garth paused, sneering at the glass on the floor, filtering several long breaths through his teeth. Ethan clutched the far arm rest, trying to still a trembling jaw. Garth sat back down.

"Fuck man, you just wanted to go fishing."

"I didn't," Ethan's voiced cracked, "I didn't know Tuck was his father."

"There's nothing to be done about it. Tuck, Bobby, and that crystal plague have taken it out of our hands." Garth was silent for a long time. "In all honesty, Bobby was probably going down either way. His path was getting narrower by the step. All of a sudden Bobs had to be perfect for the first and only time in his life, and that wasn't his way. It's nobody's way. He was bound to slip in." Garth looked up at Ethan. "You motherfuckers, outsiders and city folk, gutted us. Time and time again. Sank us and made the land soft. Now these kids, the ones born here, they're born onto vast fucking fields of shit. They spend their lives wriggling themselves deeper, then get sucked underneath. Afterwards it's like . . . were you ever actually here?"

"What happens to Bobby now?"

"First that night in jail. After that, depends which judge is working and, more importantly, how put out Deputy Culkin is. The good news is that it wouldn't really be a question if Bobby had closed his hand. Punches mean serious jail time."

"I could represent him. Starting right now. Then they couldn't speak to him, you know get a confession, if he obtains legal counsel. I'd do it Pro Bono."

Garth raised his eyebrows.

"It means for free."

"I know what Pro Bono means. But your kind and humanitarian gesture won't help him one wit tomorrow. They've caught on to that bit and start asking questions before visiting hours. And they don't let just anyone walk in and claim to be someone's attorney. Also, don't forget, Bobby doesn't want to fucking see you man. Who's to say he doesn't flip his shit again when he sees you and pick up more charges, or lose the good graces of the guards. In fact, it's definitely best if you don't go to his bond hearing tomorrow to avoid just that. And, finally and more generally, I'll point out my hesitation to put my friend's future in the hands of an attorney who just asked *what happens now.*"

Ethan had to swallow this.

"I know you don't think much of Folkston. But we do have lawyers. Lawyers who not only are familiar with the criminal system but also know the solicitors and what they like to hear."

"So what can I do?"

"Go to bed. Then finish your shit up and go home. This isn't your story. If there is a happy ending, you don't get to be a part of it." Garth stood up and disappeared down the hallway, returning with a broom and vacuum. Ethan remained still as he swept and vacuumed the area around the door. "Did I miss anything?"

"Coffee table."

"Shit." Garth rolled the vacuum over the table. Ethan considered what his mother would think of such a maneuver.

"Okay, now. You got everything you need? You need a drink or anything?"

"I'm alright. Thank you."

"Oh shit. I know what you need." Garth disappeared again, returning with a blanket. He pointed for Ethan to lay down and spread it over him. "Get your rest young one, you still have a trial tomorrow. Good night, Ethan."

"Good night, Garth."

Ethan recognized the blanket as the platitude blanket. He read the platitude nearest his chin: *The Time is Always Right to Change the World*.

Ethan rested his head on the pillow, watching the wall behind the television darken as Garth turned off the lights. This time Ethan couldn't sleep. The sound of the brick crashing through the window, followed closely by Bobby's endless primal shrieking filled the silence. When Ethan closed his eyes, his world filled with Bobby's frenetic wobbles through the sand. His father, so close, with his door closed.

Something scratched at his cheek, he propped up and checked the pillow, recognizing the rough and raised stitching of *Get Fucked*. The phrase's humor was an illusion permitted by light and distance; up close, in the dark, it was brutal and blunt. Ethan flipped the pillow before laying back down; he pulled the blanket up to his chin.

Chapter Twenty-Four

The night was long. Ethan spent it twisting about, raveling in and out of the platitude quilt, kicking out a sweaty leg when it grew too suffocating. He thought about Bobby in his cell. Ethan had only ever experienced the nation's holding facilities through field trips and television. Bobby Canterbury had apparently experienced them many times, was in one now, and, if Garth and Frank were to be believed, would be in one for quite some time.

And then what? Someplace worse? Could it really be as bad as Garth described? Sweet Bobby Canterbury marked in shame forever as a felon, cast out from society to live and die as he might?

Just last night Bobby had been sober and happy eating Gruber's. His and Frank's plan to leave was still intact.

Is that really all gone now? Did I take that from him?

It all felt too sudden and recent; as if Ethan could still identify the right move or piece together the perfect set of words to wipe the bad events from the timeline. But Ethan could not think of anything. He couldn't even attend the hearing.

Ethan watched the early sun slowly bring light to the living room. When he could clearly discern CRIMINALS BEST MULLET

OVER on Garth's Dalton Stampede poster, he returned to his allotted quarters. Garth slept on, or if awake, remained still and silent in his bedroom.

The morning breeze buzzed the cardboard window covering as Ethan tiptoed around the wreckage of the night before. It was still early; he briefly considered killing time and anxious energy with a workout—the shattered glass in the carpet changed his mind. He picked the shards from his belongings then showered until the water ran cold. He then shaved and assembled a presentable self for the day. When he was dressed and ready, he sat down on the bed with the Patricians, working the effortlessly soft fabric in his hands and studying his reflection in the black TV screen. Today, the trial was an intrusion, an obstacle to be endured before he could get back to what really mattered. Today, the Patricians were a burden he'd rather not assume. After some minutes, he surrendered, resigning himself to a long, restless day in court. Sterling Colt could scream as he pleased; Sterling Colt no longer frightened him. Ethan pushed his feet into the Patricians, stepped into his wingtips, and exited into the light.

Deborah and Frumpy patrolled the grass, not directly by the exit, but close enough that Ethan expected his passing to trigger engagement. He kept an eye on her and, when she saw him, gave a chest-high wave. She resumed watching her dog chew and defecate.

"Good morning, Deborah."

"Morning." She didn't look up.

Ethan stopped, then walked towards her, away from the courthouse. "How are you today?"

"Tired."

"Me too. I didn't sleep either. I couldn't after . . . well . . ." Deborah didn't respond. Ethan joined her in watching Frumpy sniff her shit.

"Did it upset Frumpy?"

She shrugged. "Sirens always do."

"I'm sorry Frank yelled at you."

"I shouldn't have meddled. No good in me poking my head out when someone's . . . in that way. It ain't TV; if I can't help, I best just stay out of it."

As Ethan drifted through the empty courthouse lot, his sleep deprived mind replayed the events leading to Bobby's arrest.

I did this . . .

He took the stairs to the fourth floor. When the courtroom doors jangled in their frame, Ethan slumped onto the hallway bench, checking his phone before resting his head against the wall.

Another stupid fucking delay.

The air conditioner cut in and out above him. The image of Bobby disappearing into the darkness, away from his caring friends and apathetic father, played on repeat in front of his open eyes.

I did this . . .

I did this . . .

The stairwell door opened. Ethan jolted and shook his head, not sure whether he'd fallen asleep. Cordell, the security guard, had his belt undone and was one step towards the bathroom before he noticed Ethan.

"What you doing up here now? Ain't nothing going today."

"Nothing going? What do you mean?"

"I said there's nothing going in the big courtroom today."

"Has there been another delay?" Ethan checked his phone. "Nobody told me anything."

"They don't tell me why, son. They just give me the schedule. And the schedule says there ain't nothing going in the big courtroom today."

"Have you seen any of the other attorneys?"

"Wouldn't expect to. Attorneys don't show up unless something going, something that gets 'em paid. Which there ain't today. Now, if you don't mind, I have other business needs attending." With that, he finished his journey to the bathroom.

Ethan ransacked his call history, his email, his texts: nothing. He heaved to the stairwell, taking stairs four at a time, down to the first floor whirling the immediate left into the clerk of court's office, where he came to a full stop.

Marissa stood at the front desk, leaning lazily on the countertop as she flipped through four stacks of papers as Mrs. Marsh stamped them.

"We'll be right with you, sir." Mrs. Marsh finished stamping one of the stacks then looked up at Ethan. "Oh! Good morning, Mr. McDaniel! I wasn't expecting to see you today." Marissa turned to Ethan, wide-eyed, head cocked.

"Do y'all know why the trial was delayed? Is someone sick?"

"Sick? No. Didn't they . . . oh honey." Mrs. Marsh's head slid sideways. "Mr. Lucas' case settled."

"Settled?" Ethan turned to Marissa, who nodded a scrunched face. "But . . . but what does that mean?"

"Well, in my experience, it means Mr. Paulson and that nasty Mr. Colt worked out an agreement."

"Settled . . ." Ethan's mouth kept moving, waiting for his brain to provide additional words.

"She's right, Ethan. Colt called Sires last night. It was either Mr. Lucas' testimony or that strange . . . outburst . . . but his—y'all's client, offered a lot more money."

"Nobody told me anything."

"Well, Mr. McDaniel, Ethan," Mrs. Marsh straightened her dress, "that is because you work with assholes."

Marissa shrugged and nodded again.

"So it . . . it really settled last night?" His voice broke.

"Early evening, really," Marissa said. "I'm here filing the paper-work."

"After all that, it's all just . . . over? What do I do?"

My presence really hadn't been necessary. His chin trembled.

"Don't I at least need to sign something?"

"Nope. Colt's insurer was very motivated to get it over with quickly so nothing's been asked of Standardized Integrated Insurance Company. Y'all are even getting a full release. No signature necessary. I'm sure your people will be very happy."

"Happy . . ."

Ethan could feel the dam breaking; he shuffled out of the clerk's office and out of the courthouse, collapsing on the steps in the biting sun of a morning in full bloom. The first tears squeezed out from the corners of his eyes.

"Ethan? Are you okay?"

He hadn't noticed Marissa following him. He couldn't bring himself to look up at her, vainly focusing his attention on stilling his convulsing chest.

"Ethan, don't feel too bad. You may have done nothing but that's still better than Mr. Colt. His douchebaggery essentially added value to our case. Sires joked about giving him a commission." Ethan's tremors didn't abate. "My god, Ethan, what's happening?"

"Bobby . . . Bobby . . ."

"Oh no." She sank next to him, pulling him in close. The dam disintegrated, hot tears streamed down his cheeks as a flood of de-spondent water split the bricks. Marissa, one arm firmly around his shoulder, held Ethan together as, one word at a time, he sputtered through the previous night's events.

"Ethan, that's how the world is. No one can save Bobby from having a shithead for a dad. Or being surrounded by addicts and assholes. The world seems to always be tilted against some people. Bobby Canterbury was one of them. Even if Bobby had been doing better, and was on the right track, the addiction, the disease remained. It probably would've gotten him with or without you."

He looked up at her, pleading for a more cheerful report. Her eyes were reddening as well. "But . . . I don't want Bobby to go to jail. I don't want it to be this way."

"Ethan," she brought her eyes level to his and looked straight in, "it really doesn't matter what you want. This is what's happening. There's really not a good, uplifting strand to pull out of all this." Ethan's head shuddered back down between his thighs. He had no idea how long he stayed down there, weeping, before she spoke again. "You care though. You should be proud of that. It's important. So, if you absolutely must have something good to take home, assuming it means anything to you," Marissa paused, pushing her hand through her hair, then returning her hand to his back, "I'd very much like to stay in touch with you, even if this stupid trash trial is over." Ethan lifted his head, fish-mouth gaping as the woman kissed him on the cheek and handed him his stack of settlement papers, still warm from the printer.

Ethan watched Marissa DePaul walk back to her white SUV. She waved once through the windshield, and was gone. He remained seated for several minutes, collecting himself, steadying his breath and practicing his words before making his way to the far side of the parking lot, to the spot where he'd stopped to inspect the courthouse just over one week prior. There he caught his breath and called Mrs. Warland.

"Hello?"

"Hey. The trial's over. The case just settled."

"I know. I heard from Mr. Colt's office. They said it settled last night. I was wondering why you hadn't called. I really hope you didn't agree to terms without consulting me."

"No. I wasn't a part of it at all."

"What do you mean?"

"They did it without me. Negotiated and settled. We don't have to contribute anything and it's a full release."

"That's great! We can rephrase our involvement when we tell the adjuster but they'll be thrilled. Who is the adjuster, by the way?"

"Margot."

"Oh, of course. Margot with a *T* will be thrilled."

"Yea, I guess she will."

"How are you? You sound flat. Have you already been celebrating?"

"I don't know. I just learned about it in the courthouse. I thought . . . it's all very sudden and, if I can be honest, unsatisfying. I've been here so long, worked so hard, and I really had no part in it."

"That's the way of it. Well, it'll be too late today and you've earned a quiet evening. But we can debrief and discuss when you're back in the office tomorrow. I'll take you to lunch on the firm."

"Tomorrow?"

"Yea. You don't need to be here at eight but I have some other stuff piling up that I'd like you to work on. Unless you're planning on staying in Folkston."

"No, no. Of course not. It's all just happening very quickly."

"I imagine you can't wait to get out of there."

"I . . ."

"You can say goodbye to Sires' paralegal first."

"What?"

"Teri told me y'all had developed some rapport."

"No, that's not . . . I just saw her in the courthouse."

"Good. Then pack up, drive south, and take a night off."

"Okay. Absolutely."

"Good. Nice work up there. Sterling Colt is not easy to work with and there's something to be said for successfully staying out of the way. Far too many attorneys have trouble staying out of even their own way. And, oh! How could I not have led with this, congratulations on your first trial! I'll let the trial attorneys association know! They'll issue your certificate. The firm will pay for it to get framed. That'll be another free lunch."

Ethan had forgotten about the South Carolina Trial Attorneys Association. "Thank you."

"You're officially a trial lawyer now. No one can take that away from you."

The 217 window was whole when Ethan returned. One worker in a ballcap and a drooping grey t-shirt was running something along the edges, while Garth chatted with a robust older man in khakis and a branded polo holding a clipboard.

"Oh good, you're home," Garth said. "I was worried we'd have to get your credit card over the phone." Garth introduced the older man as Mr. Cantwell of Cantwell Glass. "All they need is your payment information. I also called a cleaning company. They came by and set everything straight and vacuumed. They're washing the sheets now. They will have to call you to pay for that."

Mr. Cantwell put Ethan on the phone with his secretary who took his credit card. Then Mr. Cantwell thanked them both and left. One phone call and a swipe of the card, and the cosmetic fallout of the night was taken care of. Earl Macadoo would never even see his property damaged. He'd also finish up with a spotless new window and clean sheets.

"You're home early. And why are your eyes all red?" Garth asked, leading Ethan to his kitchen. "Have you been crying?"

Ethan filled him in on the untimely settlement.

"All that trouble, man. All that work. And I bested that old fucker with a couple of well-timed entrances."

"Bested me, too."

"So I did. Well that's it, then. You'll be leaving today."

"As soon as I get everything packed. Have they had Bobby's hearing yet?"

"They have. Frank just got back. Bobs ain't going anywhere. They read his record aloud and charged him with the enhancement, based on video evidence, as well as assaulting an officer. Frank said Bobby could barely get his head off the table. Bail is beyond our means."

"I could chip in. Or pay it. Get him out for a little while right?"

"He's better off in there. Unless Tuck goes and gets himself arrested."

"Not quite how I hoped to leave Folkston."

"I suppose you were planning on driving off into the sunset in a cloud of victory and cocaine. Folkston had other plans. You gonna say goodbye to Frank or are you just gonna bolt?"

"Oh," Ethan scrambled, "I'm not sure if there's time. It's a pretty long drive and I have to work tomorrow."

"I think you owe him that."

Ethan worked at the ends of his jacket. "I really don't want to rile him up again."

"Your ass doesn't want to face him."

"There is that. But he certainly doesn't want to see me."

"That may well be true. And I admit it's a lose-lose: if you pay him a visit, it will piss him off. But if you don't pay him a visit, he's likely to get it in his head that you're some kind of monster who somehow intended all of this. I'd consider it a favor if you let him set eyes on you again, remind him that you're just another idiot."

Ethan nodded. "Shit."

"Best get to it. Then get back to your world."

"Goodbye, Garth. It was nice meeting you and I really appreciate you taking me in. Except for the . . . well, thank you."

"Well-tiptoed counselor. Bobby's situation aside, I'm not entirely disappointed that we crossed paths. Next time work brings you to Folkston, I hope they put you up somewhere nice and you let me come try the bidet."

"Maybe at Mountain Retreat."

Garth guffawed once. "Naw, that place stinks."

"Please do let me know if there's anything I can do to help Bobby. I mean it, anything at all."

"You mean that?"

"Of course."

"Because if I call down there in a week and your paralegal tells me you're in a meeting, I'll drive down to Charleston and put my foot in your ass. I've got a well-practiced roundhouse and some big spiky boots."

"That won't happen."

"Alright then. We'll just have to wait to confirm whether you're just another condescending dickbag, or if you're actually worth a shit." Garth stood up to envelope Ethan in a musky bear hug then stepped back to look the younger man in the eye. "You ain't bad and you ain't alone. A lot of people have come through this town and fucked shit up for us, intentionally and incidentally, I do believe you're the first one who had to stick around and see the beginnings of the consequences."

"That doesn't make me feel much better."

"That was not my intention. Don't expect too much out of Frank. The world's just dealt him a pretty brutal gut punch. He won't be one for conversation."

Ethan traversed the walkway past the stairs, pausing outside Bobby's door.

How long would Bobby get sentenced? Would he be allowed to live here afterwards? What would happen to his things?

One final step brought him to Frank's door. He knocked and stepped backwards to lean on the rail, then corrected himself to stand upright.

The door remained shut.

Ethan knocked again, listening for sounds of movement. He checked the curtain.

"Frank?"

No response.

He leaned in close enough to smell the painted metal. "Frank, it's Ethan." Silence. "The case settled. I'm ... I'm leaving today." He spoke loudly; his voice ricocheted off the door. "I just wanted to tell you goodbye . . . and that I'm sorry. I'm very . . ." Ethan couldn't finish the sentence.

There was some shuffling; the door opened on an unlit room. Frank skulked out of the darkness to stand just inside the doorframe, shoulders slumped, a forlorn vampire stripped of its charm and bloodlust. For the first time Ethan could recall, Frank Besch looked like he belonged in Sapphire Courts.

"Goodbye, Mr. McDaniel, safe travels back to Charleston."

They stood in silence for several seconds. A fresh set of tears started down Ethan's cheeks. "I'm so sorry. I never wanted . . . I never imagined . . . this."

Frank's shoulders rose slightly but he said nothing. Ethan looked up and down the walkway, trying to think of something to say that wouldn't belong on the wrong side of one of Garth's pillows—it really was difficult to think of something worth saying.

"Good luck in Columbia. Good luck in school. Please let me know if I can ever help you with anything."

The figure sank back into the darkness. The door closed, resealing the vault.

Ethan hesitated for several seconds before drifting back to 217. He slid in the key, pushed, and entered. The glass was gone from the nightstand and desktop. The shattered bed frame had been reset with a brown putty almost matching the wood. Like Garth said, the cleaners had taken the sheets and left the mattress bare; Ethan could have done without seeing it in its natural state. He stepped to the desk to take down the schedules and exhibits he'd pinned to the wall on day one. He unpinned the first one, gently returning the thumbtack to its clear plastic mini-box, then examined the daily calendar it had supported—he had been wrong from the outset, if not earlier, probably even before the phantom storm disrupted the trial before it even began. Not to mention the Furry Man's interventions. But the schedule's most egregious and enraging errors were in the margins, where triplets of bullet points instructed Ethan how he would spend his evenings in Folkston, what he would be thinking about, and whom.

How could I have ever predicted how this would go? How could I have been naïve enough to try?

Ethan tugged the next page off the wall, crumpled it into a ball, and hurled it into the plastic trashcan.

If Emmett Lucas had simply washed his damn trashcans and stayed on his own property then Bobby Canterbury would still be sober and Columbia bound, not drying out in a jail cell.

Ethan thrashed the remaining schedules from the wall, leaving uneven strips of paper dangling and swaying against the wallpaper, mashing the scraps together and two-handed spiking the dry clump into the bin. It bounced off the shallow bottom, tumbling twice on the carpet before Ethan stomped it with a grunt. He stopped.

The stomp had hurt.

He sat down on the bed and inspected the carpet where Garth's cleaning crew had missed a sizable and jagged glass shard which remained embedded and upright. He lifted his right foot, still robed in a Patrician. The white skin of his sole, and the thin sock above it, appeared as if unzipped, peeled back to expose the ghostly flesh underneath. Ethan watched as the pale mass flooded, red at first, then dark purple, swelling until the blood spilled out to darken the fabric of the sock, and then the carpet.

Acknowledgements

This book should not exist. It does because Olivia, my wife, is the kindest, most thoughtful, and most patient human yet born to this earth. There are others. My family has certainly shown their support through a long, lonely process. Randall Klein, my editor, consistently takes blunt, ham-fisted ideas and coaxes them into something approaching nuanced. My cover illustrator, Caitlin Alexander, wraps my words in truly awe-inspiring art which I'm proud to show the world.

I also want, maybe need, to thank anyone who has shown support for *The Habits of Squirrels*, whether by showing up to an event, reaching out, or simply leaving a review. Another book could never have happened without this encouragement. In "Honey Jar", The Wood Brothers warn their song's subject that, "you put your lips out in the wind and hope you get some kissin' back." Writing and publishing a book is like puckering up and turning into a gale; I really appreciate y'all not leaving me hanging.

Also by

The Habits of Squirrels
A recently retired mailman goes for a very long walk.

About the Author

Brian Livingston was born and raised in Marietta, GA. He earned his BA in History at Clemson University, thru-hiked the Appalachian Trail (trail name: Mister Frodo), then earned his JD at Washington & Lee University School of Law. He works in land conservation in Charleston, SC where he lives with his wife and son. His previous works include the novel *The Habits of Squirrels*.

Those who so desire, can reach him at @brianlivingstonboks on Instagram, Author Brian Livingston on Facebook, or at brianlivings tonbooks.com